COP   1

FIC
    Matthew, Christopher, 1939-
        The long-haired boy / by Christopher
    Matthew.   1st American ed.   New York :
    Atheneum,   1980.
        248 p. ; 22 cm.
    ISBN 0-689-11051-0   RCN 0-689-11051-0
        1. World War, 1939-1945--Fiction.   I. Title.
        PZ4.M4374   823.914   79-55594

THE LONG-HAIRED BOY

THE LONG-HAIRED BOY

by

CHRISTOPHER MATTHEW

ATHENEUM
NEW YORK
1980

Dedication

To my parents who lived through those days, to the
Guinea Pigs who suffered from them, and to
Wendy and Charlotte who happily knew
nothing of them.

Acknowledgments

Although, as will doubtless be recognized, this novel has been inspired by the life of Richard Hillary, all the characters and events described in the story are entirely imaginary.

I am extremely grateful to all the kind people whom I pestered at various times for technical advice while writing the book, in particular Mr and Mrs Bill Simpson, Mr and Mrs Tom Cradock Henry, and Group-Captain Peter Townsend.

Chapter One

Hugh was making love to a girl when the telephone rang. She was young, a little on the plump side, and extraordinarily compliant. He had never met her before, nor even, as far as he could recall, seen her, yet she undressed and lay back on the bed as quickly and easily as if they'd known each other for years.

He cursed the stupid idiot who had picked this of all moments to ring him. The bed was as warm as the girl and he sighed contentedly as she opened her arms to him. Whoever it was on the other end of the 'phone could wait.

'89 Squadron, scramble!'

Even before the words were out of the telephone orderly's mouth, Hugh was awake and out of the basket chair and running mindlessly, automatically towards the row of Spitfires that stood expectantly on the grass a hundred yards away, their noses pointed upwards like greyhounds trying to catch a scent in the warm summer air.

'Start up!' Hugh yelled as he sprinted across the uneven surface of the grass, stumbling and cursing as his flying boots, only half zipped up, flapped around his calves.

He saw his fitter, Parsons, jump into the cockpit of the Spitfire, and Aldridge, his rigger, hare towards the nearby battery cart. As he arrived panting beside the plane, the Merlin engine coughed and fired, white smoke belched from the exhausts alongside the nose, and the prop started spinning. He grabbed his parachute, hauled himself up on to the port wing and into the tiny, narrow cockpit. At the same time Parsons scrambled out on to the other wing and helped him on with his Sutton harness. He pulled on his helmet, and glanced across to see Squadron Leader Dickie Bird's Spitfire already taxiing on to the runway. Parsons handed him his flying gloves but he waved them away impatiently. He was always far too hot in the cockpit and besides, he never felt he had quite the same touch on the gun button when he was wearing gloves.

Parsons tapped him on the right shoulder, crossed his fingers and jumped to the ground. Hugh felt his insides turning to water as he set up his compass, gave his instruments a quick glance, then waved his hands in front of his face. Parsons and Aldridge pulled away the chocks from under his wheels. He pushed the throttle handle forward, released the brakes and with a roar the Spitfire began to roll forward bumpily across the grass.

Dickie Bird's section took off ahead in a storm of dried grass clippings. Hugh was flying No. 2 in Bill Carmichael's section, with Peter Hemingford on his left. He completed his checks and turned into what little wind there was. Bill waved an arm at him and raised an enquiring thumb. Hugh replied and opened up. The Spitfire bounded forward, swinging from side to side.

As he gathered speed, Hugh eased the stick forward, bringing the tail up and enabling him to keep a close watch on Bill, thirty feet ahead to his left. The bumps became lighter. Hugh drew the stick back gently and suddenly he was up. Even before his undercarriage had folded under his wings, he heard Bill calling over the R/T, 'Bonzo Leader calling Dancer. Am airborne.'

The three Spitfires leaned into a right turn as they lifted away from Woodfold airfield and the Kent and Surrey countryside began to spread out beneath them. Hugh reached up behind him, ducked his head and closed the hood. The sun, even at that low altitude, glinted on the bullet-proof glass causing him to screw up his eyes. He pulled down his goggles. Normally he left them up on his forehead or hung them somewhere on the instrument panel. In that narrow, confined space, with the helmet over his ears and the oxygen mask over his mouth, they restricted his vision and produced a sense of

2

claustrophobia. He knew that just in front of his feet was the reserve tank and was aware of the devastating effect one armour-piercing incendiary bullet could have on 28 gallons of fuel, yet he was convinced he had nothing to fear from fire. He could not explain why; it was just a feeling he had. Today, though, the sun seemed stronger and brighter than usual; his eyes were sore and prickly from too little sleep, and he welcomed the relief the tinted lenses offered him.

Now the voice of the Woodfold Controller came crackling over the R/T, as calm as if he were a caddy giving advice on how to play a brassie shot over water.

'Hullo, Dickie. Dancer Control here. Vector one-three-zero degrees, repeat one-three-zero. We have seventy plus bandits for you approaching the coast between Dungeness and Ramsgate. Make angels two zero. Good luck and good hunting.'

The squadron climbed at a steady 200 mph. Ideally, the Spitfires hoped to be in a position to be able to attack the enemy from above and with the sun behind them, but despite the radar and the first class reporting by the Observer Corps down on the coast, the chances of making sufficient height in time were rarely good.

At 12,000 feet they were approaching Ashford. Hugh looked down at the familiar gold and green shapes of the hopfields and pastures of Kent, and the toylike farms and houses and cottages dozing in the midday heat.

He thought of the Georgian rectory in Norfolk where he had been born and brought up, and wondered if his parents had sat down to their Sunday lunch yet. The scene was sharp and vivid in his mind: his father in the dining room putting an edge on the old bone-handled carving knife; Muv, flustered and flushed from the heat of the oven, as she slid the roast leg of lamb out of the oven; Percy, the ancient Jack Russell, padding in from the garden with his tongue hanging out, looking for a cool place to lie. . .

     'Don't you ever cry
     Don't ever shed a tear . . .'
Peter Hemingford's voice shattered his thoughts with one

3

of his famous warbled renditions of popular songs of the day.

'Don't you ever cry
After I'm gone . . .'

Hugh looked across at him. 'Belt up,' he called over the R/T. Peter grinned and replied with an obscene gesture.

Now they were over Romney Marsh, but as yet there was no sign of the enemy in the icy blue sky. Hugh squinted ahead, his stomach twitching with fear as the sun played across the scratched windshield, constantly giving the illusion of enemy aircraft wherever they looked. He snatched off his goggles and hung them on the instrument panel.

'Tallyho, chaps!' It was Harry Lauder with his yachtsman's eyes who first spotted them. Junkers 88s, swarms of them, a couple of hundred feet higher up, with their weaving escort of Me 109s, grey and silver, like busy little pilot fish accompanying evil, slow moving sharks.

'There they are, the bastards!' shouted Peter Hemingford.

'Let's give 'em hell,' Hugh joined in.

Dickie Bird's voice grated calmly over the R/T, 'O.K., chaps. Take it quietly. Line astern, line astern. Wait till I give the word.'

Hugh automatically dropped behind Bill Carmichael and felt rather than saw Peter close behind him. He reached forward and flipped on his reflector sight. The red bead and circle of light came up on the sighting glass in front of him. He adjusted the horizontal arms to forty feet – approximately the wing span of a Junkers 88 – and turned his gun ring to 'fire'.

The squadron, apparently still unobserved, continued to gain height, the Spitfires slipping and sliding as their propellors strove desperately to bite in the thin atmosphere.

'Watch those 109s,' Dickie said quietly.

'O.K., leader,' replied Bill.

They were less than a thousand yards away from the exposed bellies of the bombers when the 109s pounced. Any feelings Hugh might have had were at once dissolved in the heat and noise and fury that ensued. The R/T crackled constantly with shouts and orders and paths.

'Look out, leader,' Peter screamed. '109s at two o'clock.'

4

'Break and give them what for,' Dickie Bird said with quiet authority. 'Now!'

The entire squadron whipped round in tight left and right hand turns and met the approaching attack head on.

'Pick your own.'

Hugh decided on one Me 109 and throttled back slightly to reduce the closing speed. Very soon he had the German in his sights, and gave him a quick three second burst. For an instant it seemed they must collide, then, to Hugh's relief, the Messerschmitt twisted away and caught the tracer from Hugh's eight Brownings in his side. He flipped onto his back, smoke and flames pouring from his fuselage, and fell away.

Everywhere he looked there seemed to be planes twisting, diving, looping, firing. Now and then, in the midst of it all, a parachute would blossom and float gently earthwards, or a wing would spin slowly past like a sycamore leaf.

Above and to his right, Hugh saw Peter diving on a hapless 109 that was darting and weaving for its life, like a frightened rabbit before a greyhound, until a long burst from Peter's guns took its tail off and it spun helplessly out of control towards the earth.

Hugh was also twisting and turning and cursing, trying hard to gain height. Suddenly Bill's voice came over his earphones, sharp and urgent.

'Watch your tail, Hugh, for Christ's sake.'

Hugh glanced up at his mirror, saw the yellow nose of the 109 and at the same moment heard the bullets smacking into his starboard wing. For several seconds he stared at the damage in amazed disbelief, hynotized almost by the pattern of the holes. But then the discipline of training took over. He slammed the stick sideways and went into a text-book half-roll followed by a controlled spin.

For a while he allowed the Spitfire to dive straight downwards, gathering speed, until it seemed that the wings must surely fall off from the buffeting. Then gradually he eased the stick back and the throttle until the weight on his shoulders was almost more than he could bear. The countryside slowly disappeared beneath him, the horizon once more came into view and the blood drained from his head so that for a second or two he blacked out.

He came to to find he had lost 5,000 feet and, apparently, his entire squadron. The sky was completely empty.

Sweat was pouring down his face and into his oxygen mask. He glanced quickly round him in every direction. A lone fighter was always easy prey. Many a pilot, left behind by his squadron and unable, through sheer inexperience, to catch up had been jumped by waiting 109s and died, alone and lost, staring about through the misty perspex, his eyes screwed up against the sun's glare, shot to pieces by an apparently invisible enemy fighter pilot. The sooner he caught up with the rest of his section, the happier he would be. He pressed the button on the top of his stick.

'Red Two to Red Leader. Where the hell are you?'

There was a pause, and then Bill's voice came crackling through.

'Red Leader to Red Two. I'm on my way home which is where you should be. Catch up as soon as you can.'

He had spotted them, about half a mile ahead just north of Ashford, when he ran into the 109s. There were six of them, approaching the squadron from the right and slightly behind. Whoever was flying Arse-End Charlie obviously had not seen them, coming as they were out of the sun.

'Look out behind you,' Hugh yelled down the R/T. 'Six Messerschmitts on your tail.' And pulling back simultaneously on the stick and throttle handle, he began to climb in a desperate attempt to get above and between the Germans and the English fighters.

'Come on, you old cow,' he shouted at the Spitfire as it juddered and skidded in its efforts to gain height.

It was only a matter of moments before the 109s were within range of the struggling Spitfires, yet despite his warning, the English pilots seemed oblivious of the danger on their tails.

Hugh had still not gained as much height as he would have liked for a really effective attack, but it had to do.

6

'Tallyho,' he bawled, and shoving his stick forward and slightly to the left, he dived on the leading 109.

The German pilots were obviously as unaware of Hugh's presence as the English were of theirs, so that he was able to get in a couple of four second bursts without any difficulty. A spurt of orange flame mushroomed round the leading German's cockpit and flared back furiously. The 109 rolled sideways, belly upwards like a dying fish, and fell away in a long trail of black smoke.

Hugh wrenched back the stick just in time to avoid colliding with the second and third Germans who, astonished at this unexpected turn of events, immediately rolled and dived away. At the same time, he heard Peter yelling, 'Bloody hell!' and Dickie calling, 'Break, break!' before he turned at the top of his climb and dived once again on the two remaining Germans who were now in hot pursuit of Bill Carmichael.

'On your tail, Bill,' Hugh shouted and pressed the gun button. Being at a slight angle to the two 109s, he was able to get in a four second burst at the leading German whose engine, to his delight and astonishment, immediately started pouring coolant. It was only a matter of minutes before it would seize up completely.

He dived below the stricken Messerschmitt, bringing his plane up in a loop until he was on his back, almost directly behind the second German. Aiming slightly above, he let go a couple of short bursts. Smoke poured from the 109's belly and pieces of fabric flew from the fuselage.

Hugh kicked himself round until he was flying the right way up. He knew that, having crippled the German, he should now break away and make for home. It had been dinned into him enough times. Instead, he followed the 109 round and gave him another short burst which missed.

'Bugger it.'

He glanced anxiously into his mirror but could see nothing. At that moment, from nowhere it seemed, bullets and cannon shells started ripping into his hood.

Before he had a chance to take stock, the whole plane was shaken by a tremendous explosion. Hugh stared wildly around

7

him, but too late, for already the cockpit was filled with a searing mass of flame, that in an instant fused one hand on to the throttle and the other on to the stick, and melted the control panel as if it were so much wax.

The whole of Hugh's face felt tight and drawn; the skin on the back of his hands was beginning to rise in huge white bubbles; both trouser legs were alight and the skin was lifting away from his calves as though they were being inflated by an invisible bicycle pump.

He reached forward into the flames to detach his radio lead and oxygen tube, but to no avail. He slumped back into his seat. He realized that he was being burned alive, yet he felt nothing. Nor did there seem very much he could do to prevent it. He had often wondered during long, sleepless hours how he would think and behave and feel at such a moment. But in fact, he felt and did nothing. Yet something told him he must make one last effort to save himself.

Ripping his right hand from the stick and leaving most of the skin still attached, he reached up to his waist to undo the safety straps. But still he was held in by the radio lead and oxygen tube. Now panic overcame him and he began to scream again and again in utter terror, 'God help me. Dear God, help me ...'

Although by now barely conscious, he succeeded in wrenching off his helmet and groped upwards for the handle to open the hood. It slid open easily. Grabbing what remained of the stick, he slammed it across to the left, and as the stricken plane turned slowly on to its back, he placed his feet against the instrument panel and pushed.

The next thing he knew, he was clear and cool and falling fast. After a moment or two of fumbling, he found the ring to his rip cord and pulled down sharply. For a while nothing happened. Then the parachute began to stream out between his legs. There was a small jerk followed by a much stronger one and both his boots fell off.

The first thing he noticed as he floated gently downwards was his Spitfire disappearing away beneath him like a fireball until it crashed in a burst of flames somewhere near a village to his left. Above him the sky was clear and blue and empty – not a single aircraft in sight. It seemed hardly possible. Had he dreamed it all?

Directly beneath him were hopfields and orchards and nearby a farmhouse with outbuildings and an oast house. A couple of cars were parked in the neatly tended gravel drive in front of the house. He only hoped he wouldn't land in a fruit tree or among the wires and poles of a hopfield. The skin hung down from his wrists and hands in strips, his legs appeared to have grown a pair of white plus-fours and he shuddered at the prospect of all those branches and sharp sticks tearing at the tender remains of his flesh.

He tugged feebly at the strings of his parachute in an effort to manoeuvre himself away towards a grassy meadow on the right of the house. As he did so, he noticed a small delivery van bouncing along the narrow track that led from the main road to the farmyard itself. It drew up in a cloud of dust in the middle of the yard and a man in khaki jumped out holding what looked like a shotgun. Hugh watched with interest, assuming that he had caught sight of a rabbit and was planning to make a quick, inexpensive contribution to the family larder. He was no more than a couple of hundred feet above the ground when, to his horror and disbelief, the man brought the gun up to his shoulder, raised the barrels skyward and aimed them carefully at him.

Hugh waved his arms frantically.

'Not me, you silly sod. I'm English,' he tried to shout. But all that came out was a pathetic, gurgling croak.

At that moment the man fired.

Had most of the flesh on Hugh's legs not been dead already, doubtless the effect of the entire contents of two barrels of a twelve bore discharged at such range would have been considerably more painful. As it was, he felt the sensation of a great number of tiny, very sharp pins being jammed into him, as though an ice-cold shower had suddenly been turned on at full pressure.

Then he was down, on his back, rolling in the deep, cool grass, scrabbling at the safety box in a desperate effort to undo

9

the harness. But the pain it caused his hands was too great and he soon gave up the idea and lay there motionless, his eyes closed against the bright sunshine, feeling faintly sick at the appalling sweet stench of his own burnt flesh.

Hugh was aware of footsteps brushing through the long grass and coming to stop beside his head. With some difficulty he opened his swollen eyelids and saw a man's weather-beaten face staring down at him in an attitude of horrified disbelief. But the sun that shone from directly behind his head was so bright that he closed them again.

He was about to say something to the fellow about the bloody fool with the shotgun when the man whispered, 'Jesus Christ,' and was promptly and very noisily sick. Hugh wondered if it was the ingredients of his lunch or his breakfast that the man was depositing so freely over the grass, and was reminded that he himself had not eaten anything since before seven.

After that there were more footsteps hurrying and a man's voice and a woman's mingled together, brisk and authoritative.

'Who is it? Is it one of ours? Who was that shooting? Is he all right?'

Then: 'Oh, my God,' hushed and reverential, followed by low, urgent muttering. 'Darling, go and ring for an ambulance. Quickly. Then bring a couple of blankets. And for God's sake don't let the children come out here. Tell Nanny.' 'But shouldn't we . . . ?' 'Don't argue. Just do as I say.' Then another voice, rustic and querulous: 'I thought he was one of theirs, you see, sir. I didn't know . . . I didn't realise, you see . . .' 'Never mind that now'. 'Shouldn't we move him indoors, sir?' 'Better not. He might be injured internally. Help me with this, would you?' 'But, all that blood and . . . shouldn't we . . . ?' 'Stop talking and help me here.'

Hugh felt them tugging and twisting at the safety box, but apparently to little effect. He lifted one hand to help, but another took him gently by the forearm and returned it carefully to his side.

'Now you just lie still, old chap. We'll have this sorted out in no time.'

Finally they succeeded in releasing the straps and easing them from under Hugh's body. They then rolled the parachute into an improvised pillow which they placed carefully under his head.

Hugh felt a perfect bloody fool lying there while the two men moved his body and shifted his head and talked about his as though he were a small child. Yet at the same time he felt a curious disinclination to help them. His brain told him not to be so bloody wet and to get up and telephone the Station Commander's office at Woodfold and let them know the form. But his body seemed to have lost all its strength; in fact, it scarcely seemed to be a part of him any longer. He had an idea it might help if somebody loosened his tie and sat him upright, but in the end he decided he really couldn't be bothered. It was so much easier just to lie there with his eyes closed, allowing himself to drift further and further away from the body in which he really felt he had no further interest.

Although he did not realize it, he was dying and doing nothing to stop it.

Later he heard the woman asking, 'Are these all right? They're from the bed in the spare room.' And he felt a blanket being laid over him. 'The ambulance should be here in any minute. Dr Irving's on his way, too.'

It was an attractive voice – low-pitched and capable. He wondered if she looked as good as she sounded. He opened his eyes to look but nothing happened. His lids had now ballooned up into grotesque proportions and become firmly stuck together as if with glue. To Hugh, it seemed that he must have gone blind. In addition, shock had begun to set in, and despite the blankets and the hot sunshine, he felt himself shivering uncontrollably.

'Poor boy,' he heard the woman murmuring. 'Poor boy.'

He tried to smile reassuringly but instead found himself sobbing like a child. He tried to pull himself together, but it was no use. He wanted to say something to the woman with the nice voice – thank you, sorry, anything really. But when he tried, all that emerged was a dismal groan, and then everything went black.

11

Chapter Two

Arthur and Iris Fleming were laying the table for supper when the 'phone went.

During the week they had their main meal of the day in the evening at seven, which gave Arthur time to walk across the fields from the bus stop, change and drink a small whisky and soda while he read the evening paper.

At weekends the routine was different. Lunch was the main meal of the day at one fifteen, while the evening meal consisted of a light snack – cold meat and pickles, cheese, apples – that sort of thing.

Iris was out in the kitchen at the time, so it was Arthur who took the call.

'I see,' he said finally when the Woodfold Station Adjutant's long and hesitant message had come to an end. He was surprised to feel so calm. 'Ashford Hospital you say. I see. About half past two. Yes, that was kind of them. No, not at all. I quite understand. When you say extensive, what does that mean precisely? I see. No, of course, you are only quoting the doctor. Critical condition. I understand . . .'

Hugh's mother entered the room with the cheese board.

'Critical condition?' she asked. 'Who's in a critical condition? Who is it, Arthur? It isn't about Hugh, is it? Where is he? What's happened?'

Arthur raised an imperious hand in his wife's direction and frowned into the mouthpiece.

'No, no,' he said, 'it's nothing. Only my wife. Yes, of course I will. Thank you very much. When may we see him? I see. But that is not to say we may not telephone the hospital for more up to date information? No. I understand. Well, thank you so much for calling. We do appreciate it. And thank you, too, for your kind sentiments, and for what you said about Hugh. It is a great comfort to us. Yes. Thank you. Goodbye.'

He replaced the receiver slowly and carefully, then turned and stared at his wife as though at a stranger.

'That was Hugh's Station Adjutant,' he said dully. 'It appears that Hugh was shot down somewhere near Ashford at around one fifteen this afternoon. He is in Ashford Hospital suffering from extensive burns and in a critical condition.'

Mrs Fleming screwed her face up tight as if in great physical pain. Hugh had said that if anything happened to him, he did not want them getting themselves into a state. He had been quite definite about that. She took a deep breath and clenched her hands tightly to stop them shaking.

'We must go to him at once,' she said. 'He may need us.'

'According to the Adjutant,' Arthur continued, 'he had already shot down one German plane when he became detached from the rest of his squadron. He was attempting to join up with them when he ran into a group of enemy fighters. Six Messerschitts against one Spitfire. He managed to destroy two of them before himself being shot down.'

'That sounds like Hugh all right,' said Mrs Fleming, her voice brisk and matter of fact.

'He will certainly be decorated, according to the Adjutant.'

'Isn't that just Hugh all over?' said his wife, addressing a spot on the wall about a foot over her husband's head.

'He managed to escape by parachute and landed safely in a farm near Ashford. I wonder if it was the Gore-Andrews' by any chance?'

'He was the same when he was a little boy,' Mrs Fleming said. 'Brave as a lion. He never ran away from anything or anyone. Like that time he met that crowd of village boys on the sea wall. You remember that, Arthur. Six of them. He came home a mass of bruises, poor little chap. You remember that.'

She turned to look at her husband for the first time since coming into the room. He was sitting in the occasional chair beside the telephone, tears pouring down his face, staring blankly at the carpet. She had never seen him cry before and for a moment she could not imagine what to do.

After a while he looked up at her and said,

'I asked him what was meant by extensive, but he didn't seem to know. What do you think it means?'

For a moment Iris Fleming looked at her husband sitting there on the occasional chair, his hands clenched firmly on his knees, his body upright, his eyes full of fear. Then she walked across and took his head in her arms and cradled it to her breast, just as she used to do with Hugh when he was small.

It was not until two hours later that they rang Susan. They had meant to try earlier, but somehow the minutes seemed to slip away without their noticing. For a while they had put off ringing the hospital, and when they did finally pluck up the courage, it was to find that there was trouble on the line between Norfolk and Kent. When they at last got through, they spoke to a sister with an Irish accent who said that Hugh was still very weak, and suggested they waited until the following afternoon before coming in to see him.

For a time they considered the advisability of setting off there and then in the Humber, and staying in an hotel somewhere on the way, but, in the end, had decided it would be better to drive into Norwich and catch the first London train the next day. They also agreed that they did not seem to have much appetite, and so they cleared away the cheeseboard and the biscuit barrel and the fruit bowl, and made a cup of tea instead. It all took time.

'I'm sure you're exaggerating, Daddy,' Susan told her father down the 'phone. 'These fighter pilots are always getting their arms and legs scorched. It's nothing out of the ordinary. According to Helena, a chap in her husband's squadron baled out of a blazing Hurricane somewhere near Canterbury a week ago and already he's back flying and none the worse for wear. I think fighter pilots have a pretty good time of it, if you ask me. They seem to get all the excitement, all the limelight, all the kudos, and most of the decorations. Men like James have risked their lives every bit as much crawling round in the mud in France, and yet no one pets them and makes heroes of them. I'm sorry, Daddy, but perhaps if you showed half the concern for us that you do for Hugh, I might be a little more sympathetic.'

Arthur Fleming sighed. Secretly he had always had a soft spot for his daughter, largely because she had never worried him as Hugh had done. He was a man who liked to have everyone's lives photographed, labelled and pigeon-holed, like identity cards. People with unsnappable lives confused and fussed him, and Susan's life with her dull, hard working estate agent husband, and her two small children, had slotted neatly into a special little pigeon hole at the forefront of his mind where he could always reach it without the slightest difficulty.

Not so with Hugh. He had never really been able to form a clear mental picture of the boy's life at school or at university, and this had always slightly irritated him.

They had been down to Eton enough times – taken tea in his room with his titled friends, proudly witnessed his 138 not out against Harrow at Lord's, picnicked with him on the river at Grantchester, and generally tried to take an active interest in his life, in so far as parents who have never had quite the same advantages of education and social unbringing as their children ever can. Whenever he had written to them announcing that he was messing with a viscount or the son of a distinguished banking family and would they be awfully decent and send down a few eggs, they had smiled fondly and sighed and packed the last dozen of their Rhode Island browns in tissue paper in a box and set off straight away for the village Post Office. It was sometimes as much as he could do to afford the school fees, yet Arthur Fleming had always taken the greatest care never to put his son in a position where he felt he could not keep his end up with his chums; and at the end of every holidays and after each school visit, Hugh would invariably find a discreet white envelope on the mantelpiece and, inside, a crisp white fiver and a note: 'To Hugh from his affectionate father, A.D.S.F.' It was the nearest he had ever come to telling

15

him he loved him. He only hoped now that it was still not too late.

Fear stabbed through him. Extensive burns. How extensive? Arms, legs, face? Why wouldn't anyone tell him anything? He wished it were already the next day and that he could already be at his son's side and know for sure. It might, as Susan had said, be less serious than it had at first appeared. And yet something in the Station Adjutant's voice – a certain forced casualness – made him fear otherwise.

The Hon. Bunny Morrell was lying in her bath in Pelham Crescent when she heard the news about Hugh. Mrs Fleming had debated long and hard with herself the rights and wrongs of telephoning her. She realized that Hugh had stopped seeing her several weeks previously, but she had grown fond of the girl in the few months that they had been going out together and coming down to Norfolk to stay, and although nothing definite had been said about marriage, she had already begun to think of her as a daughter-in-law.

Like her husband, Mrs Fleming felt happier when the lives of her friends and family were neatly and comprehensively wrapped up, like parcels. She did not care for loose ends and unresolved relationships. If people could not put their lives into the sort of order that she considered right and suitable for all concerned, then a little gentle nudging on her part might hasten things along.

Like Mrs Fleming, Bunny had never quite understood why Hugh had felt it necessary to go and break things up like that. She realized that his was the more passionate nature of the two and that, had she had a different kind of upbringing, she might well by now have permitted him full expression to his feelings. She was rather sorry in a way to have had to put her foot down, but she could not really believe that it was for that reason alone that he had suggested they should stop seeing quite so much of each other. She preferred to put the whole thing down to tiredness and strain. Deep down, she felt certain, Hugh still loved her every bit as much as he had said he did on the night of the Trinity May Ball, and she quite agreed

16

with Mrs Fleming that Hugh would have wanted her to be one of the first to hear the news. She said she quite understood about not rushing down to the hospital straight away, but that, as soon as he was up and about again, she would arrange something, and she returned to her bath in quite a cheerful frame of mind. A few superficial burns, Mrs Fleming had said; nothing to worry about. All in all, things could have been worse.

At about the same time that Bunny was lowering her slim white body for a second time into her large pink bath in Pelham Crescent, a tall, good-looking volunteer nurse by the name of Jean Cartwright was standing frowning just inside the doorway of the Saloon Bar of the Carpenter's Arms in Harpfield, a long, straggly village at the foot of the North Downs.

It had been no easy matter swapping duty with the Scots nurse from B Ward, and when she first walked into the pub to find Hugh was not there, she regretted having made the effort. Life at Redhill Hospital in the summer of 1940 had been pretty fair hell, especially since the bombing raids on southern fighter stations had started in July. Hardly a day went by when the staff were not stretched to the limit of their capabilities by the admission of yet more civilian bomb victims, burnt and injured pilots – British and German – and badly injured ground crews: the day of the first low-level attack on Woodfold was one that none of them cared to see repeated. In order to make any deal with her Scots colleague, therefore, she had had to promise double duty in return, and the fact that it all appeared to have been for nothing made her very angry indeed. She stood there for a moment, uncertain whether to go on in anyway, or to cut her losses and go home to bed. But then she saw Peter Hemingford pushing his way through the crowd towards her.

'Hullo, Jeannie,' he said, sheepishly running his fingers through his long fair hair. 'Look, I'm afraid I've got a bit of bad news about Hugh. Better sit down. I'll get you a drink. Brandy all right?"

She nodded dumbly as Peter led her to a corner seat and

quickly dived off in the direction of the bar. A couple of pilots on the far side of the room, both from Hugh's squadron, waved and smiled in her direction, but she didn't see them.

It had to happen sooner or later, she told herself. Pilots were buying it every day now – dozens of them. Hardly an evening went by in the Carpenter's Arms when she did not learn that yet another boy of nineteen or twenty with whom they had been drinking and joking the previous evening had 'had it' or 'gone for a Burton' or 'been chopped' or one of the number of euphemisms that the pilots used as part of the defence they had built around themselves against fear and the sudden death of friends. Chris Fitzgibbon had 'bought it' a couple of days previously, on a sortie over the Channel. Hugh had spotted him floating in the sea in his Mae West and had flown round a couple of times, waggling his wings, before radioing for help, but by the time the Margate lifeboat reached him an hour later he was dead. Yesterday Colin Acheson had been seen diving in flames, also into the sea. All friends, all young. One evening they were there in the pub, drinking, laughing, flirting, telling dirty stories; the next day they weren't. It was as simple as that. There was no time or place for grief or if onlys. Others were still alive and that was the important thing. But if Colin and Chris and a dozen others or more, why not Hugh? Or Peter over there, elbowing his way through the crowd with a drink in either hand, frowning and sweating with the effort? Or Bill Carmichael? Or Harry Lauder? Or Jimmy Macdonell? Or Julian Masters? The way things were going, Jean reflected bitterly, it was only a matter of time before they would all be dead.

Why she had believed so firmly that it would never happen to Hugh she couldn't imagine, but she had. To the others, maybe, but not to Hugh. And yet, why not? The only difference between him and the others was that she loved him, and why should that be enough to protect him from German bullets?

And now it had happened. No more splendidly dirty weekends at the Bell. No more snatched days of leave in the little hotel on the west coast of Scotland where they had both once nearly died of cold swimming in the clear, almost Mediter-

18

ranean-coloured sea, and revived themselves by making love, wrapped in a huge blanket, on the sand. No more lying together, whispering and giggling in the ridiculously narrow bed in her rented room above the tobacconist's shop. Never again. She repeated the words to herself several times, trying them out, like a newly married woman trying out her unfamiliar married name. They filled her with a dread, but somehow it did not seem to have anything to do with her; not yet. She absentmindedly fingered the charm in the form of a tigress that Hugh had given her, and rubbed it between her thumb and forefinger, as if this might release some magic spell to bring him back to life.

Peter put the drinks down on the little round table, and the hubbub of the room, which had seemed for a while to disappear completely, now returned with more din than ever.

'He's alive,' he said, 'but in pretty bad shape, I gather.' And he told her what had happened. Tears filled Jean's eyes.

'How bad is he?' she asked in a low, calm voice. She had already dealt with enough burnt pilots to know when she was being palmed off with any misguided soft soap. Peter knew it too.

'About as bad as it could be,' he said, staring into his beer. 'I didn't hear all the details. He's in Ashford Hospital for the time being. As soon as possible they'll transfer him to somewhere bigger – the Masonic in Hammersmith or somewhere like that. After that . . .'

'And his face? What about his face?'

Peter stared into his beer for a moment, then looked up.

'When a petrol tank goes up like that,' he said quietly, 'there's not a lot you can do about it. Any exposed flesh is automatically burnt. The more protection you have in the way of goggles, oxygen mask, gloves, flying boots and so on, the less chance you stand of injury. However, it does get very warm in those tiny cockpits. Some pilots still wear everything they've got; others risk it and leave things off.'

'And Hugh?'

'I don't know,' Peter said. 'It all depends.'

On the far side of the room, half-hidden behind the crush

19

of grey-blue uniforms and sports jackets, three young pilots were standing with half-empty beer mugs in their hands, listening intently while a fourth told one of the exceedingly bad jokes for which he was famous in the Woodfold dispersal hut. The strain and fatigue of non-stop combat showed in the greyness of their faces even from where Jean and Peter were sitting.

It had been three weeks since Goering had launched his all-out bombing assault on British airfields in the south of England, and in the previous six or seven days, the pilots of Fighter Command had been at constant Readiness or Available from 3.30 in the morning until dusk. It was nothing for pilots to make up to eight sorties a day, then taxi in as the light was almost gone and fall asleep in their cockpits even before their riggers had time to open their hoods. During combat, a pilot relied for his life on the speed of his reactions, yet by the last week of August there were very few who could remember when they had last had three decent nights' sleep in a row. Most snatched what rest they could on the hard iron beds in dispersal huts and tents; some had spent nights under the wings of their Hurricanes and Spitfires, using their parachutes as pillows; others had actually slept all night in their cockpits.

Few major airfields had escaped enemy bombing. Tangmere had been devastated by Stukas; Manston, Kenley and Croydon had been hit time and time again; a low-level attack on Biggin Hill by Ju 88s and Me 109s had destroyed workshops, the M/T yard, the armoury, the Met Office, the NAAFI, the Sergeants' Mess, the WAAF quarters and the airmen's barracks. Many ground personnel, including WAAFs, had been killed and badly injured.

During a short, four-day respite between August 20th and 23rd, as many squadrons as possible had been stood down. A few pilots had made their way up to town in an effort to revive their flagging spirits with a spot of high-spirited fun and games, but most by then were so affected by the constant physical and mental strain of combat: of non-stop flying at high altitudes, of lack of sleep, loss of friends and physical injuries, that they had been only too happy to seize the chance of slipping into the doubtful solace of sleep. Too many of them had witnessed

20

the horrors of violent death and suffered the agonies of watching friends spinning to death in blazing fighters for relaxation to come easily. For many, drink had become an important, even essential ingredient of their off-duty lives, hence the enormous popularity and ever increasing bar takings of pubs like the Carpenter's Arms.

But even as they drank and told their jokes and sang their songs, part of their minds were with their equally hard-pressed ground crews who were still hard at work in the blacked-out hangars up on the hill, inspecting, patching, plugging propellors with wax, slapping extra grease on worn parts – anything just so long as the engines were not leaking, the control wires were not frayed, and the planes were capable of taking off and getting through the following day.

'. . . so anyway the foreman asks him, "How's your sex life, then?" ' Korky Catte's story was shaping up nicely.

The three young men comprising his audience were Jimmy Macdonell, Julian Masters and Pat Lumsden. Hugh and they had been at school together and in the Cambridge University Air Squadron, and apart from the odd brief period during training, the four of them had succeeded in sticking together ever since.

Jimmy, fair-haired and broad-shouldered, with a spectacularly broken nose, had won two boxing blues at different weights and had been planning – and rather dreading – an estate management course at Cirencester in preparation for eventually taking over his father's vast estates on either side of the Spey, and his ancient Scottish baronetcy.

But if the war had saved him from the bell, as he cheerfully put it, for Julian Masters, the whole thing had come as nothing more than a bloody nuisance. After a distinguished second year as captain of the college cricket team, he had been promised a job in Fleet Street by his father's old friend, Lord Rothermere, and his frustration at not being able to get on with his chosen profession sometimes unfortunately found expression in his flying. On the other hand, occasional dashes of brilliance more than compensated for his outbursts of careless impatience, and already he had two 109s, a Dornier 17, a

21

Heinkel 111 and a DFC to show for it – all of which merely appeared to increase the air of puzzled amusement in which his features were permanently locked beneath his unruly mop of curly dark hair.

Pat Lumsden, on the other hand, like Jimmy, saw the war as nothing more than an extremely convenient and timely excuse not to have to think up ways of occupying himself after university. Not that the need to earn a living was something that concerned him greatly. His grandfather, thanks to some judicious purchasing of valuable farmland and property in Yorkshire just before the First War, had settled a quarter of a million pounds on his eldest and favourite grandson at the age of twenty-one – an event, the celebration of which must surely have qualified as one of the high points in Cambridge University's long and distinguished history.

However, even Pat had admitted that it might be considered by some rather churlish if he did not put his easily acquired Double First in Classics to some useful purpose. He had vaguely been thinking in terms of some exotic posting in the Foreign Service – the Far East perhaps, or South America – which would enable him to indulge his favourite pastime of travel, as well as to add to his already impressive list of foreign languages. But he wouldn't have to worry about that for a while now.

Six foot six and strikingly good-looking, it was a source of constant wonder to his friends and fellow-pilots that he was able to squeeze himself into the cockpit of a Spitfire at all, let alone knock down Germans with such unerring accuracy. Even the King, after decorating him with the DFC at a field investiture at Tangmere, had asked him how he managed it. 'It's easy enough, sir,' Pat had replied cheerfully, 'I just fold myself in three.'

'... "and did you do as I suggested?" the foreman asked him ...'

The three of them leaned forward expectantly as Korky approached the climax of his story. The strong Australian accent which he had tried with such conspicuous lack of success to

22

Anglicize over the previous two years, was the envy of the public-school accented members of the Mess.

'... "Yeah," said the fellow, still as gloomy as hell. "Well?" said the foreman. "It was O.K.," said the fellow glumly. "Gave the kids a laugh." '

The bellow that erupted from the corner of the bar brought a momentary hush to the high-pitched buzz of conversation. Peter looked across and grinned.

'Korky's obviously in form tonight,' he said.

'Yes,' said Jean dully, wondering, as she had wondered so often before, how it was that, no matter how many of their friends were killed or maimed, they still managed to behave as though nothing had happened.

'Don't they care?' she said, suddenly angry.

'Of course they care,' he said softly. 'We all care. It's because we care so much that we have to carry on as if everything were all right. We're not bloody heroes, you know, whatever the newspapers may say and however much the British public would like to think we are; and we never will be. We are all of us, without exception, as scared as hell. We sit there in that miserable dispersal hut on the edge of the airfield, picking over yet another cold plate of eggs and bacon and beans, dreading the moment when the telephone rings, in case the next time, it's us that won't come back. I'll tell you something. The other morning we were sitting there, about nine o'clock. The Hun was late for once. Suddenly the 'phone rang. The duty corporal answered, a dim West Country fellow with a face like a turd. All at once, from being half-asleep, we were wide-awake, tense, ready to go. The corporal was as boot-faced as ever. 'I see, sir ... certainly, sir ... right away, sir.' He put the 'phone down, turned to us and said, 'Breakfast is on its way over.' Of course, we all made a joke of it and threw cushions at him and called him every name under the sun and so on. But, you know, when I stood up a moment or two later, I found I had wet myself.'

Peter sipped at his beer.

'Oh, yes,' he said, his voice distant and remote, 'we're scared all right. Last week I gave one of our chaps a lift down here to the pub. I wasn't driving that much more dangerously than usual, but I noticed he was holding on to his seat for dear life and his knuckles were as white as his face. I didn't say anything, but just before we arrived at the pub, he laughed and said, "I'm not really as scared as that when I fly, you know."

'I told him that being frightened was nothing to be ashamed of, at which he rather broke down, so I stopped the car until he had recovered. He apologized and said he was still pretty shaken up after his narrow squeak a day or two before. He had broken away after a combat and attached himself, he thought, to a bunch of Spitfires heading for Woodfold. What he didn't realize in his tiredness was that they weren't Spitfires at all, but 109s. Anyway, they quickly turned on him, but instead of just shooting him down and being done with it, they decided to use him as target practice and play about with him like a lot of cats with a mouse. By the time he finally landed, there was hardly a square inch of his plane that wasn't riddled with holes. Not surprisingly, his nerves were equally shot to pieces. I said that surely, in that case, he had every justification on medical grounds, if nothing else, for asking to be grounded. Do you know what he said? "Don't be a clot. This country has paid good money for me to be a fighter pilot and shoot down enemy planes, and as long as I've got two arms, two legs and two eyes, that is precisely what I shall go on doing." '

Peter nodded in the direction of Jimmy Macdonell who had just let forth another of his enormous guffaws.

'That's him over there,' he said.

'Jimmy?' said Jean astonished. 'I would never have believed . . .'

'Neither would anyone else if they didn't happen to know,' Peter interrupted her. 'Don't you see? We *have* to forget, if one of us is unlucky enough to buy it. We can't afford to brood. That way we'd all be completely useless to anyone. Fortunately, nature is very kind to us. When things get really bad, she drops a nice protecting veil over us that closes the nightmare off from our minds. But most of the time, it's up to us. You do understand, don't you?'

He looked at her anxiously. Her eyes were brimming with tears.

24

'Oh yes,' she said firmly. 'I understand. I only wish the rest of us were so lucky.'

Another notable absentee from the saloon bar of the Carpenter's Arms on that warm August evening was Pilot-Officer Robin Bailey. He, too, had been shot down over the Channel the previous week, though suffering comparatively little personal injury, and was even at that moment enjoying the last few hours of a week's recuperative leave at his parents' home in Oxfordshire. Like Hugh, he had always, for reasons that he could never really explain, believed himself immune from fire. He always flew without gloves and always pushed his goggles up on to his forehead once he was airborne. Thus far, at least, his faith had been justified.

How a man who had always taken such care with his cockpit checks, his formation flying and his combat drill could ever have allowed himself to be jumped by a 109 without even seeing him was something that none of them, least of all Robin himself, could quite comprehend.

He had spent nearly three hours in the Channel and was pretty much all in when the Dover lifeboat finally found him. They had been searching ever since seeing his parachute coming down early in the afternoon, but there had been a strong sea breeze that day, and by the time they reached the spot, he had drifted considerably. In fact they had more or less given up hope and were on their way home when they spotted him.

Characteristically, he had made light of his injuries, but had still been sent home for a few days to build up his strength under the loving care of his parents. He had made no attempt to do anything more energetic than read *Vanity Fair* (for the third time), eat hugely and sleep. He had politely turned down the only invitation he had received, and his mother, taking careful note, had made no attempt to invite people to the Manor House while he was there.

He had kissed his father goodnight and was on his way up to his room when Dickie Bird rang and told him about Hugh.

'Under normal circumstances I'd have waited till you got back tomorrow,' he said, 'but seeing as you and he are so close . . .'

25

'That was decent of you, sir,' said Robin. 'How is he – mentally, I mean?'

'God knows,' said Dickie. 'I dread to think.'

Robin had wanted to weep when he got to his room, but found that the tears wouldn't come. He might have expected that, had it been anyone else in the squadron; they had all become so hardened lately to death. But to find that he could not raise a tear even for Hugh shocked him deeply He wondered if he would ever feel real emotions again.

He lay in bed for a long time with the light on, staring at the ceiling. Of all of them, Hugh was surely the most resilient and the most courageous. Outwardly he might affect an air of boredom and disinterest, and joke about his lack of skill and guts, but deep down inside he was probably stronger than any of them. Physical injury was not going to daunt him – even the crippling effects of burnt hands and legs. But disfigurement? That, for Hugh would be a different matter altogether. That was something he might never learn to live with.

Robin put his hand up to his own face and felt the outline of his jaw and the softness of the flesh over the bones. For a long time he let his fingers wander across his features, like a blind man meeting someone for the first time and trying to discern their looks. When he brought his hand down again, he saw with relief that his fingers were quite wet.

Chapter Three

Hugh was sailing home in *Sandpiper*. It had been a late afternoon tide which meant that he had been able to take her up to the beach on the last of the morning water and spend the whole of the long, hot August day walking round the island before drifting home in the evening sun.

Seal Point Island was not really an island at low tide so much as a five-mile stretch of high, grass-covered sand-dunes that lay out on the edge of the marshes like a barrier against the sea. To reach it from the village you either sailed up to it along a broad, winding creek or, at low tide, walked, scrambled and slithered your way along a muddy cockle path that wound its way for a mile or so across the marshes.

After the marsh came a wide expanse of sand, shingle, shallow rivulets and low-lying mud banks which the incoming tide, swirling round through the mouth of the creek, filled with frightening speed, cutting Seal Point off completely from the mainland, and many a summer visitor, mindless of time and dozing in some sheltered hollow in the dunes, had arrived at the water's edge just in time to see George Archer disappearing towards the village in his big blue motor-boat with his last load of holiday-makers for the day.

Beneath the dunes on the far side, stretching in either direction as far as the eye could see, was the beach. When the tide was out, the sea receded so far that the uninitiated bather sometimes found himself wondering, after paddling endlessly through the icy shallows, whether he was going to get more than his ankles wet before losing sight of land.

Hugh had spent many childhood hours wandering along

the shoreline of this vast beach, picking up shells, turning over stones and watching tiny crabs trying to bury themselves in the wet sand, revelling in the huge, empty expanse of sea and sky, but until that day, he had never walked round the whole island. To tell the truth, the solitariness of the place often made him nervous. Sometimes he would experience, for no reason at all, a strange dread that some terrible, awesome manifestation was about to occur – a vast shape was about to loom up out of the sea, or a gigantic airship was about to appear above the sand-dunes, flying very low. He had never actually seen an airship, but he had seen pictures of them in magazines and books, and they frightened him more than anything he could think of. Sometimes he would lie awake at night, unable to sleep for thinking about them. When the *Hindenburg* had burst into flames at Lakehurst, New Jersey, they had shown the ghastly event on Gaumont-Pathé News at the local cinema and he had caught a horrifying glimpse of the vast, flaming monster before he had had a chance to put his hands over his eyes. The fact that people had been burnt alive did not concern him in the least; it was the huge, blazing shape that gave him the nightmare.

And so he had put off the round-the-island project for another year. But then Charles Ackroyd had told him at the local sailing club dance that he had done it with Sally Hobson. They had taken a picnic and spooned in the sand-dunes and, Charles promised, bathed together without any clothes on. Hugh had at once proposed the walk to Amanda Dunbar. He hadn't mentioned anything about bathing, but even so she had told him she had promised to go shopping with her mother in Norwich, and why didn't he go on his own.

So he had, and was glad she hadn't come. She would only have complained and wanted to give up halfway.

It had been a grand day. After a cool, early sea-mist, it had turned into a scorcher and when he had put his Aertex shirt on to sail back, it had felt rough and prickly and he realized his back and shoulders had caught the sun. He hoped there was still some of that calamine lotion in the bathroom cupboard, otherwise he was in for a sticky and uncomfortable night.

28

Normally a tiny breeze would get up as the tide came in, but today, for some reason, the later it became, the hotter was the sun on his face. On either side of the channel, the grass the clumps of sea lavender, which usually grew damp with the rising tide, seemed to be getting drier by the second and shrivelling in the golden heat of the sun. The *Sandpiper's* single, lug-rigged sail hung limp and lifeless, and the little dinghy drifted on towards the village only on the swirling current.

Hugh usually enjoyed this part of the day more than any other, but on this particular evening he felt nervous and on edge, rather as he did sometimes on the beach.

Suddenly he was aware of a dull, throbbing sound that seemed to fill all the air around him. It grew louder and louder, so that the water seemed to be shivering with the force of the sound and the little boat shook and its stays rattled against the mast.

Hugh looked about him but could see nothing. Gradually he became aware that the sound was coming directly behind him. He wanted to look round, but dared not for fear of what he might see there. He had the distinct impression that it had suddenly turned darker and chillier, as though the sun had disappeared behind a large black cloud, and indeed, as he looked, a great dark shadow was spreading rapidly across the pale surface of the marsh.

The throbbing had now become a vast rumble, as though a terrible storm were brewing overhead. Hugh still could not bring himself to look round, for by now he knew only too well what was causing it. But he didn't need to, for now, directly above him, no more than a hundred feet up and slowly overtaking him, was a dark grey rounded shape so enormous and so overwhelming that he thought he must die at the sight of it.

On and on it came, growing ever more gigantic, until it filled the whole sky with its obscene bulk. Hugh could see quite clearly how the outer skin had been drawn tight over the struts of the superstructure. Now the cabin came into view. It was large – large enough anyway to contain a dining room, two or three lounges and smoking rooms, various walkways, and a dozen or more cabins. And yet, attached to the airship's great hulk, it seemed no larger than a sardine would, swimming beneath the belly of a whale.

Hugh wanted to cry out, to express his horror that his worst fear had at last been realized – but no sound came. He tried to cover his face with his hands and blot the nightmare out, but he was unable to move or take his eyes away from it. It was as though he had become hypnotized by the size.

And then an incredible thing happened. A great flame seemed to appear from nowhere and run, at lightning speed, the whole length of the hull. In an instant the entire airship was alight and falling on him. There were no individual flames, just one vast flame, as though someone had set fire to a model made of tissue paper and balsa wood. As the great fireball began slowly to descend on to him, he could see people at the windows of the cabin, clawing and hammering at the glass, the skin drawn tight across their faces, their eyes wide with fear. Some already seemed to be on fire, their clothes and their hair burning and their faces melting in the heat. He wanted to do so many things: to row out of the way, to jump into the water, to cry, to scream – anything. But all he could do was to sit there and wait for the end – as if that was what had been ordained for him.

The heat from the burning airship became more and more intense until he felt his whole body would burst apart like a sausage in a frying pan. He was going to die; he knew that. But at least, in the meantime, he could try and save some of the others. The channel was quite deep enough at that point for anybody to jump into from that height, if only they did but realize it.

'Jump,' he screamed up at them through the roar and crash of the disintegrating hull. 'Break the glass and jump. Now. Go on. Jump, you bloody fools. Jump!'

'There, there, darling,' he heard his mother saying calmly from somewhere in the back of the dinghy. 'It's all right. I'm here.' And reaching forward with a long thin hand, she placed it reassuringly on his shoulder.

Puzzled, he turned his head and stared blindly through the

gauze at his mother, sitting beside the bed, one hand stretched out on his shoulder. Behind her stood his father, frowning anxiously, then giving a small, embarrassed smile as his son's terror melted into relief.

'Hullo, old chap,' he said, in the same voice that Hugh remembered him using many years before when, as a small boy, he had fallen off his bicycle and cut open his head. 'What have you been up to then?'

'I thought he was looking very well, considering,' said Iris Fleming as they drove back afterwards in the taxi to their hotel on the outskirts of Ashford.

'Yes,' said her husband.

What else could he say? That it was possibly the most inane remark he had ever heard in his life?

'Yes, he was.'

The sister, the same one they had spoken to on the 'phone the previous evening, warned them when they arrived that they might be in for something of a shock. Not knowing quite what to expect but dreading the worst, the sight of the heavily bandaged, mummy-like figure lying against the pillows, with its arms propped up in front of it on pillows and only its eyes and lips visible through two narrow slits in the gauze mask that covered the whole of its face, had actually come as a relief. But to say that he was looking well . . .

'Yes,' said Arthur and gave her hand a little pat.

What she did not know and he was not going to tell her was that when he had made an excuse and slipped away from the bedside during one of Hugh's more incoherent periods, he had managed to track down one of the doctors. He had seemed little older than Hugh. At first he had made light of Hugh's injuries and talked cheerfully about having him up and about in no time. But Arthur, who was in no mood to be treated lightly, cut the young man short by saying that if he was not prepared to discuss the matter seriously, he would find someone who was. At this the doctor, irritated by the older man's overbearing manner and exhausted by too long hours and too little sleep, proceeded to describe to him, in rather more clinical detail

31

than he might normally have thought advisable, the full extent of Pilot-Officer Fleming's injuries.

'Well, the burns on his arms and legs are pretty deep and pretty extensive. Short of treating him with tannic acid, there is little more that can be done for the next few weeks other than leaving them to heal on their own. If it's any consolation, the deeper the burn, the more complete the destruction of the nerve endings, and thus the less pain the victim is likely to suffer.'

'I see,' said Arthur.

'Of course, this is only a clearing hospital, you understand. In a few days, when the initial shock has worn off, he will be transferred to a larger hospital with better facilities for dealing with cases like this. Later, after a month or two, he will have to undergo a certain amount of plastic surgery under someone like Angus Meikle at Ashbourne Wood. You may have heard of him. He's had a lot of success with fighter pilots. The arms and the legs can probably be patched up without too much trouble. The hands may be a different matter. I haven't had a chance to examine them closely, but in many cases the fire contracts the skin and the tendons, drawing them back and down – a little like the claws of a bird. Usually, with the help of massage, chaps are able to use them again, although of course they never entirely regain their full strength and suppleness. Anyway, as I say, we've slapped some tannic acid on which will help them heal.'

'And his face,' said Arthur. 'What about his face?'

Outwardly he seemed composed, resigned even. Yet the anxiety and fear behind his dry questioning was undisguisable, and the doctor, regretting his harsh outburst, now adopted a more reassuring professional manner.

'I should explain,' he said, 'that I am not really an expert on burns . . .' He hesitated.

Now it was Arthur's turn to sympathize. 'I quite understand,' he said gently. 'Even so, I should like to have some indication. The gauze over his face . . . it must indicate . . . that is, I realize it must be something serious.'

The doctor nodded grimly.

'Of course you are right,' he said. 'A severely burned face, particularly in its early stages, can be a rather shocking sight if you've never seen anything like it before. Everything swells up, you see . . . In a few days the swelling will do down and the healing process will begin. The dead skin will start to break away, and we can begin to see the true extent and depth of the burning. After, say, six weeks most of the skin will have healed, but as it does so, it tends to contract, particularly round the eyes, and this is where skin grafts are used to correct any distortion. Anyway, that is all some way ahead. The most we can say at this stage is that the left side of his face appears to be more severely burnt than the right, though precisely what effect this will have is difficult to say at present.'

'But will he be badly disfigured?' Arthur asked, his voice quavering.

'I wouldn't like to say how badly at this stage,' the doctor told him gently. 'Anyway, we've sprayed his face with a covering of tannic acid and coated his eyelids with gentian violet – to help the healing process. Now all we can do is wait and see. At present he is very weak. The more he is left to rest the better.'

The doctor paused for a moment and looked anxiously at Arthur, as though fearing that his revelations had, after all, been too blunt for the man to bear and the poor fellow might suddenly collapse on him. But Arthur remained steady where he was, saying nothing, feeling nothing, trying to force the information into his consciousness and make it make sense – or at least seem real.

'By rights,' said the doctor, more to himself than to Arthur, as though he were trying to puzzle something out in his own mind, 'his face shouldn't be as badly burnt as that. It should only be a first, or at most second, degree flash burn. He must have got trapped. If only he'd baled out straight away . . .'

'I must go back,' Arthur said. 'My wife will be worrying.'

He moved, as though in a dream, towards the corridor. Then he paused and turned. 'How long do you imagine it's going to take? I mean, when can my son expect to be restored to anything approaching normal health?'

The doctor thought for a moment. Then he said, 'As I explained, I'm not really an expert in these matters. But given that his hands recover their strength and given that there are no complications – and I see no reason why there should be – I'd say he could quite easily be flying operationally again in a year. Or even less.'

Afterwards, looking down at the white, shrouded shape of his son, lying on the bed in that cold, clinical room, as still and lifeless as a waxwork model in a medical exhibition, Arthur had not been able to resist the thought that, if the sole purpose of mending his scorched and broken body was in order to put him back into a Spitfire and begin the whole process all over again, then it might be better for them all if his hands did not recover their strength, and Mr Meikle suffered with Hugh his first real failure of the war.

'I spoke to one of the doctors,' he told Iris as the taxi turned down the tree lined road where their hotel was situated. 'They are most optimistic about his chances.'

'There you are,' she said. 'What did I say? I said things could have been worse, and they could.'

'Yes,' said Arthur staring out of the window. 'They could.'

Just then they drew up at the hotel, and what with trying to get through to Susan again in Somerset, ordering tea, and trying to plan where best to stay in London when Hugh was moved, and one thing and another, they found that they did not mention the matter again for quite two hours.

Like his mother, Hugh had very little idea of the real extent of his injuries – at least for the first couple of days. Severely dehydrated by the fire, he existed on nothing but saline drips, bottle after bottle of lemon barley water which he sipped through a straw, and three-hourly morphine injections which enabled him to float mindlessly and without great pain in a confused, dreamlike world of low, muttered voices, the smell of ether, constantly changing dressings, and the occasional conviction that he was flying against huge formations of enemy aircraft at 25,000 feet in an unresponsive and unwieldly hospital bed.

34

His only real concern was for the unfortunate farmer and his wife in whose field he had landed and whose Sunday lunch he had almost certainly ruined. He very much wanted to ring them up and apologize for being such a bore and for making such a mess of their spare room blanket, and to thank them for everything they had done for him while waiting for the ambulance to arrive, and it annoyed and concerned him that he still had not done so. Time and again he had asked Sarah, the VAD nurse, to bring him a telephone. However, despite her assurances that she would ask Sister, nothing had come of it. If only they had done what he asked, he would not have felt obliged to call her a selfish little bitch and make her cry like that. It was her own fault.

Once or twice he had dreamed that he had got up out of bed, walked along the corridor and spoken with the couple who had in turn invited him to drinks on Sunday morning. But then he had woken to find that he had done nothing of the sort and had sobbed helplessly like a child, bringing Sister Grice, not with a telephone, but a kidney bowl and a syringe which, to his immense relief, she pushed firmly into his arm.

He had raised the matter with his parents the first time they came to see him, and had even suggested they might like to call the people on his behalf and explain the problem, but they had merely sat there and smiled and told him to rest quietly and try not to speak.

Had he had the faintest idea at the time that, thanks to the combined effects of morphine and grotesquely swollen lips, most of his conversation during the first few days in hospital was rambling and incoherent, he would not have attempted to speak at all. However, convinced in his own drugged mind that he was making perfect sense at all times, he continued during his waking moments to lobby anyone unlucky enough or unwise enough to enter the room – nurses, doctors, his parents, the wretched Home Guard man, even the hospital cleaners. The fact that none of them appeared to take what he had to say seriously annoyed him no end. He was not used to being treated like a backward child and said so on several occasions. But it made no difference.

35

Apart from such traditional childhood complaints as measles, mumps and chicken pox, Hugh had never suffered a serious illness in his life, so that, added to the frustration of being confined to bed at all was that of being unable to judge to any degree the extent of his present state of health.

He realized he had been burned pretty badly. The memory of his blistered hands and legs haunted him constantly and, despite the all-pervading hospital smell of ether and old bed pans, the evil stench of fried flesh was still in his nostrils. But how badly had he been burnt and, more importantly, what had the flames done to his face? Would he be grotesquely scarred like the man who used to serve in the tobacconist's shop in Cambridge? If so, he preferred not to live. And why could he still not open his eyes? The nurses had told him that his lids had been coated in gentian violet, whatever that might have been, and that he was to lie still and not to worry. But was she telling the truth? Had he in fact gone blind and no one had yet dared break the news? Two or three times he had tried to question Sister Grice on the matter while she was changing his dressings, but on each occasion she had passed rapidly on to some other subject. The more she refused to speak about it, the more fierce became his determination to find out. Desperately he tried to force his mind to work, to devise a conversational ploy by which she would be drawn into revealing the truth, but no sooner did he set his plan in action than a further injection would suppress all coherent thought and carry him off once more on a sea of confused tranquillity.

And then, when he was least expecting it, on the afternoon of the third day, he found that he could see again. To the left of his bed, a small window framed a patch of the palest, most delicate blue sky he had ever seen. He stared at it for a long time through puffy, half-open lids, allowing the reality to sink in, before turning his gaze to the blanketed hump covering the lower part of his trunk and legs, and the bandaged hands that rested on either side of him on a pair of pillows.

His initial feeling of relief passed quickly. He did not ring the bell for the nurse, or shout for joy or weep for tears, but lay there motionless, staring ahead of him, wondering and waiting.

An hour later, Sister Grice arrived with Sarah to change his dressings. The one, he was interested to see, was short and stout and grey and every bit as hard-looking as her voice suggested; the other, slim and pretty and even younger than he had imagined.

He waited until they had started to unwrap the bandages on his hands, then said, 'How very pretty you look today, Sarah.'

Sarah spun round, her face flushed with excitement.

'Oh, Hugh,' she said, 'you can see. Oh, I am glad.'

Her eyes filled with tears and she clasped her hands together in delight.

'Nurse, would you kindly pay attention to what you are doing?' Sister Grice barked. 'This is a hospital, not a drama school.' Then, without pausing from her work, she looked up at Hugh, and the faintest vestige of a smile passed across her cliff-like features. 'There you are, you see,' she said. 'What did I tell you? Time and patience. Now perhaps you'll believe me when I say something is for your own good.'

'I'd still like to know what the damage is,' said Hugh casually. 'Perhaps you could bring me a mirror when you've finished.'

Silence. Then: 'This arm of yours is looking better already, is it not, nurse?'

Sarah's affirmative reply was timid and unconvincing. VADs were rarely taken seriously by the regular nursing staff who considered them to be nothing more than spoiled society flibbertigibbets with heads full of romantic notions of saving young officers' lives by dabbing their fevered brows with damp sponges, and occasionally lifting cups of cold water to their parched lips. In fact, most of them worked every bit as hard as their professional colleagues, and one or two, like Sarah, had shown such keenness that they were sometimes permitted to assist with dressings. Even so, they were rarely spoken to unless it was to be scolded, and it was perhaps astonishment at being asked to offer a medical opinion that caused Sarah to be so tongue-tied. But Hugh doubted it somehow. More likely, she was giving a far truer assessment of his condition than Sister was ever prepared to give.

Hugh lifted his head fractionally from the pillow. Between the starched skirts of the two women he could just make out, attached to the end of a forearm that appeared to be suffering from the last stages of leprosy, what he assumed to be his right hand. He stared at it for some time in silence, unable to believe that the shrivelled little black claw, which lay malignantly on the white sheet like a prop in a witches' sabbath, could possibly be any part of him.

'Dear God, what's that?' he cried out.

Sarah looked round at him fearfully, but the older woman continued working quietly.

'Come along now, nurse,' she murmured, 'I haven't got all day.'

Hugh shouted again.

'For Christ's sake, why is my hand that colour?'

The words came croaking and bubbling through his swollen lips.

'Now don't you go worrying yourself about things like that,' Sister Grice told him. 'That's only the tannic acid they put on to heal the skin. It always goes that colour.'

Far from feeling reassured, a chill ran through him, for he knew now for certain that indeed something terrible had happened to his face and that no one had dared tell him.

'I should be glad if you would bring me a mirror,' he said quietly.

'Now what do you want to go looking at yourself in mirrors for?' Sister Grice asked in the humouring tone of a nanny confronted with a spoiled child.

The two women now turned their attentions to his face. First they removed the thin protective gauze. No amount of self-control could disguise the expression of pity and pain that crossed the young nurse's face when the dressing was lifted away.

'Kindly stop treating me like a small child and bring me a mirror,' Hugh mumbled angrily. 'I have a right to see what they've done to me, haven't I?'

Sister Grice straightened up.

'The only rights you have in this hospital, Pilot Officer Fleming, at least so long as you are in one of my wards, are the rights that I grant you. You'll have a mirror when I say so and not a moment sooner.'

'By God, you pompous old cow...' Hugh began, but he never did succeed in giving vent to the flood of invective which he had been storing up for the previous two days. For at that moment the building was shaken by a series of huge dull explosions, each more violent than the last, that had the plaster flaking from the ceiling and Hugh's iron bedstead rattling in tune with the dressings trolley. From the corridor outside came the confused sounds of people running and orders being shouted. Sister Grice looked up briefly, swore under her breath and returned to her work. Sarah, trying hard to conceal her fear, was having difficulty in stopping her hands from shaking.

'The bastards,' muttered Sister Grice. 'Bombing hospitals. What next?'

A German pilot in trouble, more likely, thought Hugh, jettisoning his load.

The next explosion was so near and so loud that it seemed they must have scored a direct hit on the room next door. The glass in the window shattered into a thousand pieces, the ceiling split across the middle, and from the corridor came the high-pitched scream of someone in great agony.

Sister Grice threw her scissors into the kidney bowl with a clatter and strode from the room. Sarah, after a moment's hesitation, followed her. The screaming continued for a while, then stopped as abruptly as it had begun.

Hugh wondered vaguely if he should be trying to shelter under the bed, or at least beneath the bedclothes, but decided he couldn't be fished. He stared at the closed door, then up at the cracked ceiling, then at the blind flapping in the open window. What a joke it would be, he thought, if, after all that, he were done for by some snivelling coward of a Junkers pilot, who, the moment things had become too tough, had ditched his load and hot-footed it back to France. What a joke and what a relief. He smiled at the irony of it, but his face remained as stiff and mask-like as ever.

It was then that he noticed for the first time the mirror above the washbasin in the far corner of the room. Right, he told himself, if they wouldn't bring a mirror to him, then he would bring himself to a mirror – even if he were blown to bits in the attempt. He calculated the distance between the bed and the basin to be about six feet. Four good paces would do it. The only problem was how to manoeuvre himself off the bed and onto the floor. At least there were at that moment no blankets over his legs and trunk to get in the way, and he was already in a half-seated position. So, provided he could swing his legs off the bed . . .

It sounded easy enough, but when it came to it, he found that the muscles in his legs had become so weak that, try as he might, he was quite unable to shift them an inch. Pouring sweat from every part of his body, he fell back against the pillow, cursing and sobbing with the effort. After a while he lifted himself up again until he was in a position to lower his arms off their supporting cushions. He then wriggled them under his legs and, with a sudden movement, lifted upwards.

The fire had not burned quite so deeply into his arms as it had his legs, and the pain that fired up into his shoulders was so great that for a second or two a grey mist swirled in front of his eyes and he very nearly passed out. He relaxed the pressure for a moment and the mist cleared. He sat there, staring at his bandaged limbs, cursing them with a series of oaths and obscenities that even Korky Katte would have been proud of. Then, half-closing his eyes against the agony that was to come, he lifted upwards again. This time the pain was not quite so bad, and he discovered that by inching them in small movements across the sheets, he was able to move his legs until they were resting on the very edge of the bed.

Now it was a simple matter of dropping them on to the floor and standing upright. Agonizing seconds later, he was sitting up with his feet an inch or two from the floor. Holding his hands clear and wriggling forward on his bottom, he straightened his back and slowly slid down until his feet were

40

touching. His elbow banged against the iron bedstead, sending more sharp pains shooting up his arm, but now he scarcely noticed the pain any more, so much was he concentrating on the two or three short paces he would need to take across the polished parquet floor.

So desperately weak were his legs that with the first hesitant step he very nearly fell over. Somehow he retained his balance. The room advanced and receded before his eyes, and sweat poured from his forehead, down his sides and between his shoulder blades as he shuffled across the floor. It took him far longer than he had anticipated, but at last he was leaning against the basin, his hands held rigidly out at his side, panting with the effort.

He paused for several seconds while he caught his breath. Then he lifted his head and, blinking the sweat away from his eyelids, stared into the mirror.

At that moment the door behind him opened.

'Mr Fleming!' barked Sister Grice. No doubt she went on to express herself more fully on the subject of irresponsible patients who could not be trusted for a second . . . the moment her back was turned . . . etc. etc. . . . . But whatever it was she had to say was wasted on Hugh. For as the horrifying hunk of raw, suppurating, bloated, half-cooked meat that had once been his face swam in the mirror before his disbelieving eyes, he lost consciousness and crumpled sideways on to the floor.

As it turned out, the final stick of bombs that the German pilot had so hastily disposed of over the undistinguished roof-tops of Ashford had not landed in the room next to Hugh's, nor indeed, fortunately, on the hospital itself, but in the middle of the car park, thirty yards or so from Hugh's window. Apart from blowing a sizeable hole in the tarmac, and making scrap metal out of one or two of the senior consultants' cars, and blowing in most of the windows on that side of the building, the explosion had caused far less damage than had at first been feared.

One unlucky porter had been badly cut by flying glass; one of the nurses had suffered a broken shoulder when a shelf full of bedpans had broken away from the wall and fallen on top of her; and an unpopular middle-aged business man, who had recently been operated on for a hernia and who had been sitting in the corridor when the bombs dropped, had jumped so much that he had tipped an entire cup of hot tea into his lap – hence the shrieks of agony. None of the nurses had said anything, but secretly they were all rather pleased.

Hugh himself had caught his head a sharp blow against the side of the washbasin when he fell, giving himself concussion and a bump the size of a large hen's egg. But otherwise he was, according to Sister Grice, none the worse for his childish escapade.

'I marked him down as a trouble-maker the moment he was brought in,' she told Sister Macpherson as they drank tea together later that afternoon. ' "We're going to have our hands full with this one," I said to myself, and it seemed I was not mistaken.'

Her grim Irish features softened for a brief moment, and a movement almost resembling a smile played across her thin lips.

'It's just as well I'm not a few years younger, otherwise he'd have me round his little finger in no time, and before you know what, I'd be making a complete fool of myself. I daresay he's broken a few hearts in his time, and despite everything, I'll warrant he'll break a few more before he's done with.'

To the VADs and young nurses unlucky enough to find themselves assigned to her ward, Sister Grice was a woman whose heart had, for reasons they could only guess at, been turned to granite many years before, and it would no doubt have astonished young Sarah Rock to learn that the old dragon was capable of such tender sentiments.

All Sarah had ever felt, as dressings time approached yet again, was fear – not of Sister Grice or of handing her the wrong instrument or even of dropping something, which she had already done on several occasions, but of making a complete fool of herself by passing out in front of both of them. Unlike her friend Veronica in Sister Macpherson's ward, she had had no experience of burns, and had therefore never imagined, when hearing of fighter pilots being shot down in flames, that this was what it meant: hands charred like sticks, legs and arms flayed, faces melted into monstrous shapes without shape, like wax models under a blow-lamp.

Until then, she and her friends had all agreed that there was only one creature more glamorous and heroic than a fighter pilot, and that was a wounded fighter pilot. To be seen dancing close to a tall young officer with a DFC ribbon on his chest and an exciting scar down his cheek had been the ultimate daydream. But a bullet scar, not a burn scar. There was nothing dashing or heroic about a reconstructed nose, or hands that were too bent and too weak to hold you round the waist, or a pair of bloated lips that made her sick just to look at.

She found it hard to imagine that, less than a week before, Hugh Fleming had been a tall, strong, active young man, with everything to look forward to and all the girls running after him. How many girls, she wondered, would come running now?

And yet, despite her uncontrollable revulsion against the smell, the often incoherent burbling, the ugliness, the waste of it all, Sarah liked the young airman.

Perhaps it was the look in his eyes that dared her to pity him; or his determination to bend the hospital rules to his own will; or the relish with which he had told Sister Grice that she was a stupid, stubborn, bog-Irish cow – she couldn't say. All she knew for certain was that in a year's time, when the wounds had healed, and his body had regained its strength, and his mind the will to live, girls would come running again. She was sure of it.

What with all the excitement over the bomb, no one had thought to ring Mr and Mrs Fleming to tell them about Hugh's little adventure, and it had come as quite a shock to them to find him heavily sedated, with yet another bandage round the top of his head, which made him more mummy-like than ever.

However, Sister Grice had assured them there was nothing whatever to worry about, that Hugh had inadvertently banged his head while being moved to safety during the bombing and that they had thought it advisable to give him a shot of something to enable him to sleep for the rest of the day. She did not see that there was any reason at that stage to upset them with an account of his little outing to the washbasin, nor to tell them about the septicaemia which they had found was developing beneath the hard crust of tannic acid on both his hands, and which they had taken the opportunity of his accident to remove.

Nor, fortunately, had either of them asked any awkward question, but had merely sat together beside the bed, their hands clasped in their laps, watching him as he dozed – their faces set in masks of sad resignation.

When Hugh emerged from his nightmare-filled sleep later that evening, he felt lower and iller, and the pain, especially in his legs, was more intense than at any time since he had been brought in.

He told Sister Grice that he was glad to hear that his parents were taking it all so well and that he was sorry to have missed them. He said that, yes, he was feeling much better, and that, yes, Sarah's hair did look much prettier now it had been cut. He even went so far as to apologize to both of them for any unnecessary trouble he might have caused them.

In fact there was only one thought in his mind, and that was that he no longer wished to live. Of that he had no doubt whatever. His suspicions about the true state of his face had been fully justified, and he could see no reason why the world, or he himself, should have to suffer the embarrassment and discomfort of being confronted by it looking as it did. The doctors could talk to him about the wonders of modern plastic surgery until they were blue in the face, but he could see no way that any surgeon, be he the most skilful in the world, could ever make anything remotely presentable of the hideous mess that had stared back at him from the mirror earlier that afternoon. And even supposing they were to succeed in reconstructing the various pieces of skin and tissue that remained, and cobble them together with any suitable odds and ends they might collect from any of the few areas of his body that had been spared, it was perfectly obvious that he would never again hold a cricket bat, or a golf club, or even a whisky and soda with

44

hands like that – let alone fly another Spitfire. In which case, what was there for him to live for?

He cursed the pilot of the 109 for not killing him quickly and cleanly as he had been trained to do, and he cursed the stupid bomber pilot for failing to finish him off once and for all when he had the chance. He cursed the Home Guard man for not waiting until he was well within range before letting him have it with both barrels, and he cursed the ambulance for arriving so promptly at the farm and saving him from death from shock. He cursed Sister Grice for not having the humanity and the decency to add an extra dose of morphine to the syringe and be done with it. And finally he cursed himself for not having the strength or, he had to admit it, the guts to get out of bed for a second time, open the newly glazed window and dash himself headlong on to the tarmac surface of the car park below. And when he could think of no one else to curse, he cursed God and his parents for their short-sightedness and stupidity at bringing him into the world in the first place. And then he started sobbing uncontrollably like a child and, like a child, went on sobbing until at last he fell into yet another disturbed and troubled sleep.

The next morning the door opened slowly to reveal the antler-like moustaches and huge-sprouting eyebrows of Squadron Leader Dickie Bird. For a second or two the ugly, friendly features were creased in anxiety and apprehension, like those of a small boy called to the headmaster's study. But they quickly relaxed into a broad grin, the door was flung open wide and Hugh's squadron commander strode into the room, followed by the tall figures of Peter Hemingford and Jimmy Macdonell, both grinning sheepishly.

For a while they all stood about the bed looking awkward, making facetious comments about Hugh's looks and teasing him about the prettiness of the nurses, and for a while Hugh joined in the jokes as best he could, swapping quips through his dressings and making light of his encounter with the 109s in the same sort of language he might have used at Cambridge to describe a set-to with a gang of townies during Rag Week.

45

The others laughed in return, and called him a silly bugger, and told him next time to wait for the rest of them to get there before having a go, and not to be so selfish and hog all the fun.

But soon Hugh's legs had started to hurt badly, and his joints, aching from inactivity, throbbed dully, and suddenly he didn't feel like making jokes any more. The three men, too, were beginning to feel more and more out of place in the sober, unwelcoming atmosphere of the hospital room, and eventually the lapsed into an uneasy silence.

Dickie Bird then said that he was putting Hugh up for the DSO. Hugh thanked him and said that he didn't really deserve it.

There was another long silence, then Hugh said, 'How's it really going up there?"

It was Dickie who elected to reply.

'Pretty badly,' he muttered. 'Bloody badly actually. The German bombers have been concentrating on the sector stations again. They gave us two days of hell. There were a lot more killed. Planes damaged. Morale is as low as it could be.'

'How about pilots?'

They told him that Korky and Birdy Nightingale had both got the DFC, and Bill Carmichael was about to get a bar to his, and Nigel Hawkesworth had swapped his Alvis for a hair-raising and unreliable Lagonda. Oh yes, and that Jean sent her love and Bunny had rung a couple of times to ask when he was being moved to London.

Hugh said, 'Thanks, but you know what I mean.'

A look of deep sadness passed across Dickie's face.

'What else can we expect,' he said, 'when they send us boys with so little experience that they can barely land a bloody Spitfire, let alone fight in one? It's as much as most of them can do to keep in formation."

Peter said, 'One poor kid arrived the other day – he'd never even flown in a Spitfire. Bill had to go through his cockpit drill with him at eleven o'clock at night with a torch. The next morning he scrambled for the first time. He never even made it off the ground, poor little sod. Run straight into a tree. He was still in coarse pitch. Eighteen years old. Only the other day he was a schoolboy.'

'You heard about Julian?' Jimmy asked brightly. 'No, of course you didn't. How could you have done? Typical form. He only manages to land in someone's walled garden in Godstone, if you please. The owner apparently never batted an eyelid. Invited him to stay for drinks and dinner, asked a few of his own friends round so that Julian wouldn't be too bored, then sent him back to the station in a chauffeur-driven Rolls-Bentley.'

'Some people get all the luck,' said Peter.

'Some,' said Hugh.

There was another long pause while the three of them stared at different parts of the room, each wondering who was going to deliver the news that Hugh would have to hear sooner or later. It was Peter who broke the silence.

'Bad news about Pat, I'm afraid.'

There was little point in saying any more, but he felt it only proper.

'There was a big show the day before yesterday, about the middle of the afternoon. Pat was flying Arse-End Charlie. As usual we were way below height when we ran into them somewhere over Tunbridge Wells. Pat's guns must have jammed or something. Anyway, he flew straight at this 110. Never even tried to pull away. Smashed straight into him. I don't think he fired a shot. He couldn't have known a thing.'

Hugh stared ahead of him, seeing and feeling nothing. Pat, with his brilliant brain and his plans for putting it to some useful purpose. There'd be no more travelling for him now. He'd taken his last journey. What a bloody waste.

'I'm sorry,' said Dickie. 'He was a good pilot.'

'Yes,' said Hugh.

When the three pilots left, Hugh was still staring at the wall, unblinking and motionless.

His parents arrived on the stroke of three, as usual. They told him they thought he seemed a little better, and he told them about Pat. They did not say much, except how sorry they

47

were. After that they sat in silence for a bit, and then Mrs Fleming reached into her bag and brought out a copy of *Three Men in a Boat* which she read to him until it was time for them to leave.

Hugh slept for a couple of hours after they had gone, and woke to find his sister Susan sitting beside the bed. He stared at her for a long time in silence. She looked drawn and thin. Her hair was scraped back in a careless bun, and her eyes, unmade-up, seemed to disappear inside the paleness of her face. She wore a dark-blue cotton dress, patterned with white flowers, and gathered at the waist by a plain black leather belt with which her fingers played constantly.

They had not seen each other for over a year and rarely corresponded.

He was astonished and touched that she should be there at all.

'Thanks for coming,' he said at last.

'That's all right,' she said. 'How are you feeling?'

'Pretty lousy.'

'I'm sorry.'

After that, they talked, without much enthusiasm, about the problems of wartime rail travel, about the hospital and about the children.

'They're with Helena,' she told him. 'They're full of beans – considering . . .'

Hugh frowned.

'Have you seen Muv or Far?' he asked. 'They were here. Still are somewhere . . .'

'I know. I've left a message with the sister to say I've gone up to town to stay with the Bennetts. I couldn't face them now. I'll catch an early train down to Somerset in the morning.'

'Ah,' said Hugh, and for several minutes neither of them spoke.

Then, not because she had ever known him, or indeed even met him, but because she was there, Hugh began to tell his sister about Pat.

She listened without expression as he attempted to put into

words the sense of futility and waste he felt at the death of a man whose talents should have been channelled long since into areas where they could have been put to some real use. The fighting should be left to the hard-nosed professionals like Bill Carmichael and Harry Lauder and Dickie Bird, he told her— men who had been trained to shoot down enemy planes, were good at it, and would go on being good at it and surviving while their under-trained, under-gifted and over-idealistic university colleagues were killed and maimed one after another, often without firing a shot.

'Look at me,' Hugh went on. 'Less than a week ago I might have had something to offer in this bloody war – teaching, writing information films.' He gave a short laugh. 'Even playing in a night club. Whatever it was, I could have achieved far more than I've done as a pilot, and I'd still be doing it now. But what use am I to anyone now? My hands will probably never be able to hold a pen or touch a piano keyboard again, and my face is so hideous that no woman will ever want to come near me again, which puts paid to any hopes I might have had of marrying and bringing up a family.'

Exhausted by the effort of speaking, he lay back against the pillow, his breath rasping through his froth-covered lips.

'When you've quite finished feeling sorry for yourself,' said Susan, her voice low and level, 'you may be interested to know that James is still missing – though in the self-pitying mood you're in, I don't suppose that'll mean very much to you. You have always been selfish and self-centred, and surrounded yourself with people who have flattered you and told you how marvellous you are. If it wasn't your titled friends at Eton, it was that frivolous, so-called smart set you moved with at Cambridge. As far as you are concerned, no one else in this world is worth a fig if they're not part of your smug, self-congratulatory little circle of nobodies. I don't suppose you've ever stopped for a minute to think that there might be others fighting this war, apart from you and your precious pilot cronies. Well, there are, for your information. Hundreds of them – mostly like James. They may not be as clever, or as good-looking, or have such smart friends as you, but they're doing their bit just like you, and being given medals, and being wounded and killed for it, too. I'll tell you something. It's for your own good. You can take it or leave it as you wish. The fact is, all your life you've relied on your charm and your looks to get you by. Thanks to a lucky biological quirk of fate, you have been spoiled from the day you were born. Well, now all that's over and done with. No one's going to want you for your good looks now. From now on, you will have to face up to reality and discover what stuff you are really made of.'

She stood up with a sudden awkward movement, scraping the chair back across the floor, and moved quickly towards the door. She opened it and then, pausing for a moment, she turned and said quietly, with just the faintest hint of sympathy in her voice, 'It's only now that I've begun to discover who my true friends are. And so, no doubt, will you.'

And then she walked away, closing the door quietly behind her.

Chapter Four

1

Hugh and his sister had never really been friends. For as long as he could remember, they had argued and criticized each other. As a small girl, during the holidays, she had resented his passion for masculine games like cricket, bicycle polo and elaborate variations on the cops and robbers theme in which he and his cronies indulged themselves endlessly. On the rare occasions she had asked to join in, they had found some good reason why this would not be possible – it would upset the numbers; they were playing some version of the game which did not admit girls; she would only go and spoil things. From the beginning it had been made perfectly clear to her by her parents that Hugh was the good-looking one. He was the one with the brains, while she would really have to try harder if she wanted to keep up. He was the charming and attractive one; she must make more effort if she wished people to like her. The best she could look forward to in life would be a dull but honest husband, a modest but comfortable home, and polite, uninteresting children. But for Hugh – ah, for Hugh – everything and anything was possible. Beautiful women, a brilliant well-connected circle of friends, a glittering career, money, distinction.

In due course, like a prediction coming true in a fairy story, Hugh grew up to be a handsome, charming clever Etonian and undergraduate, and Susan developed into the plain, un-distinguished young woman she had always been told she would be. Her slightly prominent nose became even more prominent and her shapeless, frizzy mop of dark brown hair contorted itself into yet more shapeless and unmanageable mops. Her breasts grew alarmingly, her shoulders fell forward in sympathy, her hips widened, and her knees and calves grew in support, so that by the age of sixteen the prospect of wearing anything but baggy slacks filled her with deep anxiety.

Her career at Cheltenham was, to quote one of her housemistresses' reports, 'solid without being in any way distinguished'.

Susan had supposed that, as they grew older, brothers and sisters grew closer to one another, and throughout her early adolescent years she had clung to the firm belief that, in due course, her brother would foreswear the smutty, competitive world of public school adolescence, with its deep-seated belief in the natural superiority of one human being over another, its suspicion of women, and its thoughtless cruelty towards the less gifted and the less physically endowed.

But then one day Hugh had come across the lines from Keats's Hyperion about it being the eternal law that first in beauty should be first in might. It was an unhappy discovery both for his less gifted colleagues at school and for Susan. He quoted the words frequently, and believed in the truth of the sentiment with an almost religious devotion. He and his sister had been at each other's throats for so long that he took it for granted that this was merely one of the natural hazards of not being an only child, and her extraordinary outburst in the hospital room had not so much shocked or upset him as puzzled him.

He had never had a lot of time for James Arundel, the slow, rather humourless Carthusian estate agent she had met and married at the beginning of his last year at Eton. He was probably a decent enough fellow, and he made Susan happy, which was something. He had exchanged a few words with him at the wedding, and they had walked together across the marshes one Christmas in Norfolk. But they had very little in common, and he saw no point in pretending to be more pally with him than he really felt. He was sorry, in a detached sort of way, that he was missing in France, and had he had some sort of clue in advance, he would certainly have mentioned the matter to Susan. There was no call for accusations of callousness nor for the attack on his friends at school and at Cambridge. Possibly he had rather 'gone on', as Susan had once put it, about his various visits to Downpatricks in Ireland and in London. But then Adrian was his best friend at Eton, and Lady Downpatrick was always most frightfully gay and amusing and full of plans, and anyway, anything to do with the Downpatricks always made a good story. His parents had always shown every sign of enjoying them, and had encouraged him in his friendship.

On the half dozen occasions Adrian had stayed in Norfolk, he had always treated Susan with the utmost politeness and, as far as he could recall, never once given her cause for offence – no matter what they might have thought or said by way of a joke behind her back. Naturally they had kept themselves to themselves; men do. If Susan really thought that was being selfish or self-centred, then that was just too bad.

Hugh lay there for a long time after she had gone, staring uncomprehendingly at the accusing closed door. Had his friends always flattered him and told him how marvellous he was? If so, it was very decent of them, but it certainly didn't sound like anyone he knew. As for this – what had she called it? – smug and self-congratulatory little circle of nobodies he had mixed with at Cambridge . . . who could she possibly have been referring to? She had never, as far as he remembered, met any of them, or, for that matter, even been to Cambridge.

Looking back on those days – it seemed another world now – he had not been particularly keen on politics in the sense that he had been an active member of any of the political clubs that flourished at Cambridge. Nor was he a regular attender of the weekly political debates at the Cambridge Union. Indeed, the only occasion he had ever taken part was to second a motion, duly carried, in a May Week Debate, that women should be seen and not heard.

Which was not to say that he or his friends were totally unaware of the state of affairs in Europe. They were agreed that it was only a matter of time before war came, and when

53

that happened they would, of course, join up – not out of an unthinking sense of patriotism, nor because they were longing for some cause to fight for (as far as they were concerned, the Spanish Civil War had been a private, domestic matter, to be sorted out by the Spaniards themselves, and no concern of anyone else) but simply because they did not care for the Germans or for their regimented way of thinking, and felt it was high time they were taught a sharp lesson once and for all.

Many of them had already joined the University Air Squadron, and it went without saying that when the time came, they would join the Air Force. If they were going to have to fight, they might as well do so in the most amusing, decent, chivalrous (yes, they had even used that word) way possible.

Hugh could picture Pat Lumsden even now, almost prone in the old leather armchair in his room, his feet resting on the top of the mantelpiece, using match after match on the pipe which never seemed to draw properly, declaring in his lazy drawl, 'As I see it, being a fighter pilot is the last remnant of old-fashioned single-handed combat. It's you against the other chap. Either he kills you or you kill him. It's quick, clean and decent. It's also a damned sight more comfortable than crawling on your face in six inches of mud with bullets whistling about overhead and shells falling all around you, simply because some halfwitted general, swilling brandy in a farmhouse miles behind the lines, has decided the time has come to issue a few orders. I can't imagine a more inhuman or more futile way to end my days.'

'I agree,' Jimmy MacDonell had joined in. 'At least you know where you are in a fighter plane. The alternatives are reasonably clear cut. I mean, either you're dead, or else you finish up like a hero out of Boy's Own and pick up all the pretty girls in the Berkeley.'

'Rather like getting a boxing blue,' laughed Julian Masters.

'Exactly,' said Jimmy.

All right, so they had been cynical and effete, and had talked about war as though it were just another game to be good at. But that was not to say they were frivolous. Hugh and his friends had formed an unashamedly tight-knit group of snob-

54

bish public school hearties, intolerant of grammar-school swots and others who appeared to be trying too hard, and suspicious of anything remotely aesthetic or intellectual. Theirs was a proudly masculine club into which women were not so much admitted as allowed on an occasional guest ticket for May Balls, the Varsity Match, and punting parties on the river. Oh, women were all right in their way, and in their place, as long as they were pretty and knew how to dress and drink cocktails and laugh at silly things, but not if they were going to start jawing about politics or art. Actresses were the safest bet. They were jolly and pretty and didn't start kicking up a fuss the moment you put a hand on their knee. Some debutantes could be good fun, too. At least they didn't try to join in the conversation – like that dreadfully serious blue-stocking type Simon Cattanio had turned up with at the Trinity May Ball who had tried to get them all to join the Labour Club. Poor old Simon, they'd never let him live that down.

Hugh himself had very nearly fallen into the same trap in the early summer of their second year. Her name was Marjorie Fisher, and he'd bumped into her on the river bank of all places. It had been a perfect early May afternoon, not a cloud in the sky, and the trees heavy with blossom. She was sitting on a rug, on the bank opposite King's, painting. She was not the sort of girl Hugh would normally have addressed out of the blue. She wore a plain skirt and a jumper, and no make-up; her fair hair was cropped close around her plump features and a pair of round black spectacles were perched halfway down her nose. But Hugh had been struck by her technique, even from some distance. It reminded him of some of the water-colours he had done of the chapel during his second year at Eton, when he had won the Holiday Prize two years running, and there had been talk of his taking it up professionally one day – before he had discovered how much more fun it was to be good at games.

He had told the girl how much he liked the picture, and they had got talking. He had, he remembered, been surprised at how much easier it had been to talk with her than with the debs and society girls he usually asked down. If he had talked to them about art and painters, they would have stared at him in blank disbelief, and his friends would have ribbed him unmercifully ever after and accused him of that most heinous of offences – being a secret intellectual.

But Marjorie really seemed to understand what he was trying to say even before he had said it, and told him she'd like to see some of his paintings, and suggested they might go sketching together. Hugh had smiled his famous distant smile and said that would probably be very difficult because of his cricketing commitments.

'How could you even consider the idea of putting games before painting?' she had asked in genuine astonishment.

He had explained that these were not just any old games of cricket, and that he was expecting that year to get his Blue. But he might have announced that he played tiddleywinks for the university for all the impression it had made on her.

They had met again, a few days later, in her rooms in Girton (he could not risk bringing her into his own college), and he had taken along one or two of his water-colours, including the Holiday Prizewinner of the Norfolk marshes. She regarded them for a while in silence, then said, 'What a terrible waste.'

He frowned and asked her what she meant.

'Not the pictures, silly,' she replied. 'Playing games when all the time you could be doing this.'

He'd promised himself he wouldn't see her again. It was easy enough to find an excuse – family up for an unexpected visit, pressure of work. But then he'd found he wanted to see her again, and talk about painting and books and ideas. She discovered that he had once been a promising pianist, and persuaded him to play for her on the old upright in the college music room. It was rather out of tune, and he played a showy piece of Liszt so that it didn't really matter. She was genuinely impressed and chided him again for letting it slide, like the painting. The way she put it, it all seemed to make very good sense. But once back in the company of his friends, talking cricket and golf and flying, drinking and playing endless games of poker, his time with Marjorie Fisher seemed remote and unreal – as though it were part of his life when he was young. With them, he was at least comfortable and secure. They did not say things to him that reminded him of what he might or should have done; no one made him feel guilty about enjoying what he was good at, or question his long-held assumptions that, whatever else happened in the world, he would automatically be assured of a straight and easy passage through life.

And yet suddenly he was no longer completely happy. After all those years he had been found out. He had been reminded that he had shelved his responsibilities and chosen the easy way out, because he had known that whatever path he chose to follow, it would please his parents. They had scrimped and saved to buy the privilege and connections that Eton and Cambridge could offer, and they had not been disappointed. What more could be expected of him?

He and Marjorie met several times in the weeks that followed.

'I think Hugh's got some poppet tucked away in the town,' Adrian Downpatrick declared one day, after he had persistently refused to tell them why he had skipped nets and couldn't be found anywhere for hours.

'Sounds like a good title for a song,' Jimmy called out.

'Who is she, Hugh?'

'Is she a married woman? Is that why you can only see her in the afternoons?'

'Perhaps Hugh has a secret predilection for tarts. You might let us in on it.'

'No, I reckon she's something pretty special and he doesn't want us to meet her in case she takes a shine to one of us.'

'Which of course, she undoubtedly would.'

But despite their taunts and jibes and constant questions, Hugh had smiled and said nothing. Secretly he would have liked them to meet Marjorie, and to discover what sort of stuff their old friend was really made of. She'd certainly have given them something to think about. Marjorie had once or twice expressed an interest in meeting them, and seeing for herself who these young men were and what it was that had seduced Hugh away from the things that really mattered. But he had always found excuses why this would not be possible. So long as they remained inanimate objects of conversation and speculation, her worse fears could not be realized and he could continue to put up a case for himself. More importantly, there would be no chance of their misunderstanding his relationship with her and thus casting him out from the group.

Then one day, walking by the river, she asked him what he was planning to do after Cambridge.

He replied airily, 'Oh, you know, the usual sort of thing. Civil Service, overseas administration, you know the sort of thing. I know plenty of people. It shouldn't be too difficult to come up with something.'

She said, 'Those well-to-do friends of yours are an even worse influence than I thought. Just because they won't have to worry about mundane things like making a living, doesn't mean you are also exempt. They come from a different world from you, no matter how much you try to persuade yourself otherwise. If they don't have money themselves, they have fathers who will support them until they do. You don't. If you don't start taking life seriously very soon, all you'll finish up with is your good looks and your charming ways, and the way the world is going, they won't be enough to keep you in socks.'

Hugh laughed. 'I really don't think you need worry your head about me. Anyway, there's bound to be a war soon, and that'll take care of all our futures for a while.'

Marjorie stopped walking and looked around her at the college buildings, glowing grandly and reassuringly in the late afternoon sun.

'I certainly believe that if we win, and I cannot believe that we won't, it would free the world from the threat of tyranny.'

'And leave the world a better and happier place, fit for heroes, I suppose?'

'I can't see any point in fighting otherwise.'

'I wish I had your simple faith,' said Marjorie.

Hugh half-smiled, half-frowned at her. But she was not to be humoured.

'My belief, for what it's worth,' she said, 'is that another war will alter life in this country in a way that those who are born in after years will never fully be able to comprehend. Every-

58

thing that you and your friends and people like you have taken for granted all these years – wealth, privilege, everyone knowing his place, loyalty, service, a fair day's work for a fair day's pay, the whole idea of a society governed by an educated elite – all that will be turned on its head. Every assumption will be questioned, every cosy, comfortable belief in the status quo put under the microscope, dissected and re-structured until it is unrecognisable. Physical poverty will be abolished, only to be replaced by a poverty of spirit. Everyone's needs will be catered for, everyone's distress will be eased, and everyone's natural wish to fend for himself will seem as anachronistic and outdated as visiting cards. You may destroy one tyranny, but another will grow in its place that, in its way, will be equally destructive – I mean, the tyranny of the ordinary man, with his undeveloped tastes and his mistaken belief in his own power for good.

'You can forget breeding, charm, manners, education. From now on, a minimum of education and a very great deal of native cunning will be the sole qualifications for survival and success. That, and a profound belief in the idea that you need never worry about anything again because someone will always be there to help. And the quicker you and your cronies prepare yourselves for this bright new world, the better.'

After that, Hugh had known that he would never be able to introduce Marjorie to his friends. It was one thing to be witty and clever, but to be controversial and disturbing was unforgivable.

Lying in his hospital bed now, Hugh reflected bitterly on the irony of Marjorie's words and how much worry he would be happy to suffer rather than have to rely on others for every sort of help, as he was now having to do, and would probably have to do for some time to come.

That afternoon was the last occasion he had seen Marjorie. Both had suddenly become too occupied for painting or music – he with his elusive Blue, she with a college drama production and exams. He had missed her for a while; but then, at a debutante dance in London, he had fallen in love with Bunny,

59

and had soon forgotten all about her. This was the first time he had thought about her for several months.

He was sorry now that Susan had never met her. If she had, she might have been less hasty and sweeping in her condemnation of his Cambridge friends. No one could have accused Marjorie of being frivolous, smart or smug.

She might have been less scornful, too, of his fellow pilots had she known Robin.

2

Hugh met him first in the lounge of the Victorian hotel in Newquay which had been appropriated in the autumn of 1939 as the headquarters of the No 8 Initial Training Wing. Robin had learned to fly with the Oxford University Air Squadron before the war. He had been attested into the RAFVR in June of 1939, and in September, as a Sergeant, had reported to the Volunteer Reserve Centre in Oxford. (Hugh had gone through the same process in Cambridge.) It had been a frustrating period for all of them. There had been a good deal of marching, mainly from the station to various colleges, where they slept on mattresses, and back again, but little else. Everyone at that time, it seemed, was a sergeant, so they took it in turns to command their platoons. They never saw an aeroplane and had to be satisfied with lectures on theory which were so dull that the university pilots often cut them altogether.

Fortunately for Hugh, several of his old Air Squadron chums were there too, kicking their heels – Jimmy, Pat, Adrian, Nigel Hawkesworth – and they'd carried on very much as they had done at University, drinking, talking, playing endless games of improvised indoor cricket with a tennis ball and an old ping-pong bat. Twice, they had managed to scratch together a couple of teams for a real game on the Trinity College ground. It had been difficult to take service life seriously.

But then, at the end of September, Hugh had heard that his application for a commission had been approved based on the evidence of his proficiency certificate from the University Air Squadron, and a day or two later he had been gazetted 55383 Pilot Officer H. C. R. Fleming, RAFVR, and told to report in a fortnight's time to Newquay.

Adrian, Jimmy and Pat had been posted to Sealand near Chester, but Nigel Hawkesworth was at Newquay, as, too, were Peter Hemingford and Julian Masters. Having anticipated a spacious room overlooking the sea, and rather good hotel food, it came as something of a disappointment to find they were all to be billetted in viewless old guest houses, filled with tiny ancient individuals, huge ancient furniture and a constant and overpowering smell of cooked cabbage.

At first they had been highly amused at the quaintness of it all and had giggled endlessly, like schoolboys, at the promptness and inedibility of the 12.30 lunch and the 7 o'clock dinner, the flying ducks on the dining room wall, the hand-written rules behind the bedroom doors, the humourlessness of the landlady and the proportions of her daughter. Once, Peter had wagered a fiver with Julian that he could seduce the daughter, whose name was Daphne, in two days, and had slipped a note under his pudding plate at table inviting her to his room. Everyone had agreed it was worth five quid just for the story of how Peter, hearing a knock on his door later that night, was so excited that he rushed across the room, forgetting he hadn't a stitch on, and opened it to the landlady who announced that if there was any more nonsense she would be reporting him to his commanding officer. A couple of days later, Hugh had performed the dastardly deed himself.

For the first few days, their time was taken up to such an extent with lectures in navigation, armaments, Air Force Law, aircraft recognition and signals, long, senseless bouts of drill, P.T. and team games with rubber balls in the hotel car park and, when he was not working, with his own friends, that he scarcely bothered with any of the other officers – especially not the over-keen grammar school types, who were constantly asking questions and staying on afterwards to write up their notes – like the short, slightly balding, sandy-haired fellow he had sat next to at one of the navigation lectures.

61

In fact he would probably never have spoken to him at all had he suddenly one day not remarked pleasantly,

'I wish I found all this as easy as you obviously do. I can't remember a thing unless I pore over it like a medieval monk for hours afterwards.'

Hugh had got into conversation with him, reluctantly at first, but then more enthusiastically when he learned that he was a Balliol man, and a Wykehamist. Somehow he just didn't look the type.

For the first few days, Hugh, believing him to be as dim as he had claimed, had not taken him very seriously. Only gradually did he discover something about the man's background, and always through other people – his Winchester and Balliol scholarships, his expected double first in Greats, his family estate in Oxfordshire, his aristocratic connections.

Before long they had become close friends. Both found things to admire in the other that were lacking in themselves. Robin's unashamed passion for, and knowledge of, music and literature, his confidence in his own tastes, and his boundless enthusiasm appealed to Hugh and showed up his own cynical attitudes and second-hand theories for the poor substitutes for real thought and real feeling they were. Like Marjorie, Robin never allowed Hugh to get away with anything. When Hugh had confessed that he found it impossible to believe that he was fighting the war on behalf of anyone but the people he knew and liked and had been brought up with, Robin had replied in his quiet and unemphatic way, 'War is not a private crusade to which only the intelligent and the wealthy are invited.'

Although only twenty, Robin seemed much older than his contemporaries. This was partly due to his premature baldness, partly to his cheerful acceptance of even the most irritating rules and regulations, and partly because of his obvious determination from the outset to derive as much knowledge and experience from the different courses as he possibly could. It was true that his classically trained brain could not easily absorb all the technical information; but although his dogged eagerness inevitably came in for a certain amount of good-natured mockery from his fellow pilots (a chap who not only tried but was seen to try was rather letting the side down), there were few who, deep down, did not think his style rather fine.

For his part, Robin envied Hugh the physical confidence he derived from his tall, athletic figure and his astonishingly good looks. It was quite obvious he was going to be an outstanding pilot. He really did not have the slightest difficulty either understanding the lectures, or – and this was what Robin envied Hugh more than anything – charming women. He himself was too short and too shy to make an immediate impression. At social gatherings he seemed at times almost to disappear into the background, and he welcomed the small amount of reflected glory he derived from his new, glamorous friend.

He felt that intellectually Hugh had not made the best of himself, and his naivety and dependence on the opinions and ideas of others sometimes astonished him. But at the same time he respected Hugh's honest admittance of his own blinkered vision, his constant questioning, and his need for reassurance. Above all, he admired Hugh's fearless courage. Mentally and emotionally his defences were perhaps not as well prepared as he might have wished, but physically he was as strong as a rock.

They had remained at Newquay for nearly a month, marching up and down the front, forming threes and having their hair cut at uncomfortably frequent intervals.

Finally they received their postings to various flying training schools. To Hugh's disappointment, Robin, Peter and Julian were told to report to an obscure station on the west coast of Scotland. Hugh and a rather dull man from London University named Opie were sent to a training unit in Gloucestershire where they found Jimmy Macdonell and Pat Lumsden, both in high spirits despite an uninspiring few weeks in Cheshire and looking forward to flying at last – even if it was only in old Hawker Hind 2-seater fighter-bombers.

Here for the first time they were to experience the suspicion and disapproval that the regular members of the RAF showed towards RAFVR officers – or the long-haired boys as they were known. And here, too, they were to come into close contact with the great cross-section of raw, inexperienced young men from many different walks of life who, over the next few months, would be taught, cajoled, bullied and moulded into highly-skilled Air Force pilots.

They ranged in age from late teens to late twenties. They were lawyers, engineers, schoolmasters, merchant seamen, schoolboys. Many had joined on short service commissions – some because they wanted to be ready in the event of war, others simply because they wanted to learn to fly, others again because they feared unemployment, and the Air Force offered, if nothing else, regular employment. Some had already done a little civilian flying; several had never set foot in an aeroplane in their lives. Most took to it easily; a few were so frightened they were physically sick before going up. All were treated by their sergeant instructors with good-natured contempt.

At first, without Robin's tolerant hand to guide him, Hugh found it hard to mix comfortably with those whose backgrounds were markedly different from his own. In off-duty moments, he moved automatically towards the other long-haired boys, justifiably earning himself a reputation as a cold and superior bastard. Secretly he rather enjoyed it.

With his instructor, however, a caustic Scotsman by the name of Sergeant Gillespie, Hugh struck up a fruitful and friendly relationship, and thanks to his enthusiasm and Hugh's own natural ability, he quickly became known as one of the most brilliant, if on occasions reckless, pilots on the course.

They all had their share of amusing minor accidents and near misses.

Once, Jimmy Macdonell succeeded in landing a Harvard with his undercarriage still up. On another memorable occasion, an Irishman called O'Rourke found himself approaching the runway too high, too slowly, and with not enough power. Instead of applying full power and trying again, he put his plane down, slap on top of the C.O.'s herbaceous border.

And there were bad crashes, too: George Lowe, nineteen years old, who tried to take off in coarse pitch and flew into an oak tree; Bob Bates who, at the end of his first solo circuit, applied his brakes too hard, tipped his Harvard upside down on its back, then made the fatal mistake of undoing his harness, falling out on his head and breaking his neck.

Already, the young pilots were beginning to withdraw into a world of their own. They were finding it less and less easy to converse with the civilians who were so eager to entertain them and make heroes of them; even with their own families. People expected them to act raffishly, and occasionally they would derive a certain satisfaction from behaving as expected. But on the whole, they were really only happy back in the closed world of the Mess with its slang and its improvised rugby games – talking shop, reading comic magazines, boasting about their achievements.

Was it really any wonder that the outside world thought them rude and arrogant? And that Susan had accused them of being precious and over-glamorized? How could one persuade people otherwise, when the newspapers and popular opinion were determined to portray them as the saviours of the nation? They had never asked to be heroes.

If only, Hugh thought, turning his attention now from the closed door to the high, cold hospital ceiling, if only Susan had met some of those men: ordinary blokes like Lowe and Opie; hard professionals like Sergeant Gillespie and Tubby Saunders, the station commander; even long-haired boys like Jimmy and Pat and Nigel Hawkesworth. If only she could have seen Julian wetting his trousers on his first solo night circuit when he thought he was lost, or Adrian rushing out to be sick when his name was called for aerobatic training, or Bates lying there under his plane with a broken neck, like a stupid stuffed doll . . .

It was perfectly true that by early May (was it really four months ago?) Hugh and several of the others were rating themselves pretty hot stuff as pilots. They had completed 125 hours on five different types of aircraft, and they all passed their Wings exams with various degrees of proficiency. The news that only two were to go into fighters came as a great shock. Of the rest, six became instructors, eight were divided between bombers and coastal command, and Hugh, Jimmy and Pat were posted to No. 1 School of Army Co-operation at Old Sarum in

Wiltshire to fly cumbersome Lysanders, high-winged Stols, and twin-winged Hawker Hectors.

Fortunately they were in good company. Robin was there, and Julian, and Nigel Hawkesworth, who said Adrian had finally been forced to admit to his pathological fear of flying and had recently been commissioned in the Irish Guards, which was where he should have been all along.

Despite the frustration of being away from the centre of things, Hugh enjoyed the course, especially the morse and aerial photography. In the evenings, they sat about in the Mess, drinking beer and playing cards. Occasionally they drove into Salisbury and got tight there instead. Twice, Hugh had managed to get up to town for the night to see Bunny and take her to the Berkeley. But things were not going well between them, and he had returned angry and depressed. Robin had listened patiently, as he always did, to Hugh's tales of frustration and discontent, and said that girls who used sex as a carrot to lure men to the starting gate were not to be trusted. But Hugh was still in love and Robin's advice, for once, went unheeded.

At times it had seemed to Hugh that he would not only never achieve his ambition to fly a Spitfire, but would be lucky if he even became operational.

Then, suddenly, Dunkirk, and stories of the sorry remains of an army, without their guns, in some cases without their boots and trousers, and suddenly without hope. To the pilots at Old Sarum, this Pyrrhic victory, although blazoned across the newspapers and broadcast on the wireless, was still as remote and unreal as the Somme. It was hard to comprehend that an entire army could be destroyed just like that.

Soon the effects began to be felt more widely. Personnel were ordered to remain at all times within half an hour's call of the airfield, and suddenly invasion seemed a very real possibility.

A week later, to their amazed delight, Hugh, Jimmy, Pat, Robin and a dozen other pilots were on their way to No. 54 Operational Training Unit at Acklington in Northumberland to learn to fly Spitfires.

After all those months of training and lectures and disappointment and waiting, it was not to be wondered at that they were excited as schoolboys about to get their first game in the school XI. The Spitfire proved to be every bit as fast and manoeuvrable and exciting to fly as they had been told it would be. To Hugh, from his very first solo, it seemed impossible to make a mistake. On his second time up, he was throwing it round the sky like a veteran. After that, he began to learn how to fight in it. He was taught how to use his R/T; how to fly purely by his instruments; how to fire his eight Browning machine guns; how to fly in V formation, then line astern, then echelon port or starboard; how to evade attack with a half roll and a controlled spin; how to bring down an enemy plane with raking fire along his side.

Still he was not entirely satisfied, for still he had not been in combat; but he had good reason to be pleased with himself. He was a bloody promising fighter pilot, and he knew it.

Ten days later, the four long-haired boys were posted to 89 squadron at Tangmere.

Hugh could remember that first day as if it were yesterday. Cleaning his buttons, calling first on the squadron adjutant, then Squadron-Leader Dickie Bird. Being given his flight, then being sent off to the equipment store to draw his helmet, Irving flying suit, flying boots wth wool linings, thick leather gauntlets and silk liners. Then checking into the Mess, being allocated a room and signing his name in the membership book. Reporting to the tent that was his flight commander's office, and Bill Carmichael saying, 'You call me Sir first thing in the morning and salute me, and you do the same last thing at night. In between, you call me Bill, or any other four-letter word that occurs to you. Sergeant!' Flight Sergeant Reddish marching in. 'Pilot Officer Fleming claims to know how to fly a Spitfire, Sergeant. Better drag out one of our oldest ones, just to be on the safe side.' Learning how to fly operationally as a member of a squadron; the importance of working together as a team and understanding the squadron commander's every order; of never following an enemy plane down after hitting it; of never letting yourself be alone in the sky, even for a minute;

67

of giving yourself a stiff neck from constantly looking about you; of wearing a silk scarf to avoid chafing; of never leaving off gloves and goggles . . .

On June 25th he had flown to Church Fenton to be tested by the AOC No. 13 Group. Four days later, he learned he had been passed as operational. Pat had also been passed; Jimmy and Robin had not been so lucky and were posted to Hawarden for further training.

'Never mind,' Hugh told them cheerfully in the Anglesey Arms in Halnaker that evening. 'Things might have been worse. You might have been shuffled off into a Battle squadron. At least you're still flying Spitfires.'

Robin grinned and stroked the already luxuriant growth that had appeared on his upper lip as if to compensate for increasing baldness. 'Just you wait, chum,' he said. 'We'll be up there with you any time now. In the meantime, don't either of you go doing anything silly, like forgetting to look in your mirror. We long-haired boys have got to stick together. We'll be needed when all this is over.'

A week later, Hugh shot down his first German. To his surprise, he felt absolutely nothing at all, except perhaps a certain grim pleasure at a job well done. That same evening, he told Bunny that he couldn't see her again. He came back to the station feeling like a murderer, and the look of pain on her face haunted him for weeks.

Lying in his hospital bed now, he hoped he would not be equally haunted by Susan's words. What on earth could have persuaded her to travel all that way from Somerset like that? Was it simply for the satisfaction of seeing her superior elder brother getting his just deserts? Surely she couldn't hate him that much? Could it perhaps have been to talk about James? If it was sympathy she was after, she had certainly gone a funny way about it. Was she at that moment on her way back to Somerset – or was she putting up somewhere for the night? With Muv and Far perhaps? Very odd . . .

Hugh was getting tired again and he was finding it difficult to make his brain work coherently.

Bunny . . . Was she the clue? Someone had told him she had

telephoned, or was coming to see him or something. Peter? Susan? Susan had very much disapproved of the way he had treated Bunny. Thought he had behaved like a cad. So that was why she had come. No, that was Muv who had liked Bunny. But Susan had said he was spoiled. What *could* she have meant by it? Said he'd find out who his friends were now. Bloody fool. Why should they be any different now than they were? He knew who his friends were, thank you very much. Didn't need telling. Robin, Peter, Jimmy, the long-haired boys ... got to stick together ... Julian, Nigel, Pat ... no, not Pat ... he was dead ... poor sod ... lucky sod ...

Then Hugh fell asleep.

Chapter Five

When Sister Grice arrived the next morning to change Hugh's dressings, she had a morning paper under her arm and an unaccustomed twinkle in her eye. Her voice, however, was as severe as ever.

'Well, Pilot Officer Fleming,' she said, 'I suppose that Nurse Rock and I should be honoured to be tending the wounds of one of our nation's heroes.'

Hugh looked at Sarah who was standing beside her, grinning shyly.

'What?'

Sister Grice threw the paper casually on to the bed.

'Unless, of course, this is just another of your devious plots to get more attention than you deserve.'

'I have no idea what you're talking about,' Hugh told her.

'False modesty ill becomes you,' she said. 'Nurse, perhaps you had better put the brave man out of his misery while I make a start on these.'

Sarah picked up the paper, unfolded it and held it up in front of Hugh's puzzled eyes.

It was on an inside page, but it was unmissable. A large headline: 'ONE OF THE FEW', and underneath it, a photograph of Hugh in uniform, and two half-page columns of small print.

'Aren't you pleased?' Sarah asked him.

'What the hell's it supposed to be?'

'It's an article. About you, and how you shot down that German that day, even though your plane was on fire. It's very good; very well written. The nurses are all very excited. We

70

didn't know ... It says you've been recommended for the DSO. We're all so pleased.'

'Don't go overdoing it, nurse,' said Sister Grice briskly. 'Before you know what, we'll have him demanding all sorts of extra privileges.'

Hugh had never had so many visitors as he had that morning. Every two minutes the door would open and yet another head would poke round with a message of congratulation. Many of the nurses he had never seen before; some were even prettier than Sarah Rock. He should have been gratified, but instead their pink, giggling faces and pleasing shapes merely reminded him of his utter impotence. He wondered if he would ever be stirred by a woman again.

The article lay on his bedside table all morning, unread, until his parents came to see him after tea. He asked his mother to read it out to him, but she was too excited, and in the end it was his father who took out his spectacles and declaimed the words.

That Hugh seemed to show neither surprise nor interest, puzzled and disappointed them.

'What do you want me to say?' he asked them. 'That it is the greatest moment of my life? That it makes up for all this? Medals are being dished out by the dozen every day – especially to pilots. You only have to keep alive to win the DFC, and once you've got it, you don't become any better a pilot than the next man. It merely means you've flown more sorties. Oh, I'm quite pleased to get the medal, and if articles like this help persuade the citizenry that things are going better than they are, I suppose there's no harm in them. But it's not going to give me my face or my hands back, is it?'

His father said nothing, but Mrs Fleming said, 'Well, we're very proud of you, even if you're not. And anyway, it's not as though you won't be able to lead a perfectly normal life once these nasty burns have cleared up. They're getting better all the time. The sister told us so. It's only a matter of time. You must just learn to be patient. You should count yourself lucky. At least you're alive. Think of poor Susan, waiting for news of James. He may be lying there in France, dead.'

71

'Or not, as the case may be.'

'There's no talking to you when you're in this sort of mood,' said his mother. 'You always were a difficult boy when you wanted to be. Wasn't he, Arthur?'

Arthur still said nothing, but Hugh noticed that there were tears in his eyes, and he suddenly looked older than he could ever remember.

Exactly a week after he was shot down, Hugh was moved from Ashford to the RAF Hospital at Acton.

'Sorry, old chap,' the senior consultant had added after delivering the news of his imminent departure. 'But this is only a clearing hospital, and we do rather need the beds. Besides, you'll be much better looked after up there. Hope you understand.'

Hugh had nodded and told the doctor politely that he perfectly understood, and that anyway, Sister Grice was probably glad to see the back of him. The doctor said that was nonsense and that he happened to know that Sister Grice was very fond of him.

'Balls,' Hugh said.

But when the time came to leave, Sister Grice had joined the small crowd of nurses, doctors, patients and members of the local press who had gathered to wave their hero off, and had even insisted on coming all the way out to the ambulance with him to say goodbye, and had dabbed at the corner of her eyes with a handkerchief and, unless he had completely misheard her, promised to pray for him. For once in her presence, he had found himself completely at a loss for words.

Then at the last moment Sarah had come rushing forward to tuck a small, flat parcel under his pillow, and say that she would come and see him soon. And then she had started to cry, too, and before he knew what, tears had started to run down Hugh's face.

'Any minute now you'll have me going too, mate,' said the ambulance driver, and firmly closed the doors.

The journey took much longer than the driver had anticipated (as he frequently pointed out to his increasingly irritable patient), and after a while, not even light-hearted banter with the nurses about their sex lives could distract Hugh's attention from the pain of his badly infected hands, the soreness of his eyes and the throbbing of his legs as the ambulance jerked and jolted its way through the outskirts of London.

By the time they arrived at the hospital some four and a half hours later, he was feeling iller than at any time since the accident. Finally, to his relief, he felt a needle enter his arm, and he passed gratefully into gentle oblivion.

Within only a day of arriving at the RAF hospital, Hugh was beginning to regret the various misdemeanours and outbursts of temper which, he felt sure, had hastened his departure from Ashford. Now, in this great impersonal factory of a place, with its vast wards, its long, echoing corridors and its busy, impatient nurses, he missed the privacy of his room, and Sarah and the other nurses who always seemed to have time to stop for a chat. Being the only wounded officer in the place, he had, he realized now, been atrociously spoiled, especially after the newspaper article. Now that he was just one of dozens of Air Force casualties, he felt lost and lonely. He even, God help him, missed Sister Grice.

His mother came to visit him every day from Chiswick where she was staying with her sister, Nora. Pressure of work had taken Arthur back to Norfolk, but he had promised to return at the weekend. Sarah's little parting gift had turned out to be a charming engraved copy of A Shropshire Lad, and Hugh begged his mother to read him the simple, moving lines over and over again. They talked occasionally of Norfolk, of his old friends and of trivial family matters – mostly relating to Aunt Nora and her own age-old personal war against backache. Of his own problems they spoke rarely. If ever he made the slightest reference to his condition, Mrs Fleming dismissed it as being of little importance. For reasons that he could not quite understand, she had convinced herself that his injuries were minor ones, that his burns were merely superficial, and that any day now he'd be out and about, as though he had done nothing worse than catch his hand on a hot stove.

Hugh assumed his father must have said something to persuade her that such was the case, and wondered how much he really knew. However, he never seemed to have an opportunity to speak with him alone, and Arthur never gave the slightest hint of what he was thinking.

A few days after his arrival at Acton, Hugh was told that the famous plastic surgeon, Angus Meikle, would be coming to see him. His visit was clearly an occasion of importance for the staff, since Hugh was washed and ready to receive his distinguished visitor a good hour and a half before he actually arrived.

Meikle marched into the ward shortly before noon, a subservient retinue of housemen and nurses rushing along in his wake, for all the world like children pursuing a medical Pied Piper.

Hugh could not remember ever having seen a surgeon before, yet he realized at once that Meikle was something out of the ordinary.

'The trouble with you fellows,' he boomed, 'is that you're so damned pig-headed about wearing goggles and gloves.'

He was short and stocky, with the broad shoulders and wide forehead of a prop forward (as Hugh was later to discover, he had had a couple of seasons for Scotland), broad, blunt hands and a wide, friendly grin. He peered closely at Hugh's face, and especially at his eyelids.

'Oh no,' he exclaimed. 'Not that bloody gentian violet again. When will they ever learn? Right, we'll have that lot off straightaway and I want salt compresses applied every two hours. With a bit of luck, we may not have to graft all four lids. Now, let's look at these hands of yours, you poor old thing.'

He undid the bandages and swore.

'If you don't believe what I say about the effects of tannic acid,' he bellowed at the attendant doctors, 'just take a close look at this.'

They gathered round and made suitably long faces.

'If I've said it once I've said it a hundred times, tannic results in secondary infection and septicaemia which in turn destroys

74

the nerves and tendons, resulting in bad contraction. Look at that. And that's after only twelve days. Saline baths are the only answer, followed by moist dressings. You must allow the dead skin to fall away and the good stuff underneath to grow. These tight, dry dressings are worse than useless. They're too tight to allow the blood to flow freely, and every time you pull them off, half the living tissue comes away with them. This poor chap can count himself lucky someone had the nous to remove the tannic when they did. Even so . . . I know, I know. You haven't got saline baths. Well, use saline compresses then, until you have. Anyway, use your heads.'

Meikle turned his attention from the quaking doctors to Hugh himself, and his voice softened.

'I'd like to get you down to my place at Ashbourne Wood in Surrey as soon as possible – today if I could. But I'm afraid that, thanks to the benighted idiots into whose hands you fell, you're not anything like up to it yet. Your skin needs more time to heal on its own. Could you bear to stay here for a week or two more? I know it's like living in a barracks, but at least you'll be looked after. I'll see to that. And you're well away from the bombs. Cheer up. It's all going to be all right in the end. You'll have the girls after you again in no time. Won't he, sister?'

Sister Martin, a small, dark woman in her early thirties, with short hair, smiled and flushed prettily.

'There you are, you sexy fellow,' roared Meikle. 'You've picked one up already.'

And with that, he turned and strode from the ward, his courtiers in hot pursuit.

After a while, Hugh began, if not to enjoy being in hospital, then at least to become resigned to it. Never having needed or wanted to ask anyone to do anything for him in his life, he was surprised to find with what ease he slipped into a state of helpless old age. There was, it seemed, no action that he could perform without assistance. If he was hungry, he had to contain his hunger until someone was available to feed him (often at busy times it was another patient); if he was dirty, someone

75

had to wash him; if he fancied a smoke, he had to ask someone to put the cigarette in his mouth and light it, and stand by with an ashtray until he had finished. Having always imagined that, in such an event, he would resist all offers of aid and insist on doing everything for himself, he was astounded at his easy compliance.

One day he was told he was strong enough to get up. Remembering the last disastrous occasion, he approached the great moment with some trepidation. At first he found it difficult to stand without some kind of support, but soon he was sitting up at a table for his meals, shuffling along the cavernous corridors, and engaging passing nurses in light conversation. He still had to rely on others to bath him and take him to the lavatory and wipe his bottom and perform the dozen and one other simple actions that others take for granted. But at least he was on his feet at last and no longer a bandaged dummy in a bed.

For the first two days he carefully resisted the temptation to look into mirrors, fearful of what he might find. When he did finally pluck up sufficient courage, the face that squinted back at him was at least recognisable as human and, more importantly, as his own.

It was as though some mad artist had taken a large paintbrush, dipped it into a pot of vermilion, thrown in a handful of mud and yellow clay, then flicked it with great force and accuracy straight into his face.

The swelling had, as the doctor at Ashford had promised him it would, completely subsided, and as the skin healed, the dead layer had started to separate from the deeper patches of burn, giving his whole face a mottled, slightly scaly look. It was perfectly obvious where the bad burns were: round his eyes, down the left side of his nose, the left side of his upper lip, and his left ear, which looked for all the world as though it had been modelled inexpertly from candle droppings.

Hugh stood in the bathroom for several more minutes, examining his face dispassionately, as though he were being shown a slide at a medical lecture. Compared with what he had looked like ten days ago he was Greta Garbo; by any normal standards he was repulsive. He made himself feel sick, so what must it be like for Muv? Small wonder she had closed her mind to reality. And Jimmy and Peter and Dickie Bird? Thank God he'd been masked when they came. And for the other patients, most of whom were suffering from proper, decent war wounds – bullets in the leg, broken arms, shell splinters? Even stomach ulcers were respectable compared with this. But, as Meikle had said, given a few more weeks . . . The human body, as Muv was so fond of pointing out, is a wonderful healer. She had returned at last to Norfolk, promising to come back soon. Just so long as no one else came to see him in the meantime . . .

Two days later, Hugh was lying dozing on his bed in his dressing gown when one of the nurses woke him to say he had a visitor. Before he could do anything to stop her, into the room walked Bunny. She wore a yellow frock and a large white hat, and looked more stunning than he could ever remember.

She stood at the end of his bed, staring as though at a ghost. Her face had gone sheet white and her lower lip trembled.

'Hullo, Bunny,' Hugh said quietly. 'Well, don't just stand there like a spare part. Come and sit down.'

Bunny shook her head slowly from side to side. Hugh looked round wildly for something, a towel, a handkerchief, anything – to cover himself, to hide from her horrified gaze, to save them both further anguish. He was aware that the level of conversation in the ward had risen, and someone had turned the wireless up.

For a moment, Bunny was afraid she was going to be sick. She put her hand up over her mouth. Everything was unreal, as though in a dream. People don't look like that in real life, she told herself. She wanted to say something to Hugh; to hear him speak; to try and reassure herself that this horrible creature on the bed really was Hugh Fleming, the handsomest man she had ever known, the man she had loved and wanted to marry – still did. No, that wasn't true. Not now. Not looking like that. She had travelled over from Kensington, her heart full of love, now, even as she stood there, all that love was leaving her. The sensation was almost physically painful. She had heard of people's hearts being turned to stone, but she had never imagined that it ever literally happened. And as her love for him drained out of her, tears followed, as if to wash it clean away. She gave one huge, heart-rending sob, then turned and ran from the room.

Bunny's visit affected Hugh profoundly. At the time, he had turned to the man in the next bed and remarked with a laugh, 'Silly bitch. No moral fibre, these girls, that's their trouble.' The others had joined in the joke and made it an excuse for a general discussion on the frailty and unreliability of women, and in this way had managed to pass an amusing few minutes. But when the laughter and the talk had died away, and the ward had reverted to its usual state of mindless torpor, Hugh found that he was more frightened than at any time in his life.

Family apart, Bunny was the first person outside the hospital staff to have seen Hugh since his accident, and he cursed the little nurse for allowing her to walk in on him like that, without any warning. Of course it had been the most terrible shock. But by now he had become so used to living amongst people who took his injuries for granted, and spoke every day of improvement, and promised him a rapid return to normality, that he had begun to persuade himself, like his mother, that he really did not look as bad as all that. But he had been fooling himself. No woman had ever looked at him the way Bunny had looked at him that afternoon, and suddenly he was afraid that he might never be attractive to women again, and worse, that he might never again dare to face the outside world.

He had never, thanks to the morphine, really suffered severe pain at any time, but now that the skin had begun to heal, the itching had started, bringing with it its own special variety of undreamt-of agony that at times had him in tears and brought him, he was convinced, to the brink of madness. This, combined with an already black depression, weakened him physically and morally, delaying the natural healing process and putting skin grafting out of the question for the time being.

It was Meikle who first suggested the convalescent home.

'It's on the south coast at Bournemouth,' he said cheerfully. 'Used to be an hotel, and a jolly comfortable one, too, by all accounts. I think you'd like it there. Nice big private rooms with views, comfortable sitting rooms, good grub, lots to do – swimming pool, squash courts, golf and so on.' Hugh looked gloomily at his hands. 'Yes,' Meikle said thoughtfully, 'well, you could walk, get some fresh air into you, meet some new people. Matron's a duck. It'll do you good. Promise.'

He was driven down the following day, wrapped in gloom and a large travelling rug, and shown into a sitting room of gigantic proportions. Groups of green-covered armchairs clustered forlornly around dark wood coffee tables. Huge potted palms huddled shyly in far corners, like large, ungainly women unable to get a dance. Through the huge windows the empty, rain-swept promenade, the flat beach and the sea spread away in one vast expanse of greyness. Gazing out on it expressionlessly, like some strange religious sect awaiting the second coming, were his fellow patients, scattered about the room in small khaki clumps, smoking silently. A thin, mournful male nurse in a stained white jacket appeared from behind one of the palms and asked Hugh where he'd like to sit. The others turned their listless gaze on Hugh. They showed neither surprise nor interest in his presence, merely a vague hostility, as though daring him to disturb the ancient world of silence which they had created for themselves.

Hugh glowered at them.

'In my room,' he snapped, and left them to their grey contemplation.

Two hours later, he decided the whole thing had been a terrible mistake and set off to find the matron and ask if he could be moved back to London at the earliest possible opportunity.

He was descending the wide oak staircase into the hall, his RAF greatcoat round his shoulders, when the front door burst open and in strode a short, stocky figure dressed in baggy corduroy trousers, shapeless sports jacket and battered brown trilby. Behind him hovered a taxi driver holding a green leather suitcase with a strap round it.

79

'Oh, just shove it down anywhere,' the man told him. He bent himself slightly sideways, and with a stiff right arm, plunged his hand into the depths of his trouser pocket and came up with a pound note which he waved at the taxi driver. When the driver produced the change, the man indicated his pocket and said. 'Bung it in there, would you? There's a good fellow.'

At this moment the matron, a tiny, dark-haired woman, came bustling out from under the stairs.

'Mr Holland!' she exclaimed with Scottish delight. 'Och, am I glad to see you back. This place needs some life in it and no mistake.'

'My old darling!' said Holland, and lifted both hands in greeting. Only then did Hugh see with a shock that they were not really hands at all, but two shapeless pink stumps, scarcely recognisable as hands, except for the one or two small protuberances that were all that remained of the fingers.

At the same time, Holland caught sight of Hugh standing uncertainly on the stairs.

'Hullo, hullo,' he called out. 'A fellow flyer, I see. And not before time. Well, this is a turn-up for the books.'

Hugh continued to make his way down.

'Well now, Mr H.,' said the matron, 'what's the latest instalment?'

Holland reached up and, grasping the brim of his hat between the two little stubs on his right hand, whipped the shapeless piece of felt off his head. 'Ta-ra,' he shouted. As the light from the chandelier fell across his face, it revealed a grotesque patchwork of pink and white skin, like a cardboard jigsaw puzzle which an impatient child has shoved together willy-nilly, forcing other pieces to wrinkle and pucker and bend out of shape. The eyelids were particularly ugly and red, and far out of proportion to the brows and cheeks.

'A brand new pair of blinkers,' Holland announced proudly, indicating the eyelids with his stumps. 'What do you think? Not bad, eh?'

The matron peered at them closely.

'They still haven't quite settled in yet,' she said. 'Still, they'll shrink a lot more before they're finished.'

'I hope so,' roared Holland. 'I feel like a ruddy chorus girl who's over done it with the mascara.'

'Don't kid yourself,' Matron said with a laugh. 'Now I expect you'd like a little something after your journey. Why don't the two of you slip into the smoking room and I'll see what I can rustle up.' She gave Hugh an enormous wink. 'You have to be a really old hand to deserve this,' she said, and bustled away.

Holland extended one stump in Hugh's direction.

'My name's Tim Holland,' he said.

'Hugh Fleming,' said Hugh, half extending his own hand, then withdrawing it with an awkward laugh.

'You look to me as though you need a drink,' said Tim.

Tim Holland had been a bomber pilot in Blenheims and had been making a low level attack on a German supply column when he was shot down early in 1940.

'We were so low,' he told Hugh over a glass of Matron's whisky in front of a log fire in the smoking room, 'I could see the whites of their eyes. Almost literally. No bomber pilot likes to come face to face with his enemy like that. Puts him right off his stroke. Worse still, they had a lot of mules to pull their ammo carts. Poor bloody things, they were terrified out of their minds, jumping about, trying to break out of their harnesses and what not. Still, we dropped our load on them. I shall never forget the sight of those mules going up in the air. I still have nightmares about it. Anyway, I pulled up and away and the next thing I knew we were jumped by a couple of 109s. Got us in the port engine and down we came. There was nothing I could do. No time to bale out. Crew killed on impact; yours truly stuck in the burning, fiery furnace, turning a gentle shade of brown, like a ruddy roast chicken. God knows how I got out in the end. I certainly don't remember a thing. Well, you know what it's like. I don't have to tell you. Luckily I was picked up by a local farmer who took me home and hid me in his attic. I expected the Germans to roll up any day, but they never did. Must have assumed I was burnt to bits in the Blenheim.

'The family were bloody marvellous. A doctor came and did what he could. I can't remember what special treatments he gave me, but whatever they were, they didn't help – as you can see. He'd have done better to leave well alone. I know he slapped a lot of bandages over me. I was blind for a long time, so I couldn't really see what he was up to. Anyway, before I knew what, bits of my hands were dropping off, and then, when my eyelids did eventually open, they shrivelled up like overdone bacon. Yours'll do the same. I couldn't blink. I had to roll my eyes up into my head to sleep. They were constantly running with water. I found out afterwards I was lucky not to have lost my sight completely. Oh, don't worry. There's no danger of that for you. They'll graft new lids on long before then. Who have you seen? Meikle?' Hugh nodded. 'Good. He's the best.' He indicated his new eyelids. 'They don't look much yet, but believe me, they're surgical masterpieces. Anyway, where was I? Oh, yes. In France. Well, as soon as I was well enough to be moved, I started to make my way via the Resistance people to the south. I won't bore you with the details. Somehow I got across the Pyrenees and into Spain, and finally finished up in Lisbon. After a certain amount of argy-bargy and hanging about, I got on a plane and arrived back in England just in time to see you lads doing your bit. My wife hadn't seen me for nearly nine months. And didn't want to either, when it came to the point.'

'What happened?'

'She took one look at me and burst into tears. In the hall of the Ritz, if you please. Said she couldn't face it. I know I must have looked a pretty ghastly sight by then – terrible old French peasant clothes, watering eyes, face looking as though it had been sandpapered and what have you – but even so, I thought she was made of sterner stuff . . .'

Tim's voice trailed off and he stared into the fire.

'Anyway, that was that. Buggered off. Probably just as well. Don't altogether blame her.'

He looked up at Hugh. There were tears in his eyes, though whether for grief or from physiological reasons Hugh could not tell.

'I know what it's like,' Hugh said.

'I'm sorry.'

'Don't be. When I think what you must have been through...'

'Look,' said Tim, his voice suddenly hard, 'it's nothing to be ashamed of. Feeling sorry for yourself, I mean. We're none of us supermen.'

'They'd like us to be.'

'They haven't had their faces burnt off. They know nothing. They've been nowhere. You and I have. We've been right up to the gates of bloody hell and back, and we'll be better men for it in time. Already are. You may feel sorry for yourself now, but it won't last. Because after a while you'll realize that they're the ones who are dead – inside at least. You and I are alive. We've been through the fire, my old cock, and we've emerged – a little scorched round the edges maybe – but purged, shriven, re-born, ready to begin life anew.'

'Brave talk,' said Hugh, 'but in the meantime, what have I got to look forward to – or you, for that matter? Weeks in hospital, endless operations, hour after hour of enforced inactivity broken only by the occasional outing to the local cinema and a quick session with the physiotherapist. And at the end of it all, I'm never going to be able to hold a golf club or a cricket bat, or climb in the Coolins, or ski in St Moritz, or, at the rate I'm going, make love to women. Talk about bits of finger falling off; I think even more essential parts of me are about to fall off any day now.'

Tim poured each of them another drink.

'Look,' he said, 'I don't want to sound like a father lecturing his son, but I am an old pro of 23 and you are only a young stripling of 20. I know bloody well what you're in for over the next few months. I wish I'd been so lucky; I might be a bit more handsome than I am today. I'm not pretending it's going to be anything other than uncomfortable and boring and painful. You're going to get depressed, and not every pretty girl you meet at a party is going to rush headlong into your arms. But then looks are not everything, especially to a woman. You may not believe this, but since Brenda walked out on me, I've slept

83

with more girls than at any other time in my life, and I wasn't bad looking in my day. At first I was convinced they were only doing it out of kindness, but gradually the truth dawned on me. They did it because they liked me; because I wasn't one of these smooth faced bastards you see every evening in the Perroquet Bar at the Berkeley, with their warm smiles and cold hearts. I was a man who liked them, was interested in them and cared for them, I never used to be like that until I learnt what it was like to suffer a bit, and now I think I'm a better person for it. And so will you be, too. So cheer up, have patience, and in the meantime sit back and take your well-earned rest. You don't know how lucky you are.'

'Do you know,' said Hugh, 'you're the second person who's said that to me in the last few weeks?'

'Now you're beginning to find out who your friends are.'

'She said that, too,' said Hugh.

The next morning Hugh received a letter from Peter, telling him that Julian had been killed.

Chapter Six

Hugh stayed at the convalescent home for ten days. He spent most of the time in his room overlooking the empty sea-front, reading. On the few occasions he did venture downstairs, the Army officers made no attempt to converse with him, apart from wishing him a polite good morning. He was perfectly happy to leave things that way. At lunchtime and in the evenings, he and Tim ate together, slightly apart from the others. Tim had a talent for a good story, and his account of how he escaped from France under the noses of the Germans occupied several meals. Hugh was still unable to use his hands, and it obviously gave Tim pleasure to be able to cut up his food for him. Hugh never failed to marvel at the way he performed seemingly impossible tasks with his stumps.

After dinner, they would get rather tight on bottles of whisky of which Tim seemed to have inexhaustible supplies, and once, they behaved extremely badly with one of the potted palms and earned themselves a severe reprimand from Matron. On another occasion, Tim tried to persuade Hugh to come out with him to a local restaurant which had dancing on Friday and Saturday nights, but Hugh made an excuse and went to bed early. He wasn't ready for that sort of thing yet. The following morning, Tim was full of news about a conquest he had made in the restaurant, but somehow Hugh didn't believe him, and felt sure it had been invented for his benefit.

One source of endless entertainment for both of them was a male nurse by the name of Dickinson, a splendidly lugubrious East Anglian whose family, for reasons neither of them ever quite fathomed, held the doubtful privilege of coffin bearers to the Bishops of Barsham.

'Five of Their Graces I've seen on their way in my time,' Dickinson announced one day à propos of nothing. 'And there are not many men who can top that, I can tell you.'

He also possessed an astonishingly encyclopaedic knowledge of the London-North-Eastern Railway timetable, and as he wandered in and out of Hugh's room with various meals on trays, he would solemnly recite entire lines in a deep, sonorous voice:

'King's Lynn, Downham Market, Littleport, Ely, Cambridge, Audley End, Bishop's Stortford, Liverpool Street.'

He was also splendidly absent-minded, and on one memorable occasion during the recitation of all the stations on the Wells to Norwich line, slid a tray piled high with cups and saucers into the service lift shaft before noticing that the lift itself was not there.

But despite Dickinson's eccentricities and Tim's determined gaiety, a great deal of much needed sleep and some excellent food, Hugh missed the companionship of the hospital at Acton, and when Matron announced one morning that she thought he was strong enough to face his first operation, he did not put up any resistance. Tim left at the same time to stay with his family in Shropshire. The Army officers waved a vague goodbye from their armchairs by the window and returned to their sad contemplation of the distant horizon, but Matron seemed genuinely sorry to see them go.

'Haste ye back soon,' she said, slipping half a bottle of whisky into each of their pockets.

'And to think they say the Scots are mean,' said Tim.

Hugh arrived back at Acton to find a letter waiting for him from Jean Cartwright. It simply said she was sorry to hear of his accident, and apologized for not coming to see him sooner, and suggested a meeting in town. 'I realize this may be rather a strain for you,' she wrote, 'and I am not expecting too much, but I really couldn't bear to see you lying in a hospital bed like an invalid.'

86

Hugh had thought often of Jean, especially in the con-valescent home, and had once or twice considered asking Tim to write a letter to her. Of all the women he knew, she was the one he knew would deal with him most honestly. But Bunny's visit was still too fresh in his mind, and he had decided reluc-tantly to give it a few more weeks.

Now that she had written, he couldn't wait to see her again. Her letter was the first thing to have aroused in him the faintest stirrings of sexual longing, and that evening he per-suaded his night nurse to help him place a call to Redhill. By a miracle he caught her just as she was going off duty. The ill-concealed excitement in her soft, low voice assured him that he had made the right decision. But even so, he felt the need to warn her.

'I'm afraid I look rather a mess still . . .' he began, but she interrupted him.

'I miss you and I want you, whatever you look like,' she said. 'I've got the afternoon off tomorrow. Let's say two-thirty in the tearoom at Victoria Station. We can make plans then.'

When Hugh walked back into the ward, Sister Martin said, 'That's the first time I've seen you really smile since you came. It must be a girl. I'm so glad for you.'

By now his eyelids were beginning to contract dramatically, as Tim had told him they would. His eyes had suddenly acquired a wild, staring look, like a nervous heifer, and since he could not blink, they required frequent syringing. Water dribbled from them ceaselessly.

After lunch the next day, one of the nurses helped him on with his uniform, stuck some cotton wool pads under his eyes (all cunningly disguised with a pair of dark glasses), covered his hands with a pair of old woollen gloves, and waved him off in a taxi.

The driver was one of those naturally pessimistic men who approach each journey with the firm conviction that everything will turn out for the worst, and for whom in some curious way it always does. Thus a full and detailed account of the various misfortunes that had attended his morning's driving was interspersed with an equally gloomy forecast of the journey to come. 'I'd like to be able to promise you a straight run up the Bayswater Road, round Marble Arch, down Park Lane and Bob's your uncle, squire, but I'd only be raising false hopes in you, if you get my meaning. Last thing I heard, there'd been a bomb somewhere near the Grosvenor House and they'd blocked off Park Lane completely. Now, of course, I could drop down to Kensington High Street, and try and dodge through to Sloane Square, but I don't reckon too much of our chances, what with that unexploded parachute mine at South Ken Station and all . . .'

And so it went on. Hugh interjected the occasional grunt of assent or groan of sympathy, but otherwise allowed the dreary monologue to wash harmlessly over him while he stared out of the window, his mind on the forthcoming meeting.

Even when all the roads that he had predicted would be closed turned out to be open and empty of traffic, the driver was not to be appeased.

'I don't like this,' he muttered as they trundled down Park Lane, 'I don't like this one little bit . . .'

They rounded Hyde Park Corner, turned down Constitution Hill and swung past Buckingham Palace.

' 'ullo, 'ullo,' said the taxi driver, as they passed the Royal Mews, 'what did I tell you?'

The jam was solid as far ahead as they could see.

'What time is it?' said Hugh.

'2.45, give or take a minute,' said the driver.

'I'll walk from here,' said Hugh. 'It's no distance.'

'Please yourself,' said the driver glumly. 'I hope you have better luck getting back.'

As Hugh strode stiffly along the pavement past Gorringes, he was scarcely aware of the looks of pity that crossed the faces of passers-by before they quickly averted their gaze and hurried on. He was too concerned that Jean, thinking he had funked the whole thing, might get tired of waiting and leave. His already awkward progress was made even less easy by the unusually large crowds that pushed past him as if, like him, they were all late for an important meeting.

88

From somewhere behind him, approaching fast, came an urgent clanging of bells and two fire engines swept past and turned down towards the station entrance. These were followed a moment later by an ambulance. Then two more ambulances swung out into Buckingham Palace Road from the direction of the station and drove off at high speed towards the Mall.

Hugh now drove his unwilling legs even harder along the pavement. His mouth was dry and his heart was beating with an unspeakable dread. Sweat poured from his forehead and into his open eyes, making them sting and water even more than usual. One of the cotton wool pads dropped away from under his glasses, and his dry throat was sore with heavy breathing.

He rounded the corner to find his way blocked by a crowd of maybe a couple of hundred people staring at the station, their faces wearing that expression of dumb curiosity adopted by all bystanders of accidents – just staring at the ambulances and the fire engines and the jumble of disconnected metal girders, broken walls and smoking rubble that was all that remained of the Victoria Station tea-room.

'Oh, no,' groaned Hugh. 'Oh, no.' He pushed forward through the crowd, which parted with sounds of ill-disguised irritation, and started hobbling across the station forecourt. He heard someone calling after him, 'Here you, where do you think you're off to?' But he ran on. Everything was swimming before his eyes, and then finally the little strength that was left in his legs gave out and he fell forward, sobbing with rage and frustration. His dark glasses fell into the gutter.

Helping hands turned him onto his back, then a voice called out, 'Here's another one, Joe. Looks in pretty bad shape. Are you all right, mate?'

Hugh opened his eyes and looked up into the anxious, kindly face of an ARP warden.

'What happened?' he asked, still gasping for breath.

'Take it easy, mate. Try not to talk.'

'The tea-room,' said Hugh, 'Was it a bomb? What happened?'

'Only a ruddy German bomber,' said the warden. 'Brought down by one of your lot, I daresay. You'd have thought he'd try to put it down somewhere in the open, wouldn't you? Hyde Park, St James's. Somewhere in the open. But oh, no. Not Jerry. Slap on top of Victoria Station. The bastard. Come on, let's get you to the ambulance. You look all in. Give me a hand here, Joe.'

The two men started to lift Hugh but he shook them off.

'I'm all right,' he said angrily. 'I'm nothing to do with this. Leave me alone. I'm looking for somebody.'

He struggled to get to his feet, grunting with pain as his gloved hands scraped on the ground.

'Take it easy, mate,' said the ambulance man as they helped him up. 'Looking for someone, you say? Looking for who?'

'A girl,' said Hugh. 'We were supposed to meet in the tea-room at two-thirty. I was a bit late.'

The two men looked at each other and pulled long faces.

'If she was in the tea-room when she said she would be . . .' the ARP man said quietly.

'Sorry, old chap,' said the ambulance man.

'A whole ruddy bomber coming in on it like that,' said the ARP man. 'Bomb and all.' He shook his head.

'Perhaps she wasn't there at all,' said the ambulance man hopefully. 'Perhaps her train was late. They often are these days. Perhaps she went somewhere else by mistake. You're sure it was the tea-room, not the tea-trolley?'

'Perhaps she didn't come at all,' said the ARP man.

'Perhaps,' said Hugh and turned away.

'Here,' the ambulance man called after him. 'You sure you're all right?'

Hugh did not reply. Perhaps they were right. Perhaps her train *had* been late. Perhaps she hadn't been able to get off duty. Perhaps any moment now she would come running out from the station, her leather bag over her shoulder, and take his arm and hurry him away from this terrible scene of smoke and broken buildings and bells and sirens and people shouting and people staring. Perhaps the bomber had never crashed and all this was a dream. Perhaps . . .

Hugh felt a hand on his arm and spun round, his heart beating. But it was only the ambulance man.

90

'Excuse me, Sir,' he said, 'I hope you don't mind my asking, but this girl you was supposed to meet. I was just wondering...she...I mean I just happened to notice...she wouldn't have been wearing a gold chain round her neck, would she, with a kind of charm on it, in the shape of a cat or something?'

'A tigress actually,' said Hugh, and turned and walked away.

Hugh had known she was dead before the ambulance man said anything about the charm. He knew she wouldn't have been late, however unreliable the train services. She never was. She wasn't that sort of woman. The ambulance man might have been mistaken about the charm, but he wasn't. He wasn't that sort of man.

Hugh walked for a long time. He had no plan, and no particular aim, except to get away from the station and that stupid pile of rubble. He turned up Queen Anne's Gate and crossed over into St James's Park. He stood on the little iron bridge over the lake and looked across at the dirty white buildings of Whitehall – almost Byzantine with their minarets and domes and towers, but cold and without the inner vitality that had seemed to him to exude from every stone in Istanbul.

He had gone there one summer holidays with Adrian Downpatrick – three years ago was it now, or four? Neither had been abroad on his own before and they had both felt very much men of the world.

If he concentrated very hard, he could still recapture that sense of excitement and heightened anticipation they had both felt the moment they arrived. Everything, they had been convinced, was a prelude to some great adventure that would alter their lives for ever – whether it was haggling over some cheap souvenir in the bazaar, or watching a belly dancer go through her strangely hypnotic motions, or losing their way in the narrow back alleys with their strange mixture of smells – now sweet and spicy, now foul and menacing – or simply sitting at a café table sipping thick, sweet coffee and iced water, watching the world go by. One of their main reasons for going had been in order to acquire a unique store of sexual experience that would not only be the envy of their school fellows, but stand them in good stead for years to come. Their single-mindedness was soon rewarded in the shape of two magnificent dark-haired whores, probably from gipsy stock, who had wrapped their plump dark limbs round their hard, pale bodies, and in the course of one night, introduced them to pleasures that not even Frank Harris in his wildest dreams could have imagined.

Having had his appetite so luxuriously whetted, it had surprised and puzzled Hugh to find on his return that the sort of girls he met socially in Norfolk and London were not anxious to profit from his unique experience, and actually thought it disgusting and dangerous. And thus had been born in him the notion that in this world there are girls who don't (the ones who are to be danced with and kissed and put in taxis and eventually married, but otherwise avoided) and the girls who do (the ones who are to be danced with and kissed and make love to in taxis and never married, but to be rung up at every possible opportunity). It was a principle of life to which Hugh had adhered firmly ever since, and he had never yet seen reason to doubt it. Bunny Morrell was one of the ones who didn't, which was why he had finally been forced to boot her; Jean Cartwright was one who did . . . or rather, had been. He supposed that eventually it would sink in. He had never been in love with her nor she with him, but, by God, she had known how to *make* love to him – like the whore in Istanbul. And, by God, he missed her now.

He glanced up again at the buildings of Whitehall. One by one, lights were coming on in windows that looked out on the world like cold, heartless eyes. Behind them sat cold, heartless men who made big decisions that sent young men to their deaths and others to years of pain and disfigurement, without having the faintest idea who they were, or very much caring; like the half-witted, brandy-swilling generals that he and his friends had laughed about at Cambridge and sworn to avoid at all costs.

Hugh made a noise halfway between a grunt and a laugh. A sharp wind was getting up and it was spitting with rain.

He pulled his greatcoat collar up round his neck and hobbled off in the direction of Trafalgar Square.

'Hullo, darling. You look cold.'

The voice came out of a darkened doorway, loud and coarse, text-book style. Its owner, Hugh discovered, was slightly younger than the voice had suggested, but none the less predictable for that – cheap fur coat, fishnet stockings, heels like pencils, dyed blonde hair, eyes like a panda, mouth a scarlet slash, cheeks as red as a rag doll. They made a good pair, Hugh decided.

'How much?' he said.

The woman looked him up and down.

'A fiver,' she said, 'but seeing as how I have a weakness for RAF blue, three quid to you.'

'O.K.,' he said.

She took him by the arm. Hugh pulled away.

'What's the matter with you?' she said. 'Don't like being touched, don't we?'

Hugh said nothing as he limped beside her down Beak Street.

'Ooh, you are a poor old thing, aren't you ' she said. 'Stiff from too much sitting at a desk, are you? You look a desk type.'

Hugh reached up and pulled the peak of his cap down so that the shadow from the street lamps concealed his face.

'Well, just as long as you get stiff from something,' she said and laughed.

It was a horrible laugh, as humourless as the garish cage-bird she resembled. He would have given anything at that moment to say something cruel, to strike her across her stupid ugly face, to pull off his cap and show her his own ugliness and see her recoil, and then tell her to go to hell. He loathed her and he loathed himself for wanting her. But after all, he was as ugly and pathetic as she was and, like Jean, she wanted him – for money, it was true, not for himself; but in his condition he was hardly in a position to choose. Besides, for all her loudness and vulgarity, she excited him, and he dared not leave her now.

They turned down a narrow, poorly-lit alley and paused for

a moment in front of a red door while she fumbled for a key. Finally, she pushed open the door and he followed her up a steep, narrow staircase. There was no carpet, but there was a thin hand-rail attached to the wall on the left and, at the top, a single bulb in a red shade.

'Come on, slowcoach,' the woman called out, as Hugh struggled painfully behind her. 'Too much sitting behind a desk, that's your trouble. You need some exercise.'

Sweating heavily, he reached the top and looked around for her. She was standing in a doorway at the far end of the landing, lit from behind by an enveloping pink glow.

'Come along, darling,' she told him. 'I haven't got all night, you know. What do you think this is, blooming Maida Vale?'

Again she laughed her shrill parrot laugh.

The room was attractive in a ghastly sort of way, with its red wallpaper and pink lampshades. One side of it was taken up entirely by the bed. It had a pale pink satin coverlet embroidered with lace, and above it, she had rigged up a tent-like effect out of some white net material which was gathered at the top with a pink bow attached to the wall and spread downwards on either side of the bed. At the foot of the bed was a white dressing table with a mirror and little lamps with red shades and white bobbles. Against the other was a large white wardrobe beyond which, in a niche in the corner, stood a washbasin, concealed by a pink curtain.

'Well, come in then,' she said, slipping off her fur and throwing it across a small armchair. 'Don't just stand there like a spare prick at a wedding.'

Hugh closed the door behind him and stood uncertainly in the middle of the room. The woman moved towards him. Beneath the powder and paint and mascara her face was hard and unforgiving.

She reached up and took off his cap and looked at him intently. Hugh had underestimated her, for she did not step back in horror, or put her hand up to her face, or gasp, but said in a quiet voice, 'You didn't get that sitting at a desk, did you?'

Hugh could feel the water running down his cheek where

the cotton wool had fallen off and said, 'There's a handkerchief in my jacket pocket. I wonder if you'd mind getting it out for me.'

She did as he asked and dabbed carefully at his cheek where he indicated. Then she said he could probably do with a cup of tea. He said he'd prefer something a little stronger, if she had it, but he didn't want to put her to any trouble. She said, no trouble, and poured them both a half-tumbler of gin. He drank it down gratefully, even though he had never liked the taste of gin. Then she made a pot of tea anyway and told him to sit down and that she didn't mind if he didn't want to . . . you know . . .

Hugh sat in the little upright chair in front of the dressing table while she went out onto the landing and made the tea on a noisy little gas ring.

She sat in the small armchair and they talked.

Her name was Dorothy, she came from Port Talbot, and she had come to London to be an actress before getting into this game. Still might be one day. Comedy parts, she thought. Her Dad had been killed at Dunkirk and her mother had taken up with a paint salesman who'd got into camouflage and was doing very well for himself. Reserved occupation, you see. She hadn't seen either of them ever again; didn't want to.

Hugh did not find her or her story the slightest bit interesting, but he was glad of the tea and the warmth of the room, and anyway, he was too tired to stop her.

After a while, he asked if he could lie down for a moment on the bed. She said he was welcome and why didn't he take off his great-coat and his jacket. He asked her how much time she could spare, and she said she had all the time in the world for an airman. Had he been in the fighters or bombers? He told her fighters. In the Battle of Britain? Was he one of the Few? He said yes. Then he fell asleep.

When he awoke, Dorothy was sitting in the armchair reading *Picture Post.*

'How long have I been asleep?' he asked her.

'An hour,' she said. 'Hour and a half.'

'I must be costing you a fortune.'

She shrugged.

'Feeling better now, are you?' she asked.

'Much.'

When she stood up, Hugh saw that she was wearing a red diaphanous negligée which fell away from her body as she walked towards the bed, revealing large white breasts, a narrow, muscular waist, and heavy hips. Her legs were long and slender, like a dancer's.

'I know what you need now,' she said. She sat beside him on the bed and started to undo his shirt buttons. He made no attempt to resist.

After a struggle she finally managed to remove his shirt, then turned her attention to his trousers. He tried to raise himself up on one arm to help her, but the pain to his elbows was too great and with a little cry he fell back.

'Now just you lie still and leave this to me,' she said.

As she pulled his trousers gently down away from his hips, her eyes were wide and the redness of her mouth gleamed brightly as her tongue darted constantly over it like a snake. Something was wrong. Hugh had been with enough tarts in his time to be able to recognize the routine, the ridiculously exaggerated flattery, the simulated excitement, the carefully rehearsed performance. But this was something different. This was no act. This was for real.

It was true what Tim Holland had said. There really were women who could like him for himself. Even tarts. He felt himself bursting with pride and desire.

Dorothy laughed – not a shrill parrot laugh, but a laugh of genuine pleasure and genuine anticipation. She stood up and shrugged off the negligée which slipped like a sigh on to the red fluffy carpet.

Then she moved to the bed, placed one hip carefully beside his and leaned across him. Her breasts brushed against his chest and her lips ran lightly over his.

'You're beautiful,' she said. 'You know that? You're really beautiful.'

Hugh tried to respond, but almost at once she had moved her lips down to his chest, then to his stomach and then to his groin. She seemed almost to be purring with satisfaction as her mouth enveloped him.

Hugh called out, 'No, no. Please. I want to do it properly. I must.' She lifted her head, her lips glistened.

'All right,' she said. 'If you can.'

Her breath was coming very fast now, her stomach moved rapidly in and out and her breasts rose and fell in time.

She sat up, and placing her right knee beside him, straddled his body, then edging backwards until she was directly above him, she lowered herself slowly onto him, grinding her hips and uttering small, low moans. Hugh reached up, but then realized he was still, ridiculously, wearing his woollen gloves.

He held them up in front of him and laughed.

'Take them off,' she whispered.

'I don't think that's a very good idea,' he said.

'Yes, it is,' she said. 'Please take them off. I want you to.'

Her insistence alarmed Hugh.

'Really . . .' he began.

'If you won't,' she said, 'then I will.' And sitting upright, she took both pairs of gloves by the fingertips and snatched them away and threw them onto the floor.

By now, most of the skin had hardened, but the tannic had left bad keloid scars, drawing the skeletal fingers even deeper into the palms. Dorothy stared at them for a long time, her eyes wide with fascination. Then once more she leaned forward until her whole body was lying on top of Hugh's.

'Now then,' she said, her voice low and trembling, 'hold me with those beautiful hands of yours. Caress me. I want to feel them on my back. I want to feel them all over me, touching me, caressing me, clawing me, hurting me.'

Hugh stared up at her, his face blank with incomprehension.

'Don't you see?' She was talking now to herself, as though Hugh were not even there. 'Don't you see? I've never had a cripple before, and it's bloody marvellous. Just think. The first person to make me come in all this time, and it's a cripple. Go on. Go on. Now. Touch me, damn you. Touch me! Touch me!'

She screamed out the words at the top of her voice and her eyes were filled with contempt and loathing.

'What's the matter with you?' she screamed. 'Are you some kind of pansy or something?'

She lifted herself off him and threw herself into the armchair and burst into tears.

Somehow Hugh succeeded in dressing himself. Afterwards, he could not remember her helping him. His mind was too intent on getting away from the room to be aware of anything. But she must have done so; his hands were not capable of pulling up a pair of trousers, let alone fastening buttons and knotting a tie.

All he could remember with any certainty was that she had stood at the top of the stairs, under the single bulb in the red shade, crying and calling after him as he stumbled into the street, 'I'm sorry. I didn't mean it like that. I'm sorry.'

It had started to rain in earnest, and by the time he finally found a taxi, his shoes were soaked through. The driver, for all his optimism, lost himself twice after Shepherd's Bush, and it was nine o'clock when they finally drew up at the front entrance of the hospital.

Almost at once he bumped into Sister Martin.

'I can see I don't have to ask you what sort of an afternoon you had,' she said with a smile.

'Oh?'

'Your shirt collar is covered in lipstick.'

Chapter Seven

The following day, without any warning, Meikle marched into the ward, this time with only a sister fussing at his side. He came straight up to Hugh's bed.

'How are you feeling?'

'Pretty low,' said Hugh.

'How are those eyes?'

'Sore.'

Meikle peered at them closely.

'Can you close them at all now?'

'No.'

'Hmm. The right's not so bad. The left needs covering, otherwise you could be in trouble. Think you're up to an operation?'

'When?'

'Tomorrow.'

Hugh felt the same sick feeling in his stomach that he used to feel before take-off.

'Well...'

'Good,' said Meikle. 'That's settled then. Come down this afternoon. I'll have a car sent. See you there.'

And he swept out.

Shortly after lunch, Hugh was stumping about in a desultory fashion, gathering together his few bits and pieces – washbag, books, underclothes – when a nurse came to say he was wanted on the telephone.

'Afternoon, cock. How's tricks?'

At first he did not recognize the voice.

'My God, you're not going deaf as well, are you?'

It was Tim Holland ringing from the Ritz to say that he had

also been summoned to Ashbourne Wood by Meikle and why didn't they travel down together? Hugh, who had been dreading the journey on his own, was delighted.

'I've got a car laid on,' he said. 'I'll pick you up.'

'What a coincidence,' said Tim. 'So have I. But I think you'd prefer my driver. Look, why not get your chap to run you over? We'll have a few drinks here with my driver, then she'll take us the rest of the way, pausing en route for a little liquid refreshment.'

Tim's driver turned out to be short and fair-haired and plump. She was far from pretty, but she had an easy-going, no-nonsense manner which Hugh found immediately attractive. Her name was Nancy; she worked on a local newspaper in Shrewsbury and lived in the next village to Tim's parents.

'Bloody silly really,' said Tim as they broached a second bottle of Dom Perignon in their bedroom. 'We must have been seeing each other for years without ever actually meeting. Such a waste. If only I'd known.'

'It wouldn't have been any good,' said Nancy. 'You were different; so was I.'

'We met at a cocktail party last week,' Tim told Hugh cheerfully. 'It was, as they say, love at first sight. Or in her case, second sight.'

Nancy smiled. 'I must admit, it was a bit of a shock. I'd never come across anyone who'd been burnt like that.'

'What did you think?'

Nancy shrugged. 'Nothing much. I think I thought, So that's what it looks like. Tim was standing on the other side of the room when I first noticed him, surrounded by a small crowd of hero-worshippers listening open-mouthed while he held them spell-bound with tales of his daring exploits: How I got shot down. How I foiled the Gestapo. How I escaped over the Pyrenees.'

'Balls,' said Tim. 'If you really want to know, I was thrilling them with my theories on petrol rationing.'

Nancy made a face at him. 'I then thought, He looks kind and amusing; I wish he'd come over and talk to me. But he didn't.'

100

'Couldn't,' interrupted Tim cheerfully. 'If I don't extricate myself from this crowd of bores pretty damned soon and talk to that girl, I thought, someone else will and then I'll have lost my chance. You see, I knew as soon as I saw her, before we'd exchanged a word, that she was going to be a very important part of my life.'

'And did he turn out to be as kind and amusing as you'd supposed?' Hugh asked Nancy.

'What do you think?'

Hugh laughed.

'What I mean is,' he said, 'when it came to the point, was it his character that you found attractive, or something else?'

Nancy frowned slightly.

'What do you mean exactly? 'she said.

'It doesn't matter,' Hugh mumbled. 'Forget it.'

They finished the second bottle of champagne and then Nancy said it was time they were on their way.

'You're supposed to be there at six,' she reminded Tim.

'That doesn't apply to old hands like me,' Tim said amiably.

'But Hugh isn't an old hand,' she pointed out.

'Soon will be,' said Tim.

Nancy drove fast and well in her old Wolseley, but many of the roads leading to the river were blocked by fallen buildings and bomb craters, which meant doubling back several times before finally crossing the river at Wandsworth. There were also a number of diversions in Streatham and Wallington, so that it was already six o'clock by the time they reached Purley and dropped down to the Surrey village of Godstone. Nancy was all for pressing on, but Tim said they deserved a quick one, so they pulled up at the White Hart and Tim and Nancy sat at a table in the corner by the fire while Hugh went over and bought them all large whiskies.

While waiting to be served, he looked across at the two of them, holding hands, deep in conversation, and thought how well they suited each other, and what a miracle their meeting had been. He was not an envious man – he had never had cause to be – but he envied those two not just their love, but their friendship, too. 'Now you'll find out who your real friends are.' Until now he had happily relied on old friends like Jimmy and Pat and Julian; on Jean Cartwright, who had always been there when he needed her; on the undemanding companionship of the Mess. There had seemed no reason why they should not all be there, always. But that was at a different time and in a different place. Pat and Julian and Jean were all dead. No one could take anything for granted any more. If things went on at this rate, he would have to look for new friends, who hadn't known him before when he was young and free from care and . . . had he really once been good-looking? He couldn't remember.

And then suddenly he remembered who it was Nancy reminded him of. He had been trying to puzzle it out all afternoon. The calmness, the completeness, the assurance of one who has come to terms with who she is and is content, the utter serenity: these were the qualities that had immediately attracted him to Nancy, and these were what had immediately attracted him to Marjorie all that time ago, on a river bank in Cambridge. Tim had recognized his opportunity for happiness and had seized it with what remained of his hands. Hugh had recognized his, too, but, like a fool, he had let it slip.

Would the chance ever present itself again – as it had to Tim – and if so, would he let it go again?

One quick whisky led to another, so that it was nearly eight o'clock when Hugh and Tim finally rolled up at Queen Mary's Cottage Hospital, Ashbourne Wood.

Queen Mary's had been just another small country hospital until it was taken over at the beginning of the war by the Ministry of Health and given the title Emergency Service Hospital – a distinction it and its fellows had never sought and for which they were eminently ill-suited. They were inadequately equipped and far too small. However, the Ministry, undaunted, had provided them with a number of 'blisters' or small huts in order to meet the increasing demand for beds.

There were three wards in the main building at Queen Mary's, like many other cottage hospitals: one for women, one for children, and a third for men – half of which was for local civilians, the other six beds being set aside for service casualties.

102

Outside, in what had once been a large, ornamental garden stood the three 'blisters': one for injuries to limbs, a second for minor burns, and a third for serious burn cases and maxillo-dental injuries to the face and jaws.

This last, named after his Italian wife Francesca, was Angus Meikle's pride and joy. Not only did it house the country's first saline bath, installed, thanks to his endless bullying and badgering of the men from the Ministry, in the summer of 1940, but it had amply justified his claim that the quickest and most effective method of healing burnt skin was constant immersion in warm salt water and dressings of tulle gras – a network of large mesh dipped in Vaseline and antiseptic solution which prevented the gauze from sticking to the flesh. Moreover, it was on patients from Francesca Ward that Meikle had pulled off the most spectacular feats of plastic surgery for which his name was already becoming a by-word in the medical world.

Hugh had heard tell of Francesca Ward, both at Acton and in Bournemouth. Quite what he had been expecting he was not entirely sure: at all events not the long, low wooden chicken hut of a building into which the pretty little VAD nurse now ushered them. The walls were painted a gloomy dark brown, and down each side were twenty uncomfortable looking iron beds separated by brown wooden lockers and in places, un-decorated tea-chests.

In the centre of the room, on a plain trestle table, stood a large wireless set from which music blared at full pitch. There were also an ancient coal stove and a few upright wooden chairs with arms. Along both sides of the room there were large windows, all closed. Leading into the ward was a sort of corridor, with doors leading off into lavatories and bathrooms. Also in the corridor, set in a recess, was the famous saline bath with its elaborate assortment of pipes which kept the salt water flowing through the bath at a constant temperature of 105°.

All the beds were occupied by patients in various stages of repair. Some were heavily bandaged all over; some had just their eyes covered. Others, their faces as red as newly boiled lobsters, except for the odd pale patch of newly grafted skin,

103

wore no bandages at all. One or two lay in grotesque, almost impossible positions, their noses connected to their upper arms by pale tubes of skin. Others had similar rolls of skin which protruded from beneath bandaged foreheads and were turned down to connect with the lower part of their noses.

Hugh, slightly the worse for wear from the many large whiskies and soda, stared about him in astonished disbelief.

Since, in order to encourage the skin grafts to take, the windows were never opened and the room was maintained at a permanently high temperature, the effect was of entering a heavily disinfected Turkish bath, and it was the stuffy, oppressive atmosphere more than the condition of the patients upon which Hugh now saw fit to express his opinion.

'Jesus Christ,' he exclaimed loudly, 'it's like walking into someone's bad breath. Why doesn't someone open a fucking window and let some fresh air in?'

To a man, the patients turned and looked at him. One, who was sitting by the table, leaned forward and turned down the wireless. An air of amused expectancy hung over Francesca Ward.

It was the little nurse who broke the silence at last.

'Mr Fleming,' she snapped, 'you have already got off to a bad start by arriving two hours late, stinking of whisky, which means someone is going to have to come in specially tomorrow morning to prepare you for your operation. I don't know who you think you are, but if I were you, I'd keep my opinions to myself and get quietly into bed before I found myself in really deep water. We don't take kindly to showing off or bad language in this ward. You're in a hospital now, not a college common room.'

And glaring round the ward at the grinning faces, she marched firmly out of the room.

Hugh looked at Tim and pulled a face.

'If you think she's fierce,' Tim said, 'wait till you meet Sister Beatty.'

'I suspect I already have,' said Hugh. 'She was called Sister Grice in those days.'

Fifteen minutes later, Hugh had been undressed, washed and

104

tucked up in bed. By now the initial effects of the whisky had disappeared, his head was aching and he was feeling decidedly sorry for himself. He stared gloomily round the ward at his fellow patients.

'You must be Fleming.' Hugh turned to the speaker in the bed on his left, a grey-haired man with a flap-graft on his nose and the rest of his face a mass of red-ribbed keloid scars. 'We heard you were coming. I'm Ronald Ibbotson.'

'How do you do,' said Hugh politely but without much enthusiasm.

Ibbotson continued, 'That's Clive Unsworth on your right. Tipped his Hurricane over on his first take-off and fried for several minutes before anyone could get him out, poor chap.'

It had been eight months since Unsworth had been brought in, an unrecognizable lump of burned meat, to lie day after day in a bath of suppuration. For a long while any kind of surgery had been out of the question. But at last his skin had healed sufficiently to allow him to go away to a convalescent home for three months and build up his strength. Now he was back for the first of the fifty operations he would have to undergo before Meikle had finished with him. In so far as a face, frozen by flame, is able to express anything at all, Unsworth smiled – or at least his eyes did.

'He's been through a rough patch,' said Ibbotson, 'but he's feeling a different man now, aren't you, Clive?'

'I feel terrific,' said Unsworth. There was not a trace of irony or bitterness in his voice. Hugh marvelled at his self-control. At least he and Tim had the satisfaction of knowing that their wounds had been received while fighting the enemy; that they had done their bit. Their scars were nothing if not honourable. But Clive had never even made it into the air. He would have no tale of daring to explain his looks in years to come. He would hope people would never ask how it happened, and if anyone did, he would mutter something about a flying accident and move rapidly on to some other subject. His burns were far more serious than Hugh's and his recovery would be doubly difficult, and yet he could still say that he felt terrific and mean it. He made Hugh feel suddenly rather small.

Gradually, he learned something of the others in Francesca Ward. David Edwards in the bed opposite had been a member of the Oxford University Air Squadron when war broke out. He had lost his looks and the use of his hands in a Hurricane over the Thames Estuary in the early days of the Battle of Britain. He had spent six hours bobbing around in the healing salt water of the North Sea, blind and ready for death, before being hauled out by the North Foreland lifeboat and dunked into Meikle's saline baths for many weeks until his skin was sufficiently healed to take grafts. Like Hugh, his eyelids had contracted badly and his fingers were as stiff and brittle as dry twigs. He still had many months of operations and recuperation ahead of him before he would be ready for work of any sort, and even then there was no guarantee that his hands would be capable of any but the most simple tasks. Yet already he was convinced he was going back to flying. On the day that he was shot down, he swore that for every operation he had to undergo, he would kill a German pilot, and he talked and thought of nothing else.

In the next bed was Russell Johnson, a huge Australian fruit farmer, whose legs had been so badly burnt when his limping Blenheim had crashed on landing that he could not walk and his hands were useless. Yet his determination to get back into the war was every bit as fierce as David's. Nor were they the only two. Noel Mackinnon, six foot three, lean and fair-haired, with a first in Oriental Languages from Christ Church, who had had his Spitfire shot from under him three times in three weeks during the month of August, the last time in flames, was equally single-minded in his intention to take his revenge on the Germans. So, too, was the Czech Sergeant pilot, Victor Szepezy, lipless, lidless and minus a nose, whose incomprehensible broken English was supplemented by an equally obscure series of hand gestures. And Christian Fougerolles, a Free French pilot who had flown with 48 squadron until being shot through the jaw which was now held together by an elaborate system of steel scaffolding, thus preventing him from expressing himself quite as volubly as he might have wished on the filthiness of the Boche and the foulness of the liquid diet which he sucked up noisily through a rubber tube.

To Hugh, who had never seriously contemplated the possibility of flying again – at least operationally – or indeed of doing anything other than moving aimlessly from hospital to convalescent home and back to hospital again, this constant talk of sorties and combat and revenge and scoring seemed nothing more than idle day-dreaming. Of course the thought had crossed his mind more than once that the day might come when he would have to consider what he was going to do with the rest of his life. Doubtless something would present itself: a friend or a relation would suggest some undemanding sinecure or other. But he need not worry about that for a time yet. With loving parents and sufficient money to ensure a long and leisurely recovery, he was in no hurry. He had done his bit, won his putty medal, suffered his wounds. The idea that he should go through the whole thing again could not have been further from his mind, and the confidence of his fellow-patients disturbed and irritated him.

'Don't tell me you subscribe to this absurd cult of self-destruction,' he said to Ibbotson.

'How do you mean?' asked the older man.

'All this brave talk about getting back into the war.'

'What else is there to talk about?' said Ibbotson.

'You're as mad as the rest of them,' said Hugh.

Later, two pretty little VAD nurses came round with hot drinks. Hugh ungraciously accepted some pale, milky substance and glared at the nurse, who turned with a bright smile to Ibbotson.

'Ovaltine as usual for you, Air Vice-Marshal?'

When she had gone, Hugh said, 'I'm so sorry, sir, I had no idea . . .'

Ibbotson gave him a friendly smile.

'In the world of the limbless, the one-armed man is king,' he said gently. 'Fire is no respecter of persons, and neither is Angus Meikle. If Churchill himself were brought in here with a cigar burn on his little finger, he would be treated exactly the same as young Victor over there.' He indicated Szepezy the Czech in the bed next to him. 'Isn't that so, Vic?'

'You bloody well right, Ron,' the Czech called out.

'You'll soon get used to the idea,' Ibbotson told Hugh. 'It's perfectly true that officers have their own recreation room here and are sent to convalesce in luxurious homes on the south coast, while other ranks have their own recreation room and have to convalesce according to strict RAF medical discipline. I think that's rather a shame myself, but there we are. Here in this ward, though, there is no such thing as rank or privilege. If Russ Johnson needs wheeling to the bogs and I happen to be around, I'm as happy to do the pushing as Vic Szepezy is to cut my meat or wipe my backside. Learning to come to terms with the idea that we're all in the same boat is probably the only good thing to have come out of this whole bloody mess as far as I'm concerned.'

'And the nurses,' David Edwards called out.

'Right,' Clive Unsworth joined in. 'If it wasn't for them, we'd all have gone mad weeks ago.'

'Just because that new blonde nurse smiled at you this afternoon,' Ibbotson called out. 'Forget it, Clive. It's me she's after.'

A chorus of shouts and boos and catcalls greeted this.

'She doesn't go for the older man, Ron,' Russ Johnson roared from the other side of the ward. 'She told me so herself.'

'Next thing you know, he'll be pulling rank on us,' said Clive.

'I'd like to see him try,' said David. 'Meikle'd have you in hospital blues in no time.'

'Angus has put four sets aside as a threat to patients who show signs of being particularly obstreperous,' Ibbotson told Hugh. 'So far, no one has had to suffer this ultimate humiliation, but one of these days someone'll push him just that little bit too far and find himself walking into the town in patched and shapeless garments, like a convict.'

'In other words,' Tim Holland called out from the far end of the ward, 'if ever you feel like airing your grievances, don't.'

'When you think,' said Clive Unsworth, 'we lie about here all day, warm and well fed and waited on hand and foot by the prettiest collection of girls you could wish for outside the

J. Arthur Rank studios – what have we got to complain about anyway?'

Another man might have been relieved and reassured, happy even, to find himself, like a new boy at school, amongst others who had suffered similar if not worse misfortunes than himself, but Hugh was far from happy. Whatever the nurse may have told him on his arrival, Francesca Ward was remarkably like a college common room in Cambridge. Its inmates, with one or two obvious exceptions, were very much the sort of people one might expect to find lounging about in armchairs, drinking tea and discussing the outcome of a college cricket match. The same schoolboyish atmosphere of irreverence and mock serious debate on any subject that came up, however trivial, prevailed there as it had prevailed in the rooms of any of his friends in Cambridge. Two years ago, he would doubtless have fallen in with the general mood and soon been leading whatever campaign against authority was being mooted. Yet now he felt detached and superior to it all, as though he were his own father being forced to spend all his time with his children, and listen to their stupid bickering, and join in their puerile jokes and fancies. At Cambridge he had begun to have dreams that he was back at school – as a schoolboy, but not of schoolboy age: a mature young man of the world, used to drinking and smoking and women, who was suddenly back in the world where all three things were forbidden, bedtime was ten o'clock sharp, and the freedom to turn his back on the world was denied on pain of lack of house spirit. Now, as he lay in the darkness of the hospital ward, listening to the moans and grunts and low mutterings and the twanging of complaining bed springs beneath turning bodies, it was as though his nightmare had finally come true. He hated being there amongst all those cripples with whom he felt he had nothing in common – not even injury. He hated the smell and the heat and the noise of the raucous radio, blaring out its fatuous dance music and popular songs. He hated the clubbishness of the place and the assumption on everyone's part that he wished to become an instant and enthusiastic member. He hated the inanity of the conversation and everyone's cheerful acceptance of their lot. He didn't feel like smiling because, as far as he was concerned, there was nothing to smile about, and he was damned if he was going to pretend there was. No, perhaps the pretty little nurse had been right after all. This was not a college common room; it was a hospital.

Hugh slept so little that night and felt so wretched that the appearance shortly after six of a male orderly with a dressings trolley was positively cheering.

His name was Roy; he was a large, unsmiling Glaswegian, and he had come, he announced in gloomy tones, to 'prep' Hugh and Tim for their operations.

'Ye'll be having the wee Thiersch grafts,' he told Hugh, and proceeded to sterilize a patch of skin on the inside of his right arm. He then, with remarkable delicacy for one so large-fisted, shaved all the hair from the area.

After that, he covered it with a loose bandage and set off glumly to the far end of the ward where he went through the same dour procedure on Hugh's leg.

Soon afterwards, a nurse wheeled a stretcher to the side of Hugh's bed and helped him clamber aboard.

'This will make you feel sleepy,' she said, slipping a needle into his arm.

'You're eight hours too late,' Hugh told her. A screen was pulled round him, and after a further half hour of butterflies in the stomach, a couple of nurses appeared and, to the accompaniment of loud cheers from Tim and the others, wheeled him out of the ward, across the garden and into the main building. He had the impression of being pushed along endless corridors and through countless swing doors before finally coming to rest in a brilliantly lit world of lamps and tubes and masked men and women. The anaesthetist greeted him cheerfully, then Meikle marched in in a white skull cap and green gown.

'Welcome to the chopping block,' he said.

The last thing Hugh could remember was a pair of beautiful green eyes smiling down at him over the top of a mask, and his thinking 'Just like the farmer's wife in the field.' And then

110

a veil to match her eyes rushed up over his head and he fell into a bottomless pit.

He awoke in a panic to find he was blind. Having expected to have his left eye bandaged and his right open, this came as a deep shock. His first thought was that something terrible and unforeseen had taken place. Meikle had failed; the operation had gone wrong. In addition to being disfigured and without the use of his hands, he was to spend the rest of his life without sight. It was like those early claustrophobic days in Ashford all over again, when he had had to rely on everyone to perform the simplest tasks for him. And like then, he did not wish to go on living.

The reason he felt certain something had gone wrong was that the Charge Nurse had told him that when he woke up he would feel very little discomfort apart from a slight soreness of the eyes. Yet now it felt as though someone were pressing great lead weights against his eyes, and his eyeballs were being pierced by red-hot needles. His head hurt abominably and the inside of his arm was so sore he did not dare move it. He also felt extremely sick.

The everyday sounds of ward life advanced and receded nightmarishly – knives and forks being rattled and chinked against china, the bustling footsteps of nurses coming and going, long silences followed by outbursts of incomprehensible conversation and guffaws of laughter, the ceaseless bellow of the radio. At one point he called out to someone to switch the bloody thing down, but, as at Ashford, he did not seem able to make himself understood. Occasionally people would approach him and whisper over his head. He cursed them and they went away.

Then a woman with a pretty Irish accent announced that the operation had been a great success; Mr Meikle was delighted and everything had gone so well that he had decided to do both eyelids while he was about it.

'Is that why I'm blind?' Hugh asked her.

'You're not blind,' the voice told him. 'They're only bandages. They'll be off in a day or two. Now just you rest now.'

111

Some time later he felt well enough to ask Ibbotson who had been the owner of the beautiful Irish voice.

'Oh, that was Sister Beatty, I expect,' he told him.

'Sister Beatty? But I thought she was supposed to be a dragon from the bogs who wore barbed wire next to her skin and ate small babies for breakfast.'

'I am, and I've sometimes been known to gnaw on an airman or two for my elevenses, Mr Fleming.'

The voice came from so near that Hugh started and swore involuntarily.

'Jesus Christ.'

'Not quite, Mr Fleming, but certainly not to be under-estimated.'

Footsteps marched icily away down the ward, accompanied by stifled giggles and snortings from Ibbotson and Unsworth.

'Great help you lot are,' Hugh grumbled, and was suddenly and violently sick.

He was bandaged and helpless for five days, during which time there was nothing he could do for himself. Whether it was eating or drinking, standing or sitting, cleaning his teeth or going to the lavatory, he had to call out for help. It was, he decided on the second day, quite the most humiliating time of his life. To make matters worse, it was impossible to know who was near or available when he called for help, and thus to spread the work load. Occasionally he would find he had summoned up one of the nurses, but nine times out of ten it was Air Vice-Marshal Ibbotson who rallied to the call. The first few times, Hugh was both impressed and flattered that such a senior officer – regardless of what he had said about the absence of rank – should take so much trouble over one so junior. Nothing was too much trouble for the older man. Hugh drew the line at allowing him to wipe his bottom. However, one day, the Air Vice-Marshal happened to discover that Hugh had taken to dispensing with the habit, and from then on there was no holding him. Soon, from being touched and grateful, Hugh found Ibbotson's constant attentions faintly irritating, and he would postpone urgent tasks for hours on end rather than run

112

the risk of feeling those helpful hands once more at his elbow, and hearing that anxious, eager voice in his ear. After a while he began to imagine that some conspiracy had been hatched by the inmates of Francesca Ward simply to humiliate him, whereby whenever he called out, the others would stand where they were, holding their noses in silent laughter in one hand, while signalling Ron Ibbotson to move forward with the other. Or perhaps Ibbotson himself was not in on it after all, and they were killing themselves with laughter at both their expense as he hurried forward like a Boy Scout trying for his Endeavour badge.

At all events, the more Ibbotson helped him, the more Hugh found himself resenting that help, until by the fifth day he realized with a shock that he actually hated the man. He relied on him for everything, yet his flesh crawled and he had to make a conscious effort not to cringe whenever he came near.

Hugh never knew whether Ibbotson had the faintest inkling of his feelings, and had the situation continued much longer, he wondered how he could have avoided making them evident. As it was, on the sixth day after the operation, the bandages were removed and a mirror brought for him to admire the great man's handiwork.

'My God,' exclaimed Hugh, 'I look like a drunken panto horse. No wonder I needed all those bandages. They'd have fallen off otherwise.'

'Now that's not a very grateful thing to be saying, after all the trouble Mr Meikle's taken with you,' said Sister Beatty, who turned out to be tall, slim, fair-haired, with lovely big green eyes. 'They're as beautiful a pair as I've ever seen him give anyone, and I've seen a few in my time, I can tell you.'

'But they're far too big,' complained Hugh. 'I'll never get that lot open and shut. They'll sap my strength. I'll be an old man at twenty-five. Look . . . what did I tell you?'

By lifting his face up to the ceiling, he could just see ahead of him, but the moment he brought his face down to normal level again, the huge new lids closed, like a doll's but in reverse.

Sister Beatty explained they were always that size to begin

with, but that they'd soon shrink and that any odd bits that were left over could always be trimmed at a later date.

Two days later, Robin arrived out of the blue with the news that he and Peter had both got DFCs and been given sections, that Hawkesworth was missing over the Channel and that Jimmy Macdonell was dead.

Hugh received the news without emotion. Pat, Julian and now Jimmy, all dead. He repeated the names over and over again to himself, hoping that somehow the sheer repetition of the words would arouse some feeling within him, but it still meant nothing. Even his lack of emotion failed to distress him. Nor was he particularly pleased to see Robin. Apart from a brief letter of condolence soon after the accident, they had not communicated for many weeks.

They walked for a while in the garden and sat in deckchairs against a wall in the pale sunshine and talked. Robin told him about the squadron and how things had changed since the battle, and about the new pilots who had come in and made them all feel like old men.

Hugh listened politely but without real interest. He tried to visualize the station and recreate in his mind the atmosphere of the dispersal hut and the Mess and the Carpenter's Arms, but the images were incomplete and badly out of focus. He in turn attempted to describe to Robin some of his own recent experiences. He watched his friend's face as he nodded and smiled and frowned, but he knew that really he did not understand.

Hugh felt as remote now in his new world of hospitals and convalescent homes and operating theatres as ever he had been on a fighter station, and Robin was evidently finding it as difficult to attune himself to the language of sickness as Muv and Far and their friends in the village had when he had blinded them with RAF slang and shop back in the summer.

He wanted to talk to Robin about so many things : about his mother's strange refusal to accept the fact of his injuries and Susan's outburst that day in Ashford; about Bunny and Jean and the Soho tart; about his constant fear of impotence and rejection by decent women – so many things. And yet he felt

114

now that he could not trust even Robin to take him seriously. From now on, they would be talking to each like two foreigners with only a passing knowledge of each other's language. They knew the words, but the shades and nuances of idiom would escape them again and again. From now on, his real friends had to be people like Tim Holland and David Edwards and Noel Mackinnon and, God help him, Ron Ibbotson. Susan had scoffed at the exclusive circles in which he had immersed himself at Eton, at Cambridge and later in the RAF. He wondered what she would have to say about the even more peculiarly self-contained world of cripples and faceless men and deformed monsters in which he now found himself, and which he needed more than any other in his life before.

Hugh and Robin sat for a while in silence in the sunshine. Finally Hugh said, 'It's funny, isn't it, to think that only a short time ago we'd have had so much to talk about, but now we're like two strangers on a park bench.'

'Strangers on park benches tend to reveal things to each other that they'd never dare tell their dearest friends,' said Robin.

'You know what I mean,' said Hugh dully.

'Yes,' said Robin. 'I know what you mean. You don't want to tell me anything because you've convinced yourself I won't understand. I daresay you're right. How could I? I've never been burnt. I can't begin to imagine what it must be like. No one can. And I'd be a fool to try and kid you that I do. But that's no reason to clam up on me completely. I may not understand it all, but merely telling me may help *you* to understand better. Silence on both sides is not going to help anyone, not now and certainly not later on. Suddenly we find ourselves in different worlds, with different problems to resolve, and as long as this war continues, this gap of understanding will doubtless exist between us. But one day it's going to come to an end, and when it does, those of us who survive – the burnt, the crippled, the heroes, the cowards – we're all going to be faced with exactly the same problems: how to rebuild the world, how to make sure a war like this never happens again, how to live in peacetime, how to make a living and bring up families. Oh yes,

115

you, too, Hugh. You'll have a wife and a family one day. You may not believe now that any woman will ever want to look at you again, let alone marry you and have your children. But you're wrong. All right, so Bunny couldn't take it. I heard about it from Peter. And knowing you, I daresay your pride was hurt, even though you had already given her up as a bad job. And Jean is dead, and you're feeling thoroughly sorry for yourself. I wouldn't blame you for wishing yourself dead, too, sometimes. But you're not. You're alive like me, and we've got to go on. It's not just a matter of dreary inevitability. It's our duty and our responsibility. You're a clever man, an intelligent man, a charming man, too, when you want to be. You're also, I believe, beneath all that intellectual superiority and world-weariness, a man whose heart is in the right place. You have a lot to offer – not just to some woman, but to mankind. When this bloody war's over, we're going to need people like you in this country, Hugh, and the sooner you get that into your thick head, the better it will be for all of us.'

Hugh grunted.

'Quite what sort of job you had in mind for me,' he said, 'I can't imagine.' He lifted his hands, yellow and livid red and thin as chicken's claws. 'What would you suggest? Professional golfer? Conjurer? Croupier? The most complicated manoeuvre I have so far mastered is waving. This time next year, who knows, I might even have advanced to scratching my head.'

'There you go again,' said Robin, 'feeling sorry for yourself. Of course you can't do much yet. There are some things you used to take for granted that you may never be able to do again. Bowling off-breaks, rock climbing, a handful (if you'll excuse the expression) of trivial sporting activities. So what? You can still think, can't you? You don't need your hands for that. Besides, I'm no medical man, but I'd be prepared to bet you a hundred pounds that within six months you'll be able to use a pencil and a paintbrush and clean your teeth and brush your hair and do most of the things you used to do before the accident.'

'Like flying a Spitfire, I suppose?'

'That's up to you.'

'Everyone else in the ward can't wait to get back into the cockpit.'

'They shouldn't be blamed for that. It's probably the only thing they know how to do.'

'What makes you think I'm any different? And yet I can't think of anything I'd rather do less.'

Robin smiled and shook his head.

'You think you've changed, Hugh, but you haven't, you know. You're still the nervous duck you always were: calm and unruffled above the water but paddling like hell underneath, not knowing quite what direction you're supposed to be aiming for or how quickly you should be getting there. You believe yourself different from everyone else, with special problems of your own that no one else has ever encountered before. You could perfectly easily solve them all if only you'd have the guts to admit you're just like the rest of us – uncertain, scared, lacking in real convictions. A burnt pilot announces he wants to get back to flying. You don't. You can't understand why. There must be something wrong with you. Panic and confusion. There you are, you say, I knew all along I was different from the rest. You, too, may want to get back into flying one day – next week, tomorrow perhaps, who knows? On the other hand, you may never get the urge to go within a hundred yards of an aeroplane again as long as you live. Instead, you discover you want to be a writer, or an artist, or a teacher, or a film producer. I don't know, and neither do you, yet. But you will. When the time comes, you'll know what to do, believe me. I don't hold many firm convictions, whatever you may think; but one thing I am sure of, Hugh. Some good is going to come out of this mess, for all of us. We're all too deeply embroiled in the mire at present to have any idea of what it might be. But in the end, we'll all be better men for it, just you wait and see.'

Robin stood up to leave.

'We've lost contact rather in the last few months, Hugh. I realize that. It's no one's fault. Whatever happens to both of us from now on, let's always try to remain friends and not lose trust in each other. We long-haired boys have got to stick together, you know. There are not many of us left.'

Hugh watched the stocky, smoke-grey figure disappearing across the lawn, his cap set at a rakish angle, and thought that, for all his jauntiness, he had never seen a man who looked more tired. Then he turned and shuffled away towards the hut.

Chapter Eight

That evening, after supper, Meikle suddenly appeared in the doorway, still in his operating robes, peered about him for a moment, then marched firmly across and sat on Hugh's bed. By now the main lights in the ward had been switched off, so that the only illumination came from the half dozen or so metal bed lamps that cast a soft glow over the handful of patients who were not yet ready for sleep. He had been operating all day, there were dark patches beneath his eyes and his face was drawn. But his eyes were as bright and mischievous as ever.

'Not feeling tired?' he whispered to Hugh.

Hugh shook his head.

'Not in the slightest.'

'Me neither,' hissed Meikle with a schoolboy grin. 'Never am after operating. Let's slip out into the corridor where we can talk. There are a couple of chairs we can sit in.'

The pair of them tip-toed across the dark floor and through the swing doors.

'That's better,' said Meikle. 'Whispering always gives me a sore throat.' They settled into a couple of faded armchairs with wooden arms. 'I'm afraid you must think I've been neglecting you. Fact is, I've been run off my feet in recent weeks. The new lids are coming along nicely, I gather.' He peered closely at them.

'Hmm,' he grunted. 'Not bad, though I say so myself. A spot of trimming and they'll be as good as new. I'll do that next time you're in. I think we'd better have a go at that nose next. The left side's okay, but the right wants patching up a bit. It's a straightforward rhinoplasty job. Nothing to worry about. It's just a question of grafting a new nose with skin from the fore-head. Funny thing is, everyone assumes plastic surgery is a modern invention. In fact, it's one of the oldest forms of medicine we know of. Way back in the 4th century, a Hindu by the name of Susruta described a technique for reconstruct-ing ear lobes with pieces of skin taken from the cheek. And rhinoplasty originated in Sicily in 1412 and was performed on several vain young men unlucky or unskilful enough to lose their noses in duels.'

'Well, even if you went completely mad and grafted my left foot onto the middle of my face, I certainly couldn't look uglier than I do now.'

Meikle chuckled.

'You're as impatient and vain as the rest of them,' he said. 'They see the results for themselves day after day, and yet they all believe that, just for them, I'm going to wave a magic wand instead of a scalpel, and they're going to wake up to find they've been transformed from ugly frogs into handsome princes. I'm afraid it's never as easy as that. On the contrary, in the first few weeks after plastic surgery, everyone looks twice as hideous as they did when they were burnt. If you think you look ugly now, wait till you see what your nose looks like after I've had it on the chopping block for an hour or so. I'm sorry, there's nothing I can do about it. I wish there was.'

'In other words, I can expect to remain a lumpy chrysalis for some time to come yet.'

'Vanity, vanity,' murmured Meikle. 'Let me see. Nose, lower lids, upper lip, left ear. We may be able to combine some of those in one operation. I'll also need to do some work on those hands. Fortunately, they're not too bad. The fingers have con-tracted into the palms rather, but a couple of grafts should ease the tightness of the skin and some regular physiotherapy should do the rest. This time next year you should be able to make them do more or less what you want.'

Hugh said, 'I'd rather it was in half that time. I've got a hundred quid on it.'

'It's possible,' said Meikle, 'but a lot of it's up to you. I can heal bodies, but I can't always adjust minds.'

'I thought the whole point of suffering was that it made a better man of you,' said Hugh sardonically.

'Balls,' said Meikle sharply. 'Suffering does not build character. Why should it? In my experience it's far more likely to destroy it. Anyone who thinks it's an easy matter to show a hideously disfigured face to the world wants his brains examined. The natural reaction is to hide from the world, not to lay oneself open to expressions of disgust. Anyone can do that. Just as anyone can look at deformity and pretend he sees nothing out of the ordinary. The exceptional man is the one who can present himself to others in all his ugliness and make them genuinely believe he is no different from them. The trouble is, most people are too vain to be able to carry it off. They are thinking all the time of themselves and what others think of them, when really they should be thinking of others and putting them at their ease. But then the man who is capable of that would be an exceptional character in any circumstances.'

'I get the impression you don't have a lot of time for people who worry about losing their looks,' said Hugh.

'I'm afraid you're right,' said Meikle grimly. 'Literally so. My job and that of all my colleagues – Gillies, McIndoe, Kilner, Mowlem and the rest – is quite simply to get men fit and ready again for active service as soon as is humanly possible, not to give them fancy face-lifts. The RAF is desperately short of trained pilots and aircrew; there's no time for slow menders. If, at the end of ninety days, a man is still not fit for active duties, he is invalided out of the force, given a small disability allowance and shovelled off to some miserable Ministry of Pensions hospital to stew in his own juice. Needless to say, we've all made our feelings clear to the Air Ministry about this in no uncertain terms. Fortunately most pilots who come to us can't wait for another chance to have a crack at the Luftwaffe.'

'An attitude which you doubtless applaud.'

'I neither applaud it nor deprecate it,' said Meikle crisply. 'I am a doctor and my business is preserving life. I therefore believe it is better to live for your country than die for it. If a man has a burning desire to shoot down Germans, I say good luck to him. Let's hope he succeeds and let's hope there are many more like him. But any man who is not obliged to go shooting down Germans, doesn't wish to, and only does so for fear of losing face, would be better advised to turn his hand to something else. Because the chances are he'll only be shot down again, and either land me with a whole lot more work that I don't need or else be killed. Either way, it's a waste of everyone's time. Does that help ease your conscience a little?'

Hugh looked at him sharply.

'Meaning?'

'Meaning nothing. You obviously have doubts.'

'Doesn't everybody?'

'Yes, but not usually quite as many as you.'

'In other words, you think I'm making heavier weather of all this than I need?'

'Why the guilty conscience?' Meikle asked him, shaking his head in puzzlement. 'Everyone reacts differently to personal disaster. In the case of airman's burn, most begin by thanking God they're alive, then wishing to God they were dead, and end up hoping to God that they can soon get back to what they were doing before they were so rudely interrupted. Along the way, there are all sorts of diversions and variations and setbacks. Some hate having to have everything done for them, others revel in it. Some regret the loss of their looks, others are extraordinarily indifferent. Some get depressed at being involved in all the pain and suffering, others thrive on it. In places like this the abnormal is normal and many draw strength from finding they are not alone in their ugliness; for others it's the opposite. I can do a certain amount to help, by cutting out as many signs of officialdom and red tape as I possibly can – painting the huts a cheerful colour, replacing old iron service beds with comfortable beds, banning the wearing of hospital blues and so on. We encourage friends and visitors to come as often as possible, we recruit the prettiest VADs in the south of England, and we generally try to make patients feel they'd rather be here than at any other hospital in the country. If a patient has problems, he can come and see me and talk about them any time he wants – except when I'm

122

operating, that is. The rest is up to him. There's very little more I can do. Anyway, I mustn't keep you up any longer.'

The eyes, Hugh noticed, were glazed now with fatigue, and it was with something of a struggle that the surgeon heaved his bulk out of the old chair.

Hugh said, 'I'm sorry. You must be dead on your feet.'

'I didn't mean it like that,' said Meikle, genuinely embarrassed.

'Whether you meant it or not, I'm glad you said it. You're the second person today who has reminded me what a self-centred bastard I am.'

Meikle stood looking down at Hugh for a moment in silence, then he said, 'I have a suggestion, and I don't see why the powers that be should raise any objection. You're about ready for another bout of convalescence. Instead of taking it in Bournemouth or Torquay at one of the homes, why not go to Norfolk for a few weeks? I've had a word on the 'phone with your parents; told them the form – what to expect and so on. They sounded sweet. Obviously can't wait to get you home again. How about it? Try living in a real house for a change, with real people. Meet a few of the locals. Breathe a different air. Involve yourself in real life again. It may give you some new ideas. In fact, I'll get on to the Air Ministry straight away.' He glanced at his watch. 'Well, tomorrow perhaps. These Whitehall paper pushers work such miserably short hours.'

The following morning Meikle marched into the ward, a huge grin plastered all over his face.

'It's all fixed,' he boomed. 'A car will be here this afternoon to take you to the station. I've told your parents you're on your way. Lucky sod!'

Tim Holland, who was also on his way to convalesce with his newly grafted hand, shared the taxi.

'I hope you cope better with your family than I did with mine last time I went home. They fussed round me like a couple of old hens. Wouldn't leave me alone for a second. Every time I bent my arm or stretched my leg or broke wind, one of them was up and across asking if I needed help. Nothing

123

I said made the slightest difference. It was as much as I could do to prevent them holding my cock when I went for a pee. I tell you, a couple of weeks of that aged me thirty years. I'm surprised I didn't start dribbling.'

'There's not much chance of that at home,' Hugh told him. 'My mother seems to be under the impression I've merely singed the end of my fingers with a lighted match, and my father just sits staring at me with a pained expression on his face, as if I'd suddenly started using make-up.'

Tim gave a doubtful grunt. 'I'll give it three days. After that you're very welcome to join me at the Ritz. Nancy will be delighted to see you too. She's taken quite a fancy to you, you know.'

Hugh was astonished. 'The Ritz?' he exclaimed. 'Does Meikle know you're going to an hotel?'

'Sort of,' said Tim cryptically. 'Oh, by the way, talking of make-up, I suppose there's no point in my asking you if these are any use to you? I don't use 'em myself. Not my style.'

He reached into his pocket and produced a pair of large, round sun-glasses.

Hugh laughed.

'Where on earth did you get them from?'

'Sister Beatty,' said Tim. 'She slipped 'em into my pocket as I was leaving. Said she thought they might come in useful for the ego.'

'Sister Beatty?' said Hugh in disbelief. 'That baby muncher? I'd never thought of you as her blue-eyed boy.'

'Oh, she's a good sort underneath that fire-eating exterior, you know,' said Tim. 'As you'd find out for yourself if only you were a bit nicer to the nurses.'

'I don't know what you mean.' Hugh frowned.

'They're only simple girls, trying to do their jobs. Most of them have received very little training and they're terrified out of their wits more often than not. You are rather hard on them, you know.'

'But I'm always making jokes,' Hugh protested.

'They don't know that,' said Tim. 'They don't understand your sense of humour. They think you're being serious.'

124

'Are you sure?'

'They're all scared to death of you. But then I imagine you quite enjoy that.'

Hugh stared at him in genuine amazement.

Tim went on, 'One of them must have said something to Sister Beatty. She doesn't like her girls being unhappy. Means they don't do their work so well. Hence you are not her number one patient. I hope you don't mind my mentioning it?'

Hugh laughed and said, 'My departure was obviously better timed than I'd imagined.' But he spent most of the journey up to town in silence, staring out of the window.

They did not waste much time over their good-byes at Victoria Station. Hugh had no wish to be reminded of his last visit there more than was necessary.

Tim said, 'Don't forget. In case of emergency, just ring the Ritz.' He paused for a moment, then added, 'To play the bastard successfully with women, you've got to have the looks to carry it off. None of us can take anything for granted any more.'

And with a wave of a bandaged hand, he turned and walked off.

Hugh's father met him at King's Lynn station with the news that James Arundel was dead. At first the War Office had told Susan that he had been captured and was in a POW camp, but then they'd written again to say there had been a muddle over names. They extended their deepest sympathy.

'Naturally she's pretty cut up, as you can imagine. We suggested she come down for a few days with the children. Your mother's with her now. It was the least we could do.'

Hugh closed his eyes and rested his head against the leather seat of the old Humber. It had been a lousy journey. The restaurant car had been closed, the heating had been out of order, and he had had to share a compartment with a woman who had taken one look at him and for the remainder of the three hour journey tried to pretend he wasn't there at all.

'It isn't catching, you know,' he had told her, after her gaze had flitted sightlessly past him and out of the window for the umpteenth time.

Her mouth had set itself into an even tighter, even primer posture.

'Would you feel easier if I stopped breathing?'

At this she had stood up, gathered up her magazine and her small suitcase, and, still without looking at him, left the compartment. As schoolboys, Adrian Downpatrick and he had been known to clear an entire compartment in two minutes flat with their impressions of lunatics. Now he could do it without even trying.

'I hope you'll be nice to her,' said his father.

'Yes, of course,' replied Hugh. 'As long as she's nice to me in return.'

'If you can't be friends now . . .' Arthur Fleming's voice tailed away sadly.

'Don't worry, Far,' said Hugh, touched as he always was by his father's inability ever to say what he really wanted. 'I'm not in that much of a mood for arguing. Poor old Sue. To tell you the truth, I'm more concerned about Muv than I am about her. At least the two of us have always known where we stand. But Muv seems to have retreated into a strange, unreal world of her own. God knows, I don't want her upsetting herself over all this, but surely she must be made to understand that it's a bit more serious than a grazed knee.

'I don't know,' said his father. 'I just don't understand. She's never once cried, you know. Nothing. I'm sure it's all wrong. I feel I ought to say something, but I'm frightened of what might happen. She might break down completely. I don't know . . .'

He turned his head away and looked out of the side window, but not quickly enough to prevent Hugh seeing the tears that had welled up in his eyes.

'Don't worry, Far,' Hugh said again. 'We must just give it time. Now that I'm home, perhaps . . .'

Perhaps what? She might admit to herself that her son no longer matched up to the golden image she kept tucked away in her memory, like an old photograph? Was that what he wanted? Perhaps it might be better for all of them if the pretence were maintained. In which case, it might have been a

126

mistake to come home at all – especially with Susan there. Who knew how she might behave?

They drove for a while in silence through the dark, undulating countryside. The tyres hissed on the wet, muddy road, and a sea mist combined with the dimmed war-time headlights to make driving slow and the journey seemingly endless. Hugh's arm was hurting and he had a splitting headache.

'We were hoping,' said Arthur, 'I mean, I don't know quite what your plans are, but . . . if you could all stay on till Christmas . . . It's been such a long time since we were all together under one roof. I only wish it could be in happier circumstances, but I suppose we can't have everything . . .'

'We'll see, Far,' Hugh told him. 'We'll see.'

The Rectory was set back from the road behind a high wall with white wooden gates at either end. As the Humber drew up before one of these, Hugh automatically prepared to get out to open them, but his father put out a restraining hand and climbed out instead. As they entered the drive, Hugh found he had butterflies in his stomach, as though he were about to take off on a sortie. His father was helping him out when the front door opened and out ran Percy, barking and jumping up and down. Behind him, in the light of the hall, stood Mrs Fleming.

'Darling,' she said, clutching her hands together at her waist, 'was it a terrible journey? You must be tired. And hungry. The children are already in bed and asleep. Susan's in the kitchen getting supper. Roast chicken. Your favourite. We were lucky to get one. Ted Nudds is becoming more difficult every day. Your room's all ready. I expect you'd like to wash. Is that all your luggage? You're looking well.'

Hugh leaned forward to peck her on the cheek, but she scarcely seemed to notice.

'The weather's been quite pleasant until today. Then this wretched sea mist came up. The children wanted to wait up for you, but I said no. They're tired out from all the travelling, poor little mites. I expect you are, too. Do you really have to wear those dark glasses indoors? I'm sure it's not necessary.'

Hugh stared at her at a loss quite what to do to stop this endless flow of small talk. But then, from the far end of the

127

hall, Susan appeared, wiping her hands on her apron. She advanced a little, then paused uncertainly. Her eyes were dull and puffy and her skin was drawn and tinged with grey.

'Hallo, Susan,' said Hugh softly.

Mrs Fleming's voice died away. Her husband closed the front door quietly behind him and turned the key in the lock. Susan stared at her brother for a moment, her face empty of expression. Then she gave a little cry. 'Hugh,' she whispered. 'Oh, Hugh.' And stumbling forward, she threw her arms around him and fell sobbing against his chest. Hugh stood there stiffly for a moment or two, then slowly he brought his gloved hands up around her shoulders and held her awkwardly.

'Forgive me,' she muttered between sobs, 'I didn't mean what I said . . . I was so worried, you see . . . and then when you . . .'

'Not now,' said Hugh softly. 'Later. There'll be time later.'

And brother and sister stood there motionless, clutching each other beneath the hall light.

'It seems to me,' said their father finally, 'that everyone could do with a nice drink.'

There was a log fire burning in the sitting room. Hugh stood with his back to it, warming his fingers, as his father poured sherry for them all.

'Can you . . . er . . . ?' Arthur asked, holding out a glass. 'Or would you like someone to . . . er . . . ?'

Hugh remembered Tim and smiled as he took the glass between his two bent forefingers.

'Ah, good . . . yes . . . well . . . cheers.'

Hugh took a sip and said, 'I'm afraid there are still one or two little things I can't do for myself. Washing, shaving, cleaning my teeth, dressing, undressing and so on. I also have to remember not to close doors behind me whenever I go into a room. It can prove very embarrassing.'

They all laughed.

Arthur said, 'Well, whenever you need anything, don't hesitate to sing out.'

'Now then, Arthur,' said his wife, 'he's not an invalid. He's got to learn to look after himself. Others have. Look at that Douglas Bader.'

128

'It's incredible,' Hugh said to his sister as he sat with her in the kitchen after supper while she washed up. 'It still hasn't sunk in. Does she go on like this with you?'

Susan sighed. 'I think she's accepted that James is dead. She didn't say much. Still doesn't. She never seemed particularly upset. Of course, she never really liked him, any more than you did.'

Hugh did not reply. It was not the moment for that sort of conversation.

'There was a woman on the train coming down today,' he said, 'who was trying so hard to pretend she had noticed nothing odd about me that she finished up by behaving as though I were invisible. Why do the English find it so difficult to behave naturally?'

'They don't want to hurt one's feelings, I suppose.'

'And so they behave with such good manners that they end up being downright rude. The other day a group of us went into Ashbourne Wood for tea at the Galleon Restaurant. It's nothing unusual. In fact, by now, the locals have become so used to seeing people like us, they generally treat us pretty much as part of the furniture. However, on this occasion, no sooner had we sat down and ordered our tea and crumpets than this middle-aged woman in a hat turned to her middle-aged friend, also in a hat, and said loudly, "They really shouldn't allow them out like that." Russell Johnson immediately turned round to her and said, "Toss us a bun from time to time, lady, and we promise we won't bite you." We all laughed, because of course the woman had behaved stupidly and thoughtlessly. But at least her reaction was an honest one. I think I can cope with honesty, but I'm damned if I can tolerate pretence and hypocrisy.'

'I'll still never forgive myself for what I said to you that day in Ashford.' Susan grimaced and shook her head.

'I think that was what taught me that honesty can always be forgiven. Whatever your reasons, that's what you really felt about me at that moment, perhaps still do for all I know. I'll admit I was puzzled at the time, even hurt. There was one

129

thing in particular you said: "Now for the first time you'll discover who your real friends are." Do you remember?'

'I've been trying to forget it ever since.'

'Maybe; but believe me, that was one of the most useful things anyone's ever said to me. And the most honest.'

'I'm glad in that case,' she said. 'But don't be too hard on Muv. She's had to put up with an awful lot in the last month or two.'

'I just wish she'd be herself and behave normally, that's all,' said Hugh. 'Apart from anything else, I really do need her help. I really can't do much for myself yet.'

Susan touched his arm.

'Don't worry,' she said. 'I think I'll be here for a little while longer yet.'

They drank their coffee in silence. It was good to be home again, Hugh thought. He had feared the worst when he heard that Susan would be there, but now it seemed he had misjudged her. Perhaps after all some good had resulted through suffering for both of them.

'How are the children?' Hugh asked her, realizing with a shock that he did not even know their names.

'Full of beans. I've told them Daddy's gone away for a long time, but I don't think it's really sunk it yet. They never ask after him. Too excited at being here, I suppose. And really they're both still only babies. Would you like to see them?'

'Now?'

'Why not? They always look their best when they're asleep.'

Hugh followed his sister up the curved staircase and along the passage. A low light shone through the half open door of the old nursery at the end. Susan put her finger to her lips and beckoned him in. Timmy, aged three, lay sprawled in an attitude of blissful abandon, legs and arms akimbo, half-in and half-out of the bedclothes. Joanna, the one year old, was face down, bottom up in the cot. A small, china night-light in the shape of a toadstool glowed on the table between them.

'Aren't they adorable?' hissed Susan.

'Adorable,' Hugh agreed.

Susan moved forward to tuck Timmy in. One of the child's

130

legs had become tangled among the sheets and in her efforts to extricate it, she woke him up. He whimpered and rubbed a fist across his nose and opened his eyes very wide.

'Hallo, darling,' murmured Susan. 'Look who's come to see you.'

Hugh leaned forward slightly and, as he did so, the glow from the lamp illuminated his face, highlighting every misshapen tuck and fold and scar, his twisted lip, his half-eaten nose and his wrinkled, staring eyes. The child's eyes widened. Susan, glancing quickly at Hugh, realized what had happened and pulled her brother roughly back by the shoulder. But the damage had been done. The terrible image had already imprinted itself on Timmy's mind, and he reacted as any child reacts who has had a nightmare. He screamed, again and again and again. Moments later, Joanna had added her own cries to those of her brother. Susan tried to calm them both, but without success. Hugh stood there helplessly before finally turning on his heel and leaving the room. In the passage he passed his parents running.

'What's happened? What is it? Is someone ill?'

They disappeared into the nursery.

Hugh paused at the top of the stairs long enough to hear Timmy shrieking at the top of his voice:

'A monster. I saw a monster. He was horrible. He came into my room and tried to kill me. I saw him. I did. I did.'

Then he went down into the sitting room closing the door quietly behind him.

Later, Susan came and sat with him on the sofa. They did not speak. After a while she went to bed. Their father came down later to say that Muv was not feeling too well and had decided to have an early night, and was there anything he needed? Hugh shook his head and continued to stare into the fire. As he passed his parent's room half an hour later on his way to bed, he could hear his mother weeping as though she had never wept before and would never stop.

December, 1940, continued as damp and grey as November. Day after day Hugh was woken by his mother drawing back the curtains to reveal the same flat, uninviting prospect of the marshes and the big sand-dunes beyond, barely discernible in the mist. Time was when Hugh would have groaned at the prospect of a further day without sunshine. Weather had always mattered very much to him. As a boy it had always dictated his mood and his plans for a day. Time and again he had sat in his room, staring out of the window, debating for so long whether or not it would stay fine for a sail or a game of golf, that in the end it had rained after all, throwing him into a black mood in which no one was spared from his caustic tongue. He had been the cause of several domestic servants handing in their notice, and on more than one occasion had reduced his mother to tears. In later, undergraduate days, Susan had taken to avoiding meals altogether in bad weather, rather than run the risk of yet another tearful confrontation across the dining room table.

Now, however, he welcomed the heavy cloud and drizzling skies. They gave him the excuse he needed to remain indoors, sleeping, reading, eating rather too little and drinking rather too much, staring out of the window. The children, although resigned by now to the idea of having an uncle with a funny face, were still nervous enough of him not to pester him to play with them or to come to his room uninvited, which suited him very well. He had never felt comfortable with children, and when his offer to read them a bedtime story was shyly refused, he did not insist.

More and more, it seemed, his life consisted of trivialities. From the moment he awoke in the morning until last thing at night, hardly a minute passed without some minor, unforeseen problem presenting itself. Opening doors was the one that caused him the greatest amount of irritation. Unfortunately the majority of the doorhandles in the Rectory were round and smooth, in keeping with the period of the house, and time and again Hugh would enter a room for a book or a cigarette only to hear the door close with a smug click behind him. His hands were too tender still to enable him to gain any purchase on the slippery knobs, even between his wrists. It was either a question of waiting until someone came to rescue him, or calling for help. One afternoon, Susan and Muv and the children went shopping in King's Lynn and he was stuck in the downstairs lavatory for over three hours.

However, since the episode in the nursery, his mother seemed to have a better understanding of the sort of help he needed. Now if she pointed out something that he was capable of doing for himself, it was generally because he was, and she was always on hand every morning to help him in the bathroom, to do up the buttons on his shirt and trousers, to knot his tie and brush his hair and make his breakfast. He still found eating and drinking a problem, and either she or Susan would eat their own food first, then sit patiently for half an hour or more, cutting up his meat, pouring out his beer, and trying not to spill anything in his lap. From time to time the inevitable would happen, and a slice of toast would land, marmalade side up on his knee, or a mouthful of hot tea would dribble down his chin and into his shirt collar. Often Hugh would be unable to restrain his irritation. But Mrs Fleming never seemed to take offence, and the care and patience that the two women devoted to him frequently put him to shame. He wished there was some way in which he could express his appreciation; saying thank you never seemed enough. But if ever he showed signs of delivering any sort of speech, his mother would make some excuse about 'getting on' and hurry away. He was curious to know the mental process whereby she had finally accepted the full extent of his disability, but he didn't like to ask. Perhaps that was the best way of all of thanking her.

One day she mentioned tentatively that Major and Mrs Hobbes and their daughter had expressed an interest in seeing him. Hugh had groaned inwardly, but agreed to tea with them the following day rather than hurt Muv's feelings. It had not been a success. Major Hobbes had adopted a hearty, confidential, military manner that was purely theatrical, regaling them with endless tales of what he had once told the GOC2 at Catterick in 1919, and generally confusing them, and sometimes himself, with a great deal of out-of-date army jargon. Every few minutes he would break off to mutter asides to Hugh like 'You'll know the form' and 'I daresay you've run into this sort of thing yourself'. Occasionally he would pause to sip at his tea or bite aggressively at a slice of cherry cake, in which case his wife, a faded beauty of fifty, with pale hair that looked as though it had been washed too often and slightly over-powdered cheeks, would spring to his rescue with a series of breathless, wide-eyed enquiries about what it felt like to be one of the Few, how many Germans he had shot down, when he would be going up to the Palace to collect his DSO, and how hospitals coped with the rationing.

Their daughter Katherine, a round-faced girl, with her mother's pale blue eyes and the faintest hint of her father's moustache across her otherwise delicate upper lip, contributed little to the conversation, but made up for it by pouring tea and passing plates with skill and enthusiasm.

Mrs Fleming, realizing at once that it had all been a great mistake, passed every second in an agony of suspense, expecting at any moment Hugh's polite smile to collapse into an expression of intense boredom and his quiet, carefully considered responses to become tinged with irony.

It was for her sake alone that he contained his irritation for as long as he did. The Hobbes had been neighbours for years. He had known them all his life and could remember when Katherine and he used to sail together in local regattas. Why then would they insist on treating him in this way? Why had they adopted those silly, false voices like so many paper hats and papier mâché noses, and why were they asking him inane questions to which they really did not wish to know the answers? Why was Katherine looking at him as though he were a complete stranger? What they really wanted to know was what it was like to be trapped in a burning Spitfire, roasting to death, watching the skin lifting from your arms and legs and feeling your face tightening to bursting point. They wanted to know how it *really* felt to be disfigured and crippled, to lose your looks and your independence, and to have to put up with people staring and turning away. They wanted to know what he thought of his chances now with women, of getting married and having children and being able to lead a normal life again. They wanted to know about plastic surgery and hear about some of the really bad cases he had encountered. And why not? It was perfectly natural. So would he, in their position. It was very interesting, for God's sake. But would they come clean and admit it? Oh no. They were so concerned with sparing his feelings they'd finished up by insulting his intelligence.

'And what are your plans for the future?' he heard Mrs Hobbes fluting at him.

He considered her question for a moment, then said mildly, 'How kind of you to ask. I was thinking of becoming an actor.'

'An actor?' she said brightly. 'How very interesting.'

'Yes,' he said. 'I thought I might specialize in horror films – Frankenstein, that sort of thing. I understand they are thinking of re-making Dr Jekyll and Mr Hyde. I don't see how I can fail to win the role, do you?' He smiled politely, and seizing his cup between both hands, sipped noisily at his tea.

Mrs Hobbes stared at him, her mouth open, speechless. Katherine, to her credit, giggled. The Major cleared his throat noisily and launched into an account of his first visit to a cinema in 1919. Muv muttered something about it being time to go. Hugh thought if he didn't leave soon, he would do something violent. He wanted to shout at them, seize them by the shoulders and shake them till their teeth rattled; to tell them to stop plying him with more cups of tea and slices of cake; to tell them about Jimmy and Julian and Pat, to make them understand, and if they didn't, to slap their silly faces, seize their idiotic tea-trolley with its cut-glass cake stand and its paper doilies and throw the whole thing against the wall.

In the event, Mrs Hobbes saved him the trouble. Noticing that Hugh had accidentally slopped tea onto his trouser leg, she seized a paper napkin, leapt to her feet and in doing so tripped on the corner of the Persian rug and fell headlong with a crash on to the top of the trolley. At the same time the cherry cake, which she was holding on the cake-stand in her other hand, flew straight into her husband's face.

There was a momentary silence, as though a bomb had landed. Everyone froze. As Mrs Hobbes picked herself carefully out of the jumble of broken cups and saucers, spilt milk and

135

squashed bread and butter, Hugh opened his mouth to say something, but all that came out was a laugh. Not just a nervous giggle, but a helpless, undisguisable belly laugh. He was still giggling as he and his mother hurried away down the Hobbes's drive.

'How could you, Hugh?' she hissed, her outrage only half-meant.

'How could I not?' replied Hugh. And bursting once more into laughter, he seized his mother's arm and marched her firmly across the road to the Rectory.

It was several days before Hugh ventured out of doors again, not for fear of bumping into the Hobbes, nor because of the cold, dreary weather, but the day after the tea party he had a letter from Robin telling him that Peter Hemingford was dead, and somehow he couldn't bring himself to do anything other than sit in his room with Percy, staring out of the window. He tried to read *Pickwick Papers,* but he could not concentrate. He found his eyes travelled down the same page over and over again without registering a word, and anyway, turning the pages was a bore, so he soon gave it up as a bad job. Occasionally he would switch on the old wireless set, and tune in to ITMA or try to catch up on the progress of the war; but it all seemed a long way away now and little to do with him, so he switched off again. His parents did what they could to cheer him up, recalling old times and gossiping about village characters, and Susan tried hard to produce a tempting variety of menus; but more often than not, Hugh would pick at his food and push it away after a few mouthfuls. He grew more and more irritable. Small, unimportant things would throw him into a temper. Once, he had Susan in tears and the children screaming when she could not manage to knot his tie exactly as he asked.

'I was right all along,' she shouted at him. 'You are the most difficult person I've ever met. You're worse than the children.'

'What do you expect?' he retorted, 'since I spend my life being treated like one.' And he stormed up to his room, slamming the door behind him.

Later that day, when they were alone in the kitchen, she

said to him, 'I sometimes wonder why I bother to be nice to you. You obviously don't appreciate it. It's only a matter of time before we're back at each other's throats, like the old days.'

Hugh said nothing.

'You accept everything and give nothing in return,' she went on, emptying the washing-up bowl. 'I'd have thought the least you could do would be to relieve me of the children occasionally.'

'How can I?' he said. 'They're obviously frightened of me.'

'So would you be if someone sat and stared at you all through lunch without saying a word.'

'I don't seem to have much to say.'

'Try,' she snapped.

'I do,' he said helplessly. 'I am.'

Susan carried the plates across to the dresser and piled them on one of the lower shelves with a clatter.

'It's not easy,' she said above the noise, 'to sympathize with someone who uses his injuries to get his own way. It's not fair. Wounded war heroes aren't fair game.'

Hugh sighed.

'I know,' he said. 'I'm sorry. Look, let's go for a walk while the children are having their rest. The sun's out and Percy could do with the exercise.'

They went down to the creek and up on to the low bank that divided the salt water channel from the low-lying farm land on the other side, winding its way for nearly two miles down to the sand dunes and the sea. The muddy path on the top was just wide enough for two people to walk side by side. Percy ran ahead barking and urging haste.

They were out for about an hour, during the whole of which time Susan talked about James, ceaselessly, desperately almost, as if by recalling his every mannerism and habit and attitude she might somehow bring him back to life – or at least make nonsense of the fact of his death.

She made him sound a great deal more interesting than Hugh remembered him. Either he had sadly misjudged the fellow or she was deliberately piecing together a grander, more heroic picture of a man who, for all his undoubted kindness

137

and admirable qualities as a husband and father, was essentially small and unheroic.

But then who could blame her? She had as much right to try and salvage something from his little life and insignificant death as he had to try and make sense of his own meaningless survival. To accuse her of dishonesty now would be an act of pure spite, brought on by nothing more than jealousy on his part. Like Peter and Jimmy and Pat and Julian, James Arundel was beyond judgment. Whatever he had been in his life, he could only grow in death. Those who die for their country have nothing to lose but their lives: they shall grow not old, as we that are left grow old. However stupid and pointless and un-heroic the circumstances of their deaths, the sheer act of dying in action freezes them in a permanent posture of heroism, like statues. From the going down of the sun until the morning, we will remember them – or at least the parts of them we want to remember. They can sit there smugly on the mantel-piece, like re-touched photographs in silver frames, for all to admire; the survivors remain, uncomfortably unfrozen, des-perately fallible, warts, burns, grafts and all, trying to behave like the heroes they are supposed to be, yet always, inevitably, falling below the mark. They have the feeling they are sitting a permanent examination, which they will never be able to pass, because no one will ever tell them either the questions or the pass mark. That, as Meikle had reminded him, is up to them.

Oh balls, thought Hugh. What a load of pseudo-psychological clap-trap. Here is a young woman who wants to tell me about her dead husband and I immediately use it as an excuse to analyse my own feelings yet again. I'm becoming even more self-absorbed here than I was at Ashbourne Wood. I want to help, yet at every turn something comes up that causes me to turn my energies back on myself. I'm like a rat in a maze that always leads back to the same spot because there is no other way to go, and never will be. And all I have to look forward to in the meantime is pain and hospital wards and operations and people's pity.

That night, after dinner, on the pretext of a need for fresh

138

air, Hugh walked down to the creek. The night was still and starless and the tide was, as he had correctly judged, high.

Beside the slipway where the holiday makers hauled their dinghies up and down in the summer was a stone jetty which jutted out into the water at a point where the tide swirled past, making it, even at low tide, one of the deepest and most dangerous spots along the whole length of the creek. Legend had it that Jake's Hole, as it was known locally, had no bottom to it – a theory that had yet to be proved one way or the other.

Hugh bent down and began to fill the pockets of his RAF greatcoat with pebbles. He noted with detached interest that his fingers seemed much less stiff than usual. He then pulled down the tops of his high sea-boots, straightened up and jumped.

The icy coldness of the water knocked all the wind from his body, making him gasp and swallow a mouthful of salt water as his head went under. He felt the cold rushing into his boots, curling round his feet and pushing its way between his toes like tiny frozen hands.

Immediately he began to struggle.

Flailing his arms, he finally managed to force his head above water, choking and spluttering and gasping for breath. He cursed loudly and tried to force his head under again, but by now the water had got inside his coat, billowing it out and giving him unexpecting buoyancy. 'Go down, fuck you,' he shouted. 'Why don't you go down? Go down, you bastard. Go down.' Now his boots, completely filled with water, began to draw his legs downwards so that he was lying in the water like a doll, his coat spread out round his hips like a ballerina's skirt. Suddenly he felt his heels touch something firm. He struggled briefly and then, before he knew what, he was standing, shivering and coughing, in a little under four feet of water.

It was one of the fishermen who rescued him. The old fellow had seen him gathering the pebbles and had thought little of it, but the moment he had jumped, he had hurried across to his little flat-bottomed rowing boat.

A few minutes later, he was walking Hugh up the slipway and across to his cottage.

'If I hadna seen it with me own oyes, Oi'd've sworn bloind you gone done it a'purpose,' he told him. 'I knew we'd done roight to have that ol' hole filled in. Still, lucky for you that was only a small toide.'

The fisherman pushed Hugh in through the door. An oil lamp burned on the table and a small wood fire crackled in the tiny grate. Hugh watched as the old man closed and bolted the little door, then turned to look at him. His eyes opened wide.

'Bogger me,' he said at last, 'there must be a foo rough old devils in that creek to make a mess of you like that.'

Hugh stared at him for a moment and then, to the old man's astonishment, he burst out laughing.

Chapter Nine

Three days later, Hugh received a letter from his old house-master at Eton, inviting him down on December 18th to dine in the House and afterwards give a short informal lecture to the OTC.

Susan brought the letter up to his room. Hugh had been in bed ever since his farcical escapade in the creek. As far as his parents knew, he had stumbled in the dark and fallen accidentally in the water. He was astonished that they should have accepted such an unlikely explanation at face value, but they had. Susan had said nothing, but he knew that she did not believe him, and although he was genuinely suffering a slight chill, it was in order to avoid a conversation with her more than for medical reasons that he had taken to his bed. It also, he had convinced himself, gave Muv a much needed excuse to mother him.

Mr Blore's letter was characteristically effusive and breathless.

'The mother of one of our boys came across an article about you in a local Kent newspaper,' he had written in his neat, small hand, 'and reading that you were an Old Etonian, sent it to me with the suggestion that it might be interesting and instructive for the boys to meet one of "The Few" in person. I quite agree with her.

'Your courage and your exploits are an inspiration to all the boys in the school, especially those older ones who will themselves soon be called upon to play their part in the great struggle, and although modesty no doubt forbids you from making too much of the circumstances leading to the award of your decoration, I am sure you will agree that it can do nothing but good for young chaps to come face to face with a real-life hero, particularly an O.E. I note that you received certain injuries as a result of your brave actions. I trust you have now recovered from these and will not be prevented from undertaking what I believe to be a worthwhile and rewarding task for us all. I am sending this to your parents' home in Norfolk, since I have no way of knowing your precise whereabouts, and a letter from Lady Downpatrick, informing me of Adrian's unhappy capture and incarceration, hinted that you might be enjoying a well-deserved convalescence.

'I trust that your parents are enjoying the best of health. Please give them my kindest regards.

Yours most sincerely,

J. Radford Blore.

P.S. May I suggest you telephone here with your decision? The post is notoriously unreliable these days.'

'Will you go?' Susan asked him.

'I don't know,' he said. 'I feel such a fraud somehow. All right, so I won a gong, but it had nothing to do with bravery. I just lost my temper, that's all. I broke all the rules. By rights I should have received a severe reprimand, not a decoration. That's not what they want to hear.'

'You shot down another German.'

'He was pouring coolant. He wouldn't have made it home anyway. People cheer every time another German pilot bites the dust, and they're right. But there's a very good argument to be made for letting a few of them stagger back, full of holes, coughing up their guts. The Germans are much more demoralized by that sort of thing than they are by losing pilots altogether. That only makes them all try all the harder. They're no more heroes at heart than we are.'

Susan ran her finger nail along a crack in the kitchen table. 'You know, one of the reasons I said what I did to you in that hospital in Ashford was that I really did hate you fighter pilots for the way people hero-worshipped you and for your smug

142

belief in your own sense of superiority. You seemed to think you were God's gift to the British war effort.'

'It wasn't true,' said Hugh. 'It was only the peculiar sort of life we led. Still do, for all I know. It made us stick together that much more closely. We didn't feel comfortable anywhere else, that's all. There was nothing glamorous about it. It was other people who tried to make out we were special.'

'Let me finish,' Susan said. 'What you say may be true. One way or another I believed it. I honestly did think you and your friends were something special. It only angered me that James wasn't one of you, like Helena's husband. God how I envied her. Don't you see? It wasn't you I despised at all; it was James, for being so, I don't know, ordinary and . . .' She broke off and shook her head. There were tears in her eyes.

Hugh murmured, 'He wasn't ordinary. It's not true.'

She turned on him. 'Now who's being dishonest?'

'I mean it.'

'Look,' she said suddenly angry. 'Don't get me wrong. I'm not saying he wasn't a good man and a marvellous husband and father to the children. I loved him. I still do. Maybe I always shall. But don't you see? It was all so futile. Shot through the head by a bullet fired by a man he never saw, who probably wasn't even aiming at him anyway. Just another name on the list of dead and missing. No decoration, no recognition, nothing to make it worthwhile. The letter said something about him being a gallant officer and dying in the line of duty or some such stuff. Well, they've got to say something nice, haven't they?'

'And you really believe that I am any different or better than him?'

'Not now; then. The battle you were fighting at that time – God, it all sounds like ancient history, and it was only a few weeks ago – it seemed the most important thing in the world. Perhaps it was. Now you're just another wounded airman, like hundreds of others. You did your bit. That's what matters. But still people want to make a hero of you, especially schoolboys. You've read Blore's letter. You've heard the way people go on. Of course you must go and talk to those boys – but not about winning decorations and bagging more Germans than anyone else and being stared at in night clubs. Tell them what fighting in a war is really about: being scared and injured and perhaps killed by someone you never even see, and suddenly having your life shattered into a thousand pieces, and the arbitrariness and unfairness of it all, and the waste and the pity. Young people must not be encouraged to think that being a fighter pilot is anything other than it is – a sad necessity. It's your duty and your responsibility to tell them the truth.'

Hugh nodded slowly.

'I haven't been lectured to so often and by so many people since I was a small boy,' he said. 'It's funny. You'd think I'd be the one doing the lecturing. Everyone seems to have the answers but me.'

'None of us has the answers,' Susan said. 'On the other hand, not all of us, thank God, have had our faces burnt off and our hands reduced to matchsticks, and been forced to re-think our entire lives. People are only trying to help, you know.'

Hugh got up and walked across to the window. Through the bare branches of the trees, as skeletal against the grey sky as his hands against the window sill, he could just make out the creek. In George Loads' boatyard, the masts of the dinghies clustered together like the spears of an advancing army. The tide was low.

'My duty,' Hugh said slowly, 'and my responsibility. I'm afraid those words have never meant a great deal to me. In action perhaps. Being part of a team, doing as one was told, maintaining the disciplines. But in the end it all comes down to a matter of self-preservation. Over Ashford that day, it was my duty to catch up with the rest of the squadron. My responsibility, technically speaking, was to Uncle Dickie and my ground crew. In reality it was to myself, to save my own skin, or not. The decision was mine. It was the reason I became a fighter pilot in the first place, and the reason I am one no longer. Of course, I feel a certain responsibility to Muv and Far and you, not to cause you too much suffering, and most of the time I fail, as I failed Uncle Dickie and the rest of the squadron that day. In the end it all comes back to me. I have to find a way to go on,

144

that's all. Robin said the other day that my duty and my responsibility were simply to go on living. I think he was right. Nothing more.'

'If you really believed that,' said Susan, 'you wouldn't have filled your pocket with stones the other night and jumped into the creek.' So she did know all along; she must have spoken to the old fisherman.

'If I feel I cannot go on living, it is also my duty, and my right, not to do so,' he told her, feeling rather pompous.

'And give us an even harder time than usual,' she retorted.

Hugh mouth twisted into a sardonic grin.

'Twice I've tried to kill myself in the space of three months and twice I've failed. The fates obviously have something more interesting up their sleeves.'

Susan stopped playing with the cracks in the table and looked up sharply. 'Your flippancy is becoming less and less convincing.'

He shrugged. 'Who says I'm being flippant?'

'Oh, do grow up, Hugh,' she snapped. 'Who do you think you're fooling? I don't suppose anyone will dare tell you this, because it would be too much like hitting a man when he's down, but all this high-flown talk about duty and responsibility is merely a smokescreen for plain, simple selfishness. You were selfish as a boy, and by all accounts you were selfish as a pilot. In the past it had always paid off, or at least it hadn't caused you any noticeable harm. Suddenly, you were paid back with a vengeance. I would have thought that by now you would have learnt your lesson. You've had long enough to think about it. But all you've succeeded in doing, as far as I can see, is think up new ways of justifying the fact that you don't give a bugger for anyone – not even, to judge from the other night, yourself. Though even that little escapade sounded suspiciously to me like another device for drawing attention to yourself. Of course you think Robin's right, because he gives the sort of advice that can easily be turned round to make it mean what you want it to mean. I've never met him, as you keep reminding me, but from all that you tell me I imagine he'd be pretty disappointed to think you were quoting him as evidence that you should do

145

nothing. Even when an opportunity arises for you to put your experience to some use, you find some feeble excuse to get out of it. You feel a fraud. I'm not surprised. You are a fraud. But not in the way you implied. You're a fraud because you can't and won't face up to life. Now, shall I ring Eton, or will you?'

It was more than three years since Hugh had seen his old housemaster: John Radford Blore, M.A., Corpus Christi College, Oxford, Ist Class Honours in Classics, known to generations of Etonians as Hummer for his nervous habit of interspersing every sentence with a series of nervous hums. It had never failed to astonish Hugh that a man of his long experience as a schoolmaster, much of it in charge of a house at Eton, could actually be shy in front of small boys. Confronted by parents perhaps, but not 12 and 13 years olds. And yet in all the years he had been in his house, from new boy to Captain of House, he could not recall a moment when Hummer Blore had looked him straight in the eye or completed an entire sentence without stumbling and hesitating and going red in the face.

There was a time when that quiet, anxious voice, the short-cropped mousy hair, the narrow, pale face, constantly contorted with nerves, now smiling broadly, the next instant deep-lined with a frown, had been an even more familiar part of his life than his own father's. Yet now that he tried to recall the man, only the broadest outlines came back to him, like a caricature. It was only when the voice came on the line at last that the picture clicked again into sharp relief. The intervening years dissolved and suddenly he was back in the House again after House Prayers discussing the latest Library elections, or the declining standards of the Debate.

'This is really very good of you to . . . er . . . phone . . . mm . . . so promptly . . . ah . . . Hugh.'

'Not at all, sir. It was good of you to invite me.'

'And . . . er . . . what do you think to my . . . mm . . . proposal?'

He sounded even more hesitant and ill-at-ease than Hugh remembered, and his awkwardness seemed to infect Hugh.

'I think it's . . . mm . . . an excellent idea, sir. The only thing is . . .'

He paused, desperately searching for a phrase that would

146

not alarm the old chap and give him cause for second thoughts. He had given the matter a great deal of thought in the few hours that had passed since his conversation with Susan, and he had become genuinely excited by the idea. Perhaps this was the opportunity Robin had referred to. On the other hand, he felt it only fair to come clean straight away regarding the tone and subject matter of his talk.

An anxious humming sound came down the line.

'If it's a matter of dates, we could always . . .'

'No, no, sir. Nothing like that. It's just that . . . well . . . as you said in your letter, it might be a good thing, especially for the older boys, to meet someone like myself who's seen a bit of action. On the other hand, I wouldn't wish to give them a false picture . . . that's to say, just because I've been decorated and so on, doesn't mean . . .'

'Mmm . . . I quite agree,' Blore interrupted him, 'quite agree. The picture must be accurate or nothing.'

'I mean, I've seen some pretty nasty things in my time,' Hugh pointed out. 'That's to say, there's nothing very heroic about being shot down in flames in a Spitfire, you know.'

'Of course, of course,' Blore jumped in. 'I am sure I can leave it to your discretion to describe only those incidents you feel happy to re-live. Let me just say, however, that you need have no fear on the boys' account. They breed them even tougher now than in your day, believe it or not.'

He chuckled in a series of long, breathy mumbles. Hugh did not join in.

The date was confirmed, an invitation extended to stay the night, and travel arrangements agreed.

Hugh went back to bed, fearful suddenly of the task he had undertaken, yet overwhelmed by a sense of enormous relief that at last here was the opportunity he had been waiting for to talk about Jimmy and Julian and Peter and the rest who had died. To explain that all those big words like Duty and Patriotism and Courage and Right were meaningless compared with the death of frends and the loss of feeling.

Almost certainly they would not understand; how could they? But they would listen, and anyway, just by telling some-

147

one, it might relieve some of the guilt *he* felt at being alive and hailed as a hero when better men than he – yes, even James Arundel – were dead and already half-forgotten.

As she hurried down Eton High Street towards the river, a cold wind whipped at Eileen Parsons' face, making her eyes water and reddening her nose. She pushed her hands deeper into her coat pockets in search of warmth and feeling, and bent her head yet lower against the weather. It was the second time that week that the manageress of the haberdashery where she worked had decided to re-arrange the knitting wools, and consequently the second time she had missed her bus and been forced to walk to the station for the short journey to Staines. No doubt she would also now have to walk the mile to the semi-detached with the small front garden where she lived with her mother and father. Her elder brother had also lived there before joining up in the RAF. That was a long time ago, before the war started, when jobs had been scarce and the services had offered a regular wage, even if the work was rather humdrum.

She lifted her head during a brief lull in the wind and saw a tall, grey-blue figure on the far side of the road, his hands jammed into the pockets of his RAF great-coat, his cap tilted at a rakish angle.

Eileen glanced quickly about her to check there were no cars coming, then crossed the street. As he approached, she could see that he was even taller than she had first thought and his shoulders were broad and square. She ducked her head again, judging the precise moment when he would pass. As he did so, she looked up eagerly. But the smile died on her lips as though frozen by the wind, and her eyes filled, not with laughter, but with horror and disbelief.

It was, as she told her parents later, so unexpected. He'd been so handsome from a distance in his uniform that it had never occurred to her that he was going to turn out like that. She had not meant to stare at him so, but really she could not help herself. The wind had lashed his skin into a hideous patchwork of red and yellow and white, like a badly made rag doll, and

148

his eyes, half-lidless still, had stared out angrily at her above a nose that seemed to have partly rotted away and a lip that was twisted upwards in a permanent sneer. It was almost – the thought was to recur to her often in years to come – as though he had set out to frighten her on purpose.

Hugh had noticed the girl at about the same time she had spotted him. Something about the way she walked made him guess that she would be pretty, and he would have broken a school rule and crossed to the right hand side of the street for a closer look had she not crossed over to his side first. His eyes were streaming from the cold, but he carried himself more erect than ever, looking straight ahead. She had turned out to be every bit as pretty as he had surmised – her hair blowing about her wide freckled forehead and over her dark eyes, her little nose pink from the wind. Her modest, downward glance at the pavement had made him smile, and he was still smiling when they drew level and she looked up.

She had had no time to disguise her expression. Shock, fear, pity – all superimposed themselves on the half-smile that remained. The spell was broken and in an instant he was brought back ruthlessly to reality. For during those few brief moments, as they had approached each other, Hugh had forgotten the way he looked, and that he was no longer the young man he had been the last time he had walked up this street, and for all Meikle's skill could never be again.

A sense of deep longing overcame him then, and his heart seemed physically to ache as he plodded on up the street towards the Burning Bush, his head lowered once more against the cold wind.

'May I help you?'

The voice was unchanged, the face a little thinner, the hair greyer than he remembered. The kindly grey eyes that were capable of reducing even the most senior and powerful boy to a quivering jelly in seconds, observed him curiously and without recognition.

'It's me, Ma'am!' Hugh told his old house matron. 'Fleming. Hugh Fleming.'

She frowned up at him, her head cocked slightly on one side, as though faced by a very good confidence trickster.

'Hugh?'

She moved slowly towards him, shaking her head slowly from side to side. Somewhere in the far recesses of the House a voice echoed dismally through the corridors. 'Bo-o-o-y!' And moments later came the unmistakable sound of small frightened feet running, trying not to be the last to respond to the senior boy's shout.

Mrs Gascoigne stood in front of Hugh, a tiny figure looking up at him. Tears gathered in the corner of her tired grey eyes.

'You poor boy,' she said softly at last. 'You poor, dear boy. What have they done to you?'

She went to take his hands in hers, but seeing Hugh's grimace, drew back sharply.

'You poor, poor boy,' she repeated, and putting both arms round him, she held him close to her, as his mother might have done, had she been a different sort of woman. Hugh, feeling rather foolish, wondered how the three small boys, who had suddenly appeared in the corner and now stood staring at the pair of them, were ever going to be able to look Mrs Gascoigne in the eye again without bursting into shrieks of laughter. But then he realized it was not her they were gazing at with such wide-eyed solemnity, but him. If they were shocked by his appearance, they showed no signs of it. On the contrary, Hugh had the feeling that some profound form of communication had developed between him and the small boys; it was almost as though, without either of them saying a word, they had understood everything. They were not frightened, or sorry, or revolted, like most people he met; nor did they try to give the impression they had not noticed anything was wrong. They had looked at him, understood what had happened, and accepted him for what he was.

Hugh was suddenly more moved than at any time since he had been shot down. Yet he felt no desire to weep or regale the boys with a dramatic speech or resort to any of the obvious devices that others – and, he realized now, he himself – had used to protect themselves in the last three months whenever a similar confrontation had taken place. He did not even allow himself the satisfaction of a smile. He simply returned their gaze over Mrs Gascoigne's grey head and thought how much he owed Susan for persuading him to come there. He felt certain that no small boy could understand such things; but he was wrong, as he had been wrong about so many things lately. Children have a way of cutting through the self-deception and the false emotion which adults throw up to conceal their true feelings. They are rarely deceived and rarely confounded by what older people convince themselves are insoluble problems. And it only proved to Hugh how old he had become in the last few years that he should have believed otherwise.

'Bo-o-o-y!'

The long, drawn-out cry echoed again through the building. Hugh shivered with remembered fear. Had he really once shouted like that, without realizing, or caring, that small boys dreaded the sound of it like young men once dreaded the whisper of 'press gangs'? Was it possible that decent men like Peter Hemingford and Adrian and Jimmy Macdonell could have been so callous? If the call terrified him now, what did it do to the three children who, without a sound, turned and ran for their lives along the gloomy corridor.

Mrs Gascoigne stood back from Hugh, drew a small lace handkerchief from her pocket, made a couple of quick dabbing motions at her eyes, then blew her nose with neat economy of sound and effort.

'What you must think of me,' she muttered, treating herself to one last disapproving sniff. Hugh gave an awkward little laugh.

'Have you seen M'Tutor yet?' she asked.

'No,' said Hugh, 'but he is expecting me.'

'So I understand. You're to dine with us and lecture to the OTC in School Hall afterwards, I hear.'

Hugh thought he detected a faint note of disapproval in her voice.

'I think it's a jolly good idea, don't you?'

'They tell me you won a medal.'

'All pilots get one of those. It goes with the job.'

151

She regarded him sternly.

'DFCs perhaps,' she snapped, 'Not DSOs. I may have a few more grey hairs than when you last saw me, but that's no reason to go treating me like an old fool.'

Hugh felt himself reddening.

'I'm sorry, Ma'am,' he said. 'But it's hard to get excited about medals when chaps like Peter Hemingford and Jimmy Macdonell and God knows how many others are dead. They're the ones everyone ought to be shouting about. Besides, heroes are handsome.'

'Don't you think I don't grieve for you all?' There was bitterness in her voice as well as sorrow. 'I remember you all as well as if you were my own children. And the ones who came after you. And I daresay in a few weeks from now I'll be weeping for some of my boys here now. You'll see them this evening for yourself in School Hall, hanging on your every word, wishing the time would pass quickly so that they can go off and fight for their country and win DSOs and DFCs like you. You remember Johnny Waterlow? He had a brother called Andrew. One of the best all-round sportsmen the house has ever seen. Member of Pop, Captain of Cricket. We were almost certain of winning the House cricket with him. What happens? In the middle of long leave, his mother rings up M'Tutor to announce that he won't be coming back after all. He'd volunteered for the RAF. Six weeks later he took off on his first sortie and his Hurricane was blown out of the sky before he'd even fired a shot.' She shook her head. 'Such a waste,' she said sadly. 'And to think he could have won us the cricket cup for the first time in twelve years.'

Hugh stood looking at her, at a complete loss for words. She took him gently by the arm and gave a quick smile.

'Thank God you're alive, my dear,' she said. 'You'll give a marvellous lecture tonight, I'm sure. But please don't make it too good, otherwise we might lose them all.'

And with that, she hustled off along the corridor, her leather shoes clacking on the stone floor. Hugh turned and walked in the opposite direction until he came to the housemaster's door.

Announcing his presence was another simple task for which

he had yet to find a solution. His hands were still very stiff and his knuckles exceedingly tender. So, for that matter, were his elbows. Once or twice recently he had been forced to resort to a sharp kick, but it had to be done carefully to achieve the right effect and even then it sounded rude. He looked round for a passing boy, but there was none in sight. He wondered perhaps if he should give a Boy Call.

At that moment the door opened in front of him and there was Hummer Blore. Unlike Mrs Gascoigne he had not changed in any particular.

'Oh . . . mm . . .' he said slightly flustered, 'I'm so sorry . . . mm . . . I was expecting someone else. . .'

Hugh smiled. Hummer took a step backwards.

'Good gracious me,' he exclaimed, 'Fleming . . . Hugh . . . mm . . . I didn't realize . . . I mean, I thought . . . I'm so sorry . . . mm . . . won't you come in and . . .?'

He took several more steps backwards into his room, his voice dying away into a meaningless series of hums and hahs, until he found himself up against the desk and could retreat no further. Hugh advanced slowly into the room, feeling like a robber who has cornered a bank manager in his office, and closed the door behind him.

Hummer finally managed to get away from the desk and moved crab-like across to the fireplace around which were arranged the familar deep leather armchair, two upright wooden chairs with arms and plain wooden side-table with two shelves. It was strange. One moment Hugh had the strongest feeling that only a few days had passed since he had last been invited to 'draw up a pew'; the next, he felt as old as the white-haired O.E.s he used to come across tottering on sticks round the House on the Fourth of June, announcing in quavering tones that nothing had changed since their day except the manners.

The two of them continued to shuffle and weave about the chairs for a while longer in a series of clumsy manoeuvres punctuated by nervous laughter, until at last Hugh sank gratefully into the welcoming depths of the leather armchair and Hummer scuttled towards the far side of the room where a half-empty bottle of sherry and several assorted glasses stood on top of a low wooden bookshelf, flanked by a pile of exercise books and a framed photograph of Hummer's mother.

'Sherry . . . er . . .?'

'Thank you, sir,' said Hugh politely.

'I would like to be able to offer you something a little . . . how shall we say . . . mm . . . stronger. But these days . . .'

'Sherry will be fine for me, sir.'

It was rather sweet for Hugh's taste and the tiny glass was difficult to handle, but he quickly took it between his two gloved hands and sipped at the sickly liquid.

'It's extraordinary how adaptable the human body can be when it has to be,' said Hummer solemnly.

They talked for a while about old times and Hugh's contemporaries. Peter's death had for some reason not reached Blore's ears.

'Hemingford,' he said gazing pensively into the fireplace. 'He had the makings of a very good little diver.'

After a while they lapsed into an uneasy silence. Then Hugh said, 'About the lecture, sir. I've been thinking about it, and . . .'

Hummer cleared his throat noisily and stood up, his back to the fireplace, warming his hands behind him over the dull coals.

'Ah, yes. The lecture. Mmm . . . the thing is, Hugh . . . mm . . . I don't know quite how to put this but . . . aah . . . there's been a bit of a muddle over dates. Silly, really. No one's fault . . .just a combination of circumstances . . . anyway the fact is, I'm afraid I've . . . mm . . . brought you here on somewhat false pretences . . . mm . . .'

Hugh frowned at him.

'I'm sorry, sir, I don't think I quite follow you.'

The little man was becoming more nervous and embarrassed by the second.

'I tried to ring you in Norfolk. . . several times in fact . . . but the line seemed to be out of order . . . you know how it is . . . mmm . . . wartime, and so on . . . ha, ha . . .'

'I'm sorry, sir, I still don't quite understand. Are you trying to tell me the lecture is off, or what?'

'Let me put it this way . . . aah . . . Hugh. It would be difficult

. . . impossible really . . . to re-arrange things at this late stage. I'm sure you understand.'

His evasive behaviour was beginning to irritate Hugh.

'I'm afraid I don't understand,' he replied sharply. 'M'Dame seemed to have no doubt the lecture was on when I spoke to her a few minutes ago. We talked about it at some length. If there had been any change of plan, surely she . . .'

'She couldn't have known,' Hummer said hastily. 'It was something that came up at the last minute.'

He wrung his hands together pleading silently with Hugh to do something, say something, make some decision that would relieve him of further misery – anything rather than press him for further explanation. Hugh sensed that if he were to get up out of his chair, announce that he had thought better of the idea, and leave without further ado, it would be one of the kindest favours anyone had ever done Hummer Blore.

But Hugh was an expert now at recognizing deceit when he saw it, and whatever his motives and however great his shame in front of one of his own pupils, one thing was certain : the man was lying. Hugh would not have given a damn one way or another had those three boys not looked at him the way they did. He had set his mind on talking to the OTC that evening. For the first time he could rely on people who would listen to what he had to say and afterwards ask the questions they really wanted to ask, that no one else had dared to ask, and to which perhaps he had never himself dared find the answers. Now it was all off, and he wanted to know why.

'I would rather you were honest with me, sir,' Hugh said quietly to the unhappy housemaster. 'Very few people are these days.'

Now that Hummer knew the game was up, he stopped trying. His shoulders sank, his eyes closed with relief and shame, and he lowered himself slowly into one of the upright arm-chairs. He looked suddenly very old.

Hugh felt like a private eye in an American film – 'Wanna tell me about it Blore?' But he said nothing.

Hummer sighed a deep sigh. He looked up but his eyes did

155

not meet Hugh's. They rested their attention on a point somewhere to the left of him and slightly below.

'I had no idea, you see . . . mm . . . no idea at all . . .'

Hugh still said nothing.

'When it said injured, I assumed it meant, oh I don't know,
a limp perhaps, an arm in a sling, a few superficial scars, not
. . . The article didn't say anything about you being burnt . . . I
mean, how was I to know . . .?'

His voice tailed off miserably, and he hung his head like a
scolded dog.

'You couldn't have known,' Hugh told him gently. 'I should
have realized when you wrote; I should have said something.
It must have come as a terrible shock. But that need not affect
our plans for the lecture. Small boys, even eighteen year olds,
accept this sort of thing much more easily than adults. You
yourself said that today's generation is even more resilient than
ours, and that's saying something.'

'You don't understand,' Hummer interjected.

'But l do, sir. I really do. Much more than you imagine. And,
more importantly, so do they. That's what I was going to tell
you. Don't you see? War is not heroic; scars are not honours to
be worn like house colours. It isn't all a game. That's what I
want to tell them, and I know they'll understand. M'Dame said
just now she was afraid I might persuade them all to rush off
straight away and join up. But it's the very opposite I want to
achieve. Don't you see?'

Hugh was breathing fast with excitement, and sweat had
started to break out on his forehead and upper lip. He leaned
forward expectantly.

'You don't understand, my dear boy,' Hummer repeated. 'It's
not the boys I'm worried about. It's all the parents I invited to
come along, too. If I let you loose on them, there'd be the most
frightful outcry. We've got quite enough on our hands as it is
without setting ourselves up as a complaints bureau. No, I'm
sorry, Hugh, really I am. But I'm in charge of the OTC in the
absence of the serving officers, and that is my decision. I'm sure
you appreciate my position . . . mm . . . there's nothing personal
in it, I assure you . . . mm . . .'

'Like hell there isn't,' snapped Hugh angrily. 'You're just like all the rest of them. You think it's catching. Well, how do you think I feel? I have to live with it.'

Hugh struggled to his feet, sweat pouring now from his brow. Blore hurried forward, then at the last moment drew back and stood there watching, wringing his hands pathetically.

'But you'll dine with us anyway, I hope?'

'Thank you, sir,' said Hugh coldly, 'But I wouldn't like to put you all off your food.'

'Mmm,' mumbled Hummer Blore, but no words emerged.

Later, after dinner, he described the events of the early evening to Mrs Gascoigne over a cup of coffee.

'Fleming always was a hot-headed and impetuous boy,' he remarked thoughtfully. 'I said so more than once in his report.'

'Yes,' she said. 'Thank God.'

For the life of him he could not understand what she meant.

Chapter Ten

The more Hugh thought about it on the train up to town, the less inclined he felt to return to Norfolk. He loved the place as much as ever, and the healthy combination of Norfolk air and Muv's and Susan's cooking had brought a fresh spring to his step and added a much-needed inch or more to his waist. Between them, they had worked out a design for living together which was more agreeable than at any time in the past. But the seaside village was oppressively small, especially in winter when the visitors had gone. Everyone took far too unhealthy an interest in everyone else's affairs, and Hugh was finding his newly acquired notoriety hard to shrug off. It irritated him that every time he poked his nose outside the Rectory gates, a knot of local inhabitants would gather, with all the promptness of extras on a film set, and, with an unconvincing air of casualness, would whisper together as he passed. Few of them actually spoke to him, and if ever he showed signs of trying to converse with them, they would mumble excuses and shuffle off into the wings. After a while he began to be convinced they must know something he didn't, and wondered if the old fisherman down by the creek had been making his suspicions widely known.

As time went by, he began to feel an outcast in the village he had known and loved all his life, as though – and the thought recurred yet again – as though he were the carrier of some fatal disease.

He had had every intention of staying on at the Rectory until Christmas – indeed had virtually promised he would – but that would inevitably have meant socializing with the locals, the Hobbes and the like dropping in for drinks, and invitations to do likewise. He felt less up to playing the local hero now than ever, and his reluctance to emerge from the house would doubtless have attracted accusations from Susan of self-indulgence. It was all bound to end in tears and, on balance, he decided it would cause Muv and Far less pain to have to spend Christmas without him than with everyone getting on each other's nerves.

At Waterloo he took a taxi to the Ritz, only to learn that during his absence Tim and Nancy had been married and had left that very afternoon to spend Christmas in the country. The news made him sad and envious and he cursed himself for his lack of generosity.

The entrance hall was full of uniforms and life. He stood for a while and watched the comings and goings between the restaurant, the bar and the street entrance, as officers of all services, many of them as young as he and most with women at their sides, set about the business of enjoying their precious off-duty hours. He wondered why he found it so difficult to enjoy himself any more, and laugh and make silly jokes, and throw himself into absurd projects as he had once done at Cambridge. He had never really found anyone or anything amusing since that little group had been broken up. Like a diamond under a hammer, the brilliant, individual fragments had floated about, occasionally coming together (usually at different stages of training) to glimmer palely for a while before again dispersing, but never quite to recapture the glory and genius of the original, complete gem. Now, with so many of those bright lights extinguished, the only world in which he had been really happy and felt himself to be most completely himself, and upon whose continued existence he had, he realized now, been relying for all this time for his own continued existence, had gone for ever. And with it, it seemed, had gone his capacity for friendship, tolerance, enjoyment – even love.

And yet, he thought as he looked around him, there must be thousands like him who had lost friends and loved ones, and looked back with longing on a way of life that had gone for ever. Yet somehow they seemed to be making the best of things.

They could still laugh and make new friends and think up fresh ways of diverting themselves. However much they might regret the passing of the old life, they seemed to be accepting the new order of things with an enthusiasm that was beyond his comprehension or capability. He was twenty-one years old and he felt a relic from a bygone ago.

Few people who passed him in the hall regarded him with more than the vaguest interest. Most were too intent on enjoying themselves even to notice him. The only person to acknowledge his presence was another pilot of about Hugh's age with a small blonde ATS girl on his arm. He smiled and nodded as he strode by, and it was only when he had gone that Hugh realized he, too, had been burnt. It was as though an Englishman walking in the African rain forest had suddenly come upon another Englishman in trouble with a tribe of head hunters, but not wishing to seem rude by poking his nose in uninvited, had tip-toed by. For a moment Hugh was tempted to run after the fellow and invite him for a drink and a chat, if only for the sake of hearing someone speaking his own language. But by then the man had disappeared through the swing doors and been swallowed up in the night.

Instead, Hugh rang Ashbourne Wood. Luckily, Meikle had just finished operating. He did not seem unduly surprised to hear Hugh's voice, nor that Hugh was anxious to know if his nose operation could be brought forward.

'I could probably manage next week,' Meikle told him. 'Any good to you?'

'I was rather hoping you might be able to find me a spare bed straight away.'

'Hmm. Tricky,' Meikle grunted. 'Tell you what. If you don't mind taking pot luck, come down tomorrow. If the worst comes to the worst, Francesca can always find a bed for you at the cottage in the meantime. We can't go letting down our old customers. We never know when we might need them.'

The clerk at the reception desk hummed and hahed and pulled a few faces and talked about the problem of finding rooms in London in wartime, but finally came up with a modest single for one night. The restaurant manager was also persuaded to find him a quiet table in a corner where he ordered smoked salmon, an omelette (food that required cutting was still beyond him, but he had devised an inelegant, though reasonably efficient, method of eating with a spoon or a fork), and a bottle of claret. After that, he drank several brandies in the bar and then rang his parents to tell them of his decision. They said they understood, but he could tell they were deeply disappointed and he felt lousy about it. He drank two more brandies in the bar before finally dragging himself up to his room where he passed a reasonably comfortable night despite sleeping in most of his clothes. (Buttons, shoe-laces, even zips had yet to be mastered and this was the first night he had ever spent out of reach of understanding hands.)

The following morning, feeling extremely hung-over, he set off for Ashbourne Wood.

By chance, a bed had suddenly become vacant in the men's ward in the main hospital building. Hugh was delighted, since, more than anything else, he had been dreading the thought of the radio as it vomited out popular song after popular song. Even the knowledge that his graft stood slightly less chance of taking there than it would in the warmth of Francesca Ward seemed comparatively unimportant. All that mattered was that he was back again amongst his own sort. He was, God help him, home.

That afternoon, Meikle marched in, stood beside Hugh's bed with his hands on his hips and said, in broad imitation of an American gangster, 'Couldn't take it, huh?'

Hugh grinned sheepishly.

'I don't know what you mean,' he said.

'I don't blame you,' Meikle told him. 'It's never easy at first trying to be a normal person again. You've lasted longer than many.'

'That's damning with faint praise.'

'You know your trouble, don't you?' said Meikle as he leaned over to examine him more closely. 'You're too bloody intelligent for your own good.' He straightened up. 'You think too much.

The best treatment for your complaint would be a nice, kind girl with big tits and the plainer the better.'

Hugh frowned enquiringly. Meikle shrugged.

'The plain ones are always much more fun,' he said. 'Stands to reason. They have to try that much harder. When did you last meet a beautiful girl with a sense of humour?'

'There are one or two round this building I could name,' Hugh said.

'Ah,' said Meikle, his eyes twinkling, 'they're different. They've been specially trained by me.'

He then alarmed Hugh by announcing that he had changed his mind about operating on his nose.

'Oh, don't worry,' he said. 'I'm not going to boot you out in the snow. It's just that I think a couple of new lower lids would make a better Christmas present than a new nose. That can wait till the New Year, when you haven't got so many social commitments. See you tomorrow, on the slab. Same time, same place.'

And with a cheery wave he disappeared, like some latterday Merlin.

Hugh's spirits sank at the prospect of another five days of helpless blindness, especially when he looked round at the uncongenial collection of fellow patients on whom he would largely have to rely from now on.

He was, he quickly discovered, the only action casualty in the ward and the only RAF officer. Half the beds appeared to be occupied by Army types suffering from a variety of mild complaints, a couple by local civilians, and the rest by very old men who rarely moved, but stared incuriously ahead of them, occasionally transferring their gaze whenever someone entered the room, before lapsing once more into a state of motionless, mindless torpor. One of them, he never quite succeeded in pin-pointing the suspect, broke wind at approximately half hourly intervals. He never made a sound, but what he failed to achieve in dramatic expression he made up for more than adequately in pungency.

'Here it comes, lads,' the patient two beds along from Hugh (an employee of the gas board who had broken his leg falling off his motorbike) would sing out, at which the army officer in the next bed, who had recently undergone an undignified though extremely painful operation for the removal of a pile, would reach into his locker and produce a tub of talcum powder which he would sprinkle liberally into the air around his bed. He was a man of about thirty, with a large moustache and receding chin, who, when he was not being facetious, was complaining. After lunch Hugh put on his dressing gown and slippers and went for a walk in the corridors. Detached though he had been in Francesca Ward, at least he had been amongst men who had been through similar experiences. It was possible to feel some sort of sympathy with others who had been injured in action, but not with men who suffered from chronic wind and pimples on their bums.

At the far end of the corridor there was one old leather-covered bench seat. Sitting on it, his elbows on his knees, a cigarette smouldering between his fingers, was a young man in dressing gown and slippers. Hugh recognized him as one of the patients from his ward, and asked him what he was in for. The young man pulled on his cigarette and replied, without looking up, 'Why should you care?'

He spoke in a light, educated voice.

'I'm sorry?' said Hugh politely.

The young man continued to stare at the polished brown linoleum beneath his feet.

'Nothing,' he muttered.

'Ah,' said Hugh cheerfully. 'Which service are you in?'

'I'm not,' said the young man. 'I work on the land.'

'You mean you're a farmer? You have land in the neighbourhood?'

The young man gave a short, bitter laugh.

'That's a joke.'

'Oh?'

The young man looked up sharply, his face flushed.

'If you must know,' he snapped, 'I'm a labourer. A manual labourer. Pulling up carrots, humping sacks, menial tasks that require not the slightest skill or intelligence.'

'Makes a change anyway,' said Hugh with a laugh.

'Don't patronize me,' the young man snapped.

Hugh was astounded and slightly bewildered.

'But I . . .' he began.

'I'm not a fool,' the young man interrupted, grinding his cigarette beneath the heel of his slipper. 'I know what you're thinking. It's all right for you people with your honourable scars, received in battle, defending your country. You think you're God Almighty now, I suppose, looking down from your exalted position as one of the nation's heroes. You can say what you like about anyone else, but no one can touch you. If you want to say what you think of me, say it, but don't patronize me. I can't bear it.'

Hugh stared at him.

'What the hell are you on about?' he said. 'I asked you a perfectly simple question. If you don't want to talk, that's fine by me.'

He started to get up, but the young man took him by the arm.

'Please don't go,' he muttered. 'I'm sorry about what I said. It was inexcusable. It's just that . . .'

His voice tailed away miserably.

Hugh said, 'Look, are you allowed out or anything? Into the town, I mean? We could have tea or something.'

Like Hugh, he was to be operated on the following morning – though for what, he did not say.

'I don't know. Is it all right? I mean, shouldn't we ask someone . . .?'

Hugh, feeling more like the boy's father than a contemporary, led the way to Matron's office, where solemn promises were elicited on pain of death that they would be back in time for 'prepping' at six thirty. Hugh and the young man dressed hurriedly and set off down the narrow country lane between damp ghostly woods towards the little market town.

They headed straight for the Galleon Restaurant with its oak beams and horse brasses and gleaming copper and round tables laid with tea cups and pots of jam and carefully folded napkins. The log fire was already crackling in the corner, and

164

sprigs of holly and paper chains added to the warm welcoming atmosphere.

Mrs Endicott bustled forward, red-faced and smiling, wiping her wet hands on her apron as she came, and showed them to a table for two near the fire.

'It's just like old times having you back,' she said. They gossiped about old customers. Ronnie Ibbotson had gone to the south coast to convalesce; so had David Edwards. Noel McKinnon had been in the day before with Russell Johnson. Hugh told her about Tim getting married, and Mrs Endicott said she'd never have thought he'd settle down, that one.

'There's something different about the place,' said Hugh looking round the room. 'Something missing. I know. That nice big mirror that used to hang over there.'

'We took it down,' Mrs Endicott lowering her voice. 'We've taken down all the mirrors, not just here but in all the pubs and restaurants and hotels in the town. We all got together and decided. We thought it would be a kindness to all of you. It's not much but it helps.'

And smiling shyly, she hurried off to fetch them tea and scones and cakes.

The young man seemed more depressed than ever, and it was some time before Hugh was able to get him talking at all. Finally he confessed that his name was Dick Barclay, that he was twenty-two, had been educated at public school and Oxford, where he had gained a First in Classical Mods before the war put an end to an obviously outstanding university career, and that he was a coward.

'You see, I am a pacifist,' he explained staring into his tea as it grew colder. 'It wasn't some badly thought out, half-baked undergraduate whim. I'd come across plenty of those wishy-washy left-wing intellectual types, and they made me sick. No, this was something I'd worked out for myself after a lot of serious thought. I really believed it was my duty not to raise my hand against a fellow human-being. I really believed it. I thought of registering as a conscientious objector, but I could not face the thought of being submitted to the scrutiny of a lot of men who would never really understand what I was

165

talking about and would almost certainly end up by sending me to prison. It wasn't as though I didn't want to do something to help. So I wrote to the headmaster of my old prep school in Somerset and proposed myself as a classics master who was also prepared to help out with games and so on. To my relief, he offered me a post straight away.'

He sipped at his tea, pulled a face and continued.

'Oh, it was all right at first. I think I could be quite a good teacher if I put my mind to it. But gradually I began to have my doubts – not about teaching, but about my decision. When I began to realize what sort of man Hitler really was, and that he meant what he said, I did not see how I could honestly maintain the position I had taken up. It just didn't make sense any more, not in the light of events. On the other hand, I knew I could still never bring myself to kill anyone. Anyway, then I got very ill – pneumonia or something – and had to go home to recuperate. The doctor recommended a long convalescence at home, but I couldn't stand it. Not with my father looking at me the way he did, and my mother trying to make excuses to him on my behalf. I had to get away. Then I remembered Andrew; he's the chap who has this farm on the other side of Crowborough. We were at Oxford together. I rang him up and asked him if he needed any help and, well . . . here I am.'

Hugh said, 'But you still haven't told me why you're in Queen Mary's.'

Dick hung his head. A lock of hair flopped over his forehead.

'In-growing toenail, if you can imagine anything so pathetic,' he muttered.

'That's nothing to be ashamed of. I had one of those once. It was bloody painful.'

'You see,' said Dick wretchedly, 'you're still patronizing me. The fact is, I resent the way you look, just as I resent anyone who's been injured in action. No, resent's not the word. I envy you. I think you're lucky. I'd rather live with your scars than mine. Yours will gradually disappear in time; mine will be with me for the rest of my life.'

Dick looked up at him. His eyes were filled with fear. The

possibility that, after all, Hugh might still reject him was more than he could bear.

Hugh was also seized with a sudden fear, for he knew that whatever he said to Dick now would either give him hope for the future, or it would destroy him altogether. What possible use was a man like Dick to any of the services? On the other hand, what use was he to himself or anyone else in his present condition? What sort of answer was he hoping for anyway? That, yes, he should join up? That, yes, he had been right all along, and that he had nothing to envy? He looked at Dick in his baggy tweed jacket and ill-fitting corduroy trousers, his long thin fingers nervously pushing back the lank lock of hair that persistently dropped over his forehead, his eyes full of expectation. And suddenly a feeling of enormous anger swept over Hugh that this useless, pathetic figure should load all his guilt and responsibility onto him and put him on the spot simply because the fellow didn't know his own mind. Others, equally sensitive, equally averse to killing, had managed without making everyone else's lives a misery in the process. And then the wave of anger passed, as quickly as it had come, leaving him tired and drained of emotion. He would have liked to help, but not now. He did not trust himself to give a good, well-balanced answer.

'I'm sorry,' Hugh heard himself say. 'I don't know how to advise you. You'll just have to work it all out for yourself.'

They walked back together through the darkened streets and along the little damp lane to the hospital. Neither of them said a word. They were, as Matron pointed out, in excellent time for their 'prepping'.

Chapter Eleven

The following morning at nine, Hugh climbed once more aboard the trolley for the short, stomach-churning ride to the theatre.

Johnny Walker, the anaesthetist, said cheerfully, 'Welcome back.' Hugh felt the needle slide into his arm and he lost consciousness.

He awoke to the familiar sense of claustrophobia and helplessness. The bandages seemed, if anything, tighter than before and his eyes prickled damnably. It was extraordinary to think that only a few hours before he had been living the life of a normal, healthy human being (well, almost) – dining in the Ritz, taking tea in the Galleon, catching trains, hailing taxis, washing, shaving, lighting his own cigarettes; and to be plunged once again into this appalling state of childish dependence seemed to him to be both unjust and unnecessary. He was not ill like most of the others in the ward; he did not even need to be there. He had come of his own free will. It irked him to be lumped together with all the rest of them and made to eat the same food and conform to the same idiotic hospital routine. He missed being in Norfolk and regretted his hasty decision over Christmas.

Still, he had to admire the lengths to which Meikle and the nursing staff went to make the patients feel at home. One evening some of the nurses and doctors got up a scratch choir and went round the wards singing Christmas Carols. Hugh actually tried to join in the familiar tunes with the rest, but a huge lump came into his throat and he suddenly found himself blubbing like a child behind his bandages. His eyes stung like hell and for a while he feared for the safety of his new lids.

Another time, Russ Johnson and Noel McKinnon came over to see him from Francesca Ward with hair-raising tales of some of the new cases that had been brought in, and a half bottle of whisky which they slipped into his dressing gown pocket with best wishes for a happy Christmas. They were both off to Bournemouth for the festive season which annoyed Russ no end since he had recently fallen in love with the little dark nurse with whom Hugh had had words at the beginning of his first visit. However, Meikle badly needed the beds, and there was a strong chance she might be able to get away for a couple of days and join him down there.

Hugh felt even more cut off from real life after they'd gone. The Army officer's complaints increased daily, as did his apparently inexhaustible supply of pointless jokes. Dick Barclay, despite considerable pain, was always at hand to take Hugh to the lavatory or cut up his meat at lunchtime, just as Ibbotson had been, but otherwise he rarely spoke or intruded on Hugh's hours of solitary contemplation, so that Hugh gradually began to acquire a sort of respect for the young man that he had never felt for Ibbotson.

On the afternoon of Christmas Eve, Hugh had a short, largely tearful conversation on the telephone with his parents who told him he was in their thoughts and in their prayers. The following morning his bandages were removed just in time for the ceremonial carving of the turkey by Angus Meikle who visited each ward in turn, dressed in full operating clothes, wielding a knife and fork and cracking jokes in execrable taste about stuffing birds, well-covered breasts, and slices of skin. After that, a huge flaming Christmas pudding was brought in and more Christmas carols were sung with Meikle himself leading the singing in a loud and tuneless baritone. In order that the more seriously ill should not feel hard done by, no alcohol was served. However, such was the air of general confusion and excitement that Hugh succeeded in demolishing the whole of Russ and Noel's present, and thus survived the celebrations in a state of numbed bliss.

169

After lunch, the nurses came round to each bed and handed out little presents and kisses on the cheeks to all the patients. The fact that some of them had difficulty disguising their reluctance at making such close contact with Hugh completely escaped his notice.

On New Year's Eve, 1940, Hugh set off to Bournemouth for a couple of weeks' convalescence in order to build up his strength for the forthcoming operation on his nose.

The old hotel was much as he remembered it, although by now most of the green armchairs were occupied and the potted palms had been relegated to the billiard room and other more suitable recesses of the house.

It also enjoyed a much more lively atmosphere, generated largely, it seemed, by Mackinnon and Johnson who, despite their various handicaps, had succeeded in turning the place into a kind of preparatory school for delinquents. Pillow fights, boisterous games of sardines, murder and trying-to-get-round-the-room-without-touching-the-floor, and raucously bawdy sing-songs round the piano were commonplace, and on one occasion a donkey was inveigled out of winter retirement and introduced into the dining room with hilarious results, earning Dickinson half a bottle of whisky from Noel, Russ and Hugh, and the dressing down of his life from Matron. In many ways, it was like Cambridge all over again, and Hugh realized that he was enjoying himself for the first time in years. There were times when he thought he had never laughed so long and so loudly in his life, and it was a sad day when Matron finally announced that enough was enough and packed Noel and Russell off to another convalescent home which, she promised them, would be like a German POW camp compared with hers.

However, the atmosphere that the two of them had created prevailed in a slightly watered-down version for several days after their premature departure, and it was with some regret that Hugh returned to Ashbourne Wood to collect a new nose.

This time he was assigned a bed in Francesca Ward. Many of the old faces had gone – David Edwards, Ibbotson, Mackinnon and Johnson – but Szepezy was still there, still struggling with his new lips and the intricacies of the English language; and Fougerolles, his jaw still encased in scaffolding; and Clive Unsworth, who had recently undergone the first of dozens of operations to re-build his face.

Even more badly burnt was one of the newcomers, a sergeant pilot named Andrews, whose cockpit hood had jammed on his Hurricane, causing him several minutes of roasting before he was at last able to fall free. Hardly an inch of his body had not suffered third-degree burns, and only by holding him very gingerly by his armpits and his heels could the nurses move him at all. It was a wonder he had lived.

Several times a day he would be lifted across to the saline bath, uttering high pitched screams for which he would afterwards apologize profusely. At such moments, someone would stroll across to the wireless and turn up the volume and everyone would start talking with unnatural vivacity.

Although only half his nose had been burnt away, Meikle told Hugh that he would cover the shrunken remains with a rhinoplasty, which was normally used to replace an entire nose.

First he created a new lining for the nostril in question by folding down a thin flap of skin and gristle from what was left of that half of the nose, and turning it inside out to form a new lining and a foundation for the new nostril. Next he raised a flap of living skin and flesh from Hugh's forehead, twisted and rolled it into a tube, and attached one end of it to the left side of his nose.

Meikle's assistant, Bob Jolly, then removed a patch of skin from Hugh's stomach to cover the large gap left on his forehead.

It was a grotesque and frightening sight that greeted Hugh when the following morning he peered into the mirror. He was, he thought, almost as unrecognisable as he had been that very first time he had seen himself in Ashford, and he let out an involuntary shout so that a nurse came running to see what had happened. He was reminded of the diabolical creatures dreamed up by Hieronymus Bosch, and for several days he lay in bed, hating Meikle for what he had done, hating himself, and hating everyone else in the ward for their remorseless flow of ribald comments.

Only Meikle's sympathy touched him, perhaps because, for

171

all his bluff throwaway manner and rugger club language, deep down he was as sensitive about his handiwork, if not more so, than his patients.

'It does make you look a bit like the Hunchback of Notre Dame, I must admit,' he said with a grin, 'but it'll settle down in time, I promise you. I've tried to make it look as distinguished as the original. Thank your stars there was enough good skin left on your forehead to do it like this, otherwise it would have been a case of raising a flap from your chest, attaching it to your arm, then freeing it at the chest end and attaching it to your conk. They're not so easy to get right and I've lost a hell of a lot through infection.'

'I know I shouldn't complain. It's a bloody miracle really.'

'Steady, old chap,' said Meikle. 'You'll have me on nodding terms with J. C. himself at the rate you're going.'

Two weeks later, Meikle cut the pedicle from Hugh's nose and returned the remains to their proper place on his forehead. Far from improving his looks, the fat white object in the middle of his face looked exactly like a piece of liver sausage that someone had stuck there for a joke. It was impossible to avoid it, since wherever he looked he could see it out of the corner of his eye, pale and shapeless and utterly humiliating. Nor did it show the slightest sign, as Meikle had promised, of settling into anything remotely approaching a normal nose, and jokes about Dumbo were wearing thin. He had not set foot outside the hospital since the operation and was horrified when a few days later Meikle told him he was sending him off to Bournemouth for another couple of weeks' convalescence.

His intelligence told him he ought to be ashamed of himself. Day after day he watched Andrews being lifted in and out of the warm salt water, crying out with the pain, but otherwise silent and uncomplaining, and prayed that the boy's dumb acceptance of his fate might teach him the better to accept his own condition. He could imagine his mother telling him to pull himself together and remember there were others far worse off. But no matter how often he repeated the proposition to himself, all he felt was anger at Andrews' lack of anger.

Then, one afternoon, the boy called for a bedpan. Three

nurses finally arrived – two young and pretty VADs and Beryl, an older volunteer nurse whose large, rather protruding teeth had inspired amongst the patients many a tasteless joke.

Lifting Andrews' pitiful body onto a bedpan was a particularly awkward operation requiring a complicated combination of skill and strength. One of the VADs took his right, the other his left side, while Beryl slid the pan beneath him.

The exercise having been satisfactorily completed, the two VADs gingerly lifted the boy once more while Beryl seized the lavatory roll in one hand and the bedpan in the other.

At that moment she sneezed. It was a loud, wholehearted sneeze. Her head went back, then abruptly forward again, and with a great roar, her teeth flew straight out of her head and into the bedpan.

As one of the VADs later reported (for all this had taken place behind screens), the boy, who had not moved a muscle in weeks, laughed so long and so loudly that for a while they feared for his life – so much so that morphine had to be brought and the boy kept in a state of deep sedation for much of the following day.

Hugh was immensely cheered by the incident. Like Mrs Hobbes falling into the tea trolley, it served as a healthy reminder of the absurdity surrounding the disabled.

How could any grown man stand there with a straight face while another solemnly struggled to undo his fly buttons? His new nose was ugly and humiliating, but the very fact it so closely resembled a sausage invested it with comic potential. Andrews' bravery and solid acceptance of his suffering was for Hugh as irritating and humiliating as his new nose; laughing, he was a revelation.

During the journey by train to Bournemouth, fellow passengers regarded him with the customary variety of expressions, ranging from undisguised horror to eye-dropping embarrassment and forced naturalness. But now they amused Hugh more than they offended him. So much so that he deliberately changed compartments several times purely in order to try and guess how many different people would behave when they glanced up casually and caught sight of him.

After a while, however, the novelty of his little game began to wear off. He regretted that Tim was not there to join in the fun, and he spent the rest of the journey staring out of the window.

At Bournemouth Station he was unable to find a porter and as a result had to wait for a long time for a taxi. Then the taxi driver went to the wrong address, so that by the time he finally arrived at the convalescent home, dinner was over, the kitchen was closed and he had to make do with cold spam and a soggy, tasteless tomato.

The lounge was as full as he had remembered it, but not with anyone he recognized. He missed Noel and Russ, and the nice Scottish matron had been replaced by a humourless, sour-faced creature with a chest like an overstuffed bolster, who reminded him of Sister Grice at her worst. Even Dickinson seemed to have lost a large measure of his anarchic sense of humour.

After only half an hour, Hugh retired to his room – not the spacious double room overlooking the sea front that he had had on his last two visits, but a dark pokey box at the back overlooking the service area.

But even that was preferable to the sombre atmosphere of the lounge, and ignoring the matron's daily advice to 'take advantage of the nice sea air', he remained determinedly in his room for the next few days, reading and sleeping, descending only for meals and sometimes not even then.

Even the news that the famous English film actress Loretta Stone would be paying a visit failed to entice him from his self-imposed exile.

Quite what it was that persuaded her to make the special detour to his room he never quite discovered. Later, when he put the question to her, she had laughed her famous tinkling laugh and said something about having a soft spot for the boys in blue; but he always suspected she had simply been curious to meet a man who had shown such little curiosity about meeting her. Not that he was totally unaware of her fame and her fast growing reputation as one of Britain's leading young

174

stars, and it was more self-consciousness than genuine indifference that persuaded him to remain where he was during her visit.

He was reading Gosse's *Father and Son*, a book that in some ways reminded him of his own uncomprehending relationship with his father, when she arrived with Matron.

As soon as she entered the room he remembered her, despite the heavy make-up.

'You came with Jimmy Macdonell to a Trinity Ball,' he said.

A haunted look came into her face as if she had been caught out in a lie.

'Yes,' she said slowly, almost suspiciously, 'but . . .'

'Who am I? How do I know?' he smiled. 'I've changed a bit since then. So have you, for that matter.'

Matron chipped in with, 'I didn't know you and Mr Fleming were friends.'

'Fleming?' said Loretta Stone. 'Not Hugh Fleming?'

She had taken a course in elocution since Hugh had last seen her, and a lesson or two in poise and charm, too, to judge by the curiously stiff, unnatural way she held herself.

Hugh nodded.

'Do I call you Loretta now?' he asked, 'or Jean?'

'Joan.'

'Sorry. It was a long time ago.'

'You're telling me.'

'If you'll excuse me for a moment,' Matron said, 'I'm sure you two have a lot to talk about.' And since neither of them denied it, she stumped from the room.

'Jimmy's dead, you know,' Hugh said after she had gone.

'I didn't,' she said. 'I'm sorry. I liked him. I liked you all. We had a lot of fun in those days.'

'Yes.'

They reminisced about Cambridge and London and the times they'd had; about Jimmy and Julian and Pat and Peter. Her face grew longer and sadder, the conversation more halting.

'Adrian Downpatrick's still alive,' Hugh said during one of the long silences. 'Do you remember him?'

She shook her head numbly.

175

'He's in some POW camp,' he added lamely.

'At least he's alive,' she muttered.

'There are not many of us left from those days.

'We've all changed.'

'Some more than others.'

'Oh, I didn't mean . . .' She went red beneath the make-up.

'I know,' said Hugh gently. 'Believe it or not, I was referring to you. You've done well, I hear.'

She laughed.

'You sound surprised,' she said.

'Why should I be? I'm afraid I've never seen you act, but you're very pretty. More charming even than before.'

'They teach you that,' she said. 'But thank you anyway for the compliment. I'm not used to people being so straight. They usually come out with some stuff about how intelligent I am, as though that's bound to get me into bed.'

Hugh laughed.

'That's nothing to what they try on me.'

'To get you into bed?'

'Hardly. I think I'm going to have to think up better ideas than that for building my career.'

Loretta Stone flushed.

'That was unkind.'

'I'm sorry,' said Hugh. 'I didn't mean it like that.'

'Yes you did,' she replied hotly. 'Everyone thinks the same about film actresses. Why else did you invite us down to Cambridge? And don't say it was because you enjoyed our company or I'll hit you with my handbag. I liked Jimmy. He was good fun. But I doubt if we exchanged more than a dozen intelligent words the whole time we knew each other.'

'We must have seemed an arrogant bunch,' said Hugh wistfully.

'Don't kid yourself, ducky,' said Loretta Stone. 'As far as me and Dawn and the rest of us were concerned you were just a lot of spoiled kids who hadn't the first clue what life was all about. But you had plenty of money and fast cars. A free meal means a lot to a girl who hasn't eaten for a week or two.'

Hugh nodded, then grinned.

'I'd tell you how intelligent you are if I didn't want my intentions misunderstood.'

'I'm also not a bad actress, if you really want to know.' It was a straightforward statement of fact. Clearly no comment was either expected or hoped for. Even so, he said, 'I believe you,' in a quiet, serious voice. It sounded like a line in a script, badly written and badly acted.

'I really believe you are trying to get me into bed,' she said with a sly smile.

For a moment Hugh felt himself completely off-balance. He would have sworn that she was propositioning him, and yet he was not sure. Was this Joan from Hackney talking? Or was it Loretta Stone using her training and talent to good effect to make Hugh feel he was the one she desired, the same way she made thousands of other men feel every day in cinemas up and down the country? Time was when he would have gone ahead and let her seduce him anyway – or at any rate give her the impression it was happening that way round. Now, with his big nose and his scarred face and his bent hands, he was shy and unsure of himself. He covered his confusion with a light laugh.

'What's so funny about that?' she said. 'You never had any trouble in the past, if I remember rightly.'

'It seemed to matter then. Now I have more important things to worry about.'

'Sounds grand,' she said. 'Such as?'

The moment of doubt and uncertainty had passed, and he suddenly felt certain he could trust her. Hesitantly at first, he tried to explain to her his sense of uselessness and his need to find something to do; his conviction that he must have been spared and put through all the pain and suffering for some purpose; but what? He told her what Robin had said about recognizing the moment when it came, and about his disappointment at Eton.

'I seem to be unable to focus my mind on anyone or anything except myself and my own problems, for the simple reason that I can find nothing else.'

177

The actress sat listening to him, saying nothing, smoking a cigarette. When he had finished, she said:

'I can think of something. It's not very much – but it could lead to something. They're starting a film down at Bramham Studios about fighter pilots. It's fictional but it's based on true events. They've got a very good writer, but they need someone to advise them on the technical side of flying – you know, someone who's actually been a pilot and knows what it's like. I don't know if you'd be interested. They'd pay well and you'd be doing something useful.'

Hugh did not need any further urging. The combination of film-making and flying appealed to him at once, and Loretta told him she'd ring the producer, who was a friend of hers, as soon as she got back to town.

Hugh accompanied the actress along the corridor to the top of the stairs.

'I'd better go and sign a few more autographs,' she said.

'I'll collect mine another time,' said Hugh.

She reached up and kissed him.

'I'm sorry you didn't try to get me into bed,' she murmured. 'I always did fancy you best of all of them.'

A day went by, then another, and Hugh became convinced it had all been a lot of typically vacuous theatrical talk, and he cursed the girl for raising his hopes. He was angry, too, at himself for having taken the project seriously.

But then, on the third day, Dickinson came to his room with the message that he was wanted on the telephone.

'It's that Loretta Whatsername what was here the other day. Says it's urgent.' He winked suggestively and nudged Hugh in the ribs. 'You're a quick worker and no mistake!'

'Sod off, Dickinson,' said Hugh quietly, and walked calmly down the corridor.

The news was good. Her producer friend (boy friend? wondered Hugh with a stab of jealousy) had expressed himself extremely enthusiastic about the idea and wanted to know how soon Hugh could make himself available. Hugh promised to talk to Matron and Meikle and ring her back.

Both were, to his surprise, extremely enthusiastic and said that, as far as they were concerned, he could leave at the end of the week. The next thing was to get permission from the Air Ministry. He remembered that the head of his college at Cambridge was a close friend of one of Sir Walter Monckton's assistants at the Ministry of Information, and after a couple of telephone calls, Hugh found himself with an appointment to see the Director-General himself.

Monckton listened attentively to what Hugh had to say. The young man's enthusiasm was so engaging that after a while he was scarcely aware of the pitifully thin fingers which he jabbed in the air to make his points, and the cruelly misshapen features which perspired in his effort to explain the usefulness of the job he had been offered.

When he had finished, Monckton made two telephone calls: one to Mr George de Brownfield, the producer of *The Boys in Blue*, and the second to an air marshal in the Air Ministry, by the name of Hoggart.

Five minutes later, Hugh was being congratulated by Sir Walter on his appointment as technical adviser to the film, and shown personally to the lift.

It was, he told himself, as he strode down Whitehall in the pale winter sunshine, probably the most successful day of his life.

Loretta (he had begun to think of her now only in her present incarnation) said why didn't he come round to her flat for some lunch and afterwards they could drive down together to Bramham Studios. She would ring George.

She lived at the top of an Edwardian block in Rutland Gardens, Kensington. The flat, which was on two levels, had, Loretta explained proudly, been decorated and designed personally by – and she she mentioned an interior designer who was evidently enjoying a vogue but who meant so little to Hugh that two minutes later he could not for the life of him recall his name. Even the choice of books seemed to have been left to him, and not a cushion nor an ashtray was an inch out of place. It was like walking into an exhibition.

An unsmiling butler in white jacket and gloves served chilled champagne and, for an encore, smoked salmon, some hot beef dish and a bottle of extremely expensive claret. Hugh wondered if the famous decorator had chosen the menu, too.

After that, they moved across to one of a pair of impeccable sofas where the butler served them with coffee and brandies and Egyptian cigarettes. Loretta smoked one through an onyx holder. She seemed neither ill at ease nor especially at home in these strangely artificial surroundings. It was as if the entire thing, flat, meal, butler and all, were some sort of theatrical event in which she was playing a well-rehearsed, professional, and not entirely convincing, part. Hugh had a vision of the whole place being dismantled, walls, furniture and all, after they had gone, and reassembled somewhere else to impress another visitor to another actress.

He had quite expected her to carry on with her self-confessed seduction where she had left off after the butler had left, and was mildly disappointed when, after a short while, she announced it was time to leave. However, on the way down to Bramham in the chauffeur-driven Humber, she hooked her arm into his and chattered away about the future, for all the world as if they had just left Caxton Hall. Hugh, a little light-headed after all the wine, was thoroughly enjoying himself. Indeed, as the man at the gate of Bramham Studios waved them through with a cheery salute of recognition, and passers-by pointed and whispered as they entered one of the big sound stages, he was beginning to feel positively proprietorial about her.

The building was bigger than an aircraft hangar. At the far end, a battery of lights illuminated with unnatural brilliance what Hugh could see, as he approached on tip-toe, was a dispersal hut – or rather, a cross section of a dispersal hut of which the nearest wall had been removed, exposing its interior to lamps, camera and film crew.

As Loretta and Hugh approached, a young man in an open-necked shirt hurried towards them, kissed Loretta and nodded at Hugh. 'Terry Hughes. Second Assistant,' whispered Loretta. Hugh smiled and nodded back.

'I expect you recognize this only too well, Mr Fleming,' Terry murmured, indicating the set.

Hugh said, 'It was never quite as bright as this indoors.'

Terry chuckled and beckoned them closer as a number of young men in uniform with spotted scarves round their necks walked forward into what was, Hugh had to admit, an extraordinarily lifelike set. Even the old wood-burning stove with the chimney going up through the roof was exactly as he remembered it at Woodfold.

Hugh had feared that, at the sight of such familiar scenes so faithfully reproduced, he might suffer some sort of unpredictable reaction. He did not expect to faint, or throw a fit or anything as dramatic as that, but he certainly did not expect that he would observe it with quite such dispassion. He cast a professional eye over the scene before him – checking for any little inaccuracies or oversights or exaggerations.

'Very good,' he whispered to Terry.

'Take up positions,' a disembodied voice called out of the darkness surrounding the set.

'Chair?' said Terry.

'What?'

'Would you like to sit down while we shoot this scene?'

Hugh shook his head.

Terry said, 'Fine. Careful you don't trip over any of the cables. You can meet John after this scene. He's looking forward to it.'

'Who's John?' Hugh asked.

'He's the director.'

'Which is your friend?' he asked Loretta.

'George? Over there, with the grey hair.'

She indicated an elegant, swarthy man of about fifty with long, wavy, grey hair, sitting in an upright canvas chair on the far side of the set.

'Take up your positions, *please*,' the voice came again, tinged now with impatience.

The young men in uniform began to spread themselves around the hut – some lying on their backs on the iron beds reading books, other slouched in the basket chairs that stood around the stove. Except for the brilliant lighting, Hugh could easily have imagined himself back at Woodfold dispersal with Peter and Jimmy and Harry Lauder and Bill Carmichael and the rest – and yet there was something missing, something wrong, something that didn't ring true that he couldn't quite put his finger on.

'They'd probably be reading comics,' he whispered to Terry.

'What?'

'Quiet on the set, please.'

'Those men on the beds. They'd be more likely to be reading comics than books.'

'Comics? You mean Beano and Dandy and things?'

'Yes.'

'I said *quiet please*. Are you ready – Bob? Arthur? Eddie?'

One or two of the actors looked across to where Hugh and Loretta and Terry were standing beneath one of the huge lamps.

'Any problems?'

The actors shook their heads and returned to their original positions.

'Okay. Sound.'

'Sound running.'

'And ... *action*!'

There was a long moment of silence, then the telephone on the set rang, bringing Hugh's heart into his mouth so that for a moment he thought he was going to be sick. As the actor playing the orderly picked up the receiver, the pilots looked up expectantly.

'Dispersal,' said the orderly. 'Yes ... I see ... right ...' Suddenly a voice shouted, 'Okay, hold it, everybody. Sorry about that. Technical problem. Sorry. Position One, if you would be so kind and we'll go again.'

The actors, wearing expressions of bored indifference, strolled back across the set. And then it was that Hugh realized what was wrong: they didn't care. Not about their acting, but about the news the orderly was going to give them. Was it an order from Group that was going to mean death and pain and mutilation for some of them and grief and exhaustion and

182

more fear for the rest? Or was it someone ringing to say that tea was up? Hugh could remember several of them, himself, Peter, Corky Catte, Robbie McTurk, being sick in the few seconds between the telephone ringing and the orderly delivering the verdict. But these actors looked no more frightened than patients in a waiting room.

It wasn't their fault. How could they know what it felt like? They were actors, not pilots. The stripes on their wrists and the ribbons on their chests were assigned by a wardrobe mistress, not put up by a C.O. The nearest they had probably ever been to a Spitfire was when they had climbed into some cardboard replica on a set. To them a German pilot was just another actor in a different costume using a different accent. Damn them for their comfortable existences and their fat contracts and pretending so casually and easily to be Peter and Jimmy and others, each of whom had been worth a dozen of them any day.

And yet, could one honestly say their contribution to the winning of the war was any the less useful than his? They at least had the talent and the looks to amuse and entertain, perhaps even instruct, a hard-pressed nation at war. He could only stand on the sidelines and criticize.

Still, if he was going to do his job at all, he had better do it properly.

'I have one slight reservation about this scene,' he whispered to Terry, 'and that is . . .'

'Not now,' hissed Terry. 'They're just about to shoot again.'

'But it concerns this scene,' Hugh emphasized.

'Surely it can wait. You said yourself it was looking good.'

'But this is to do with the atmosphere and the acting, not the set.' Hugh's voice rose in exasperation.

'Mr Fleming,' Terry replied, his voice also rising angrily. 'You are here as a technical adviser, not as a dramatic coach. Now, *please* . . .'

By now, several of the actors had started to get up out of their positions and move to the side of the set to see what all the trouble was about.

'Come on now, everybody, first positions, *please*,' the disembodied voice boomed out again. 'We haven't got all day. Now, can we please have silence on the set. QUIET.'

But the argument between Hugh and Terry was, if anything, increasing in ferocity.

'There's no point in my being here at all if no one's going to take a blind bit of notice of what I say. I happen to know something about this, you know.' Hugh was shouting now. He turned to Loretta. 'If this idiot can't understand what I'm talking about, perhaps you could speak to the director?'

Loretta whispered, 'Hugh, please. Don't make a scene. It's not important.'

'Not important?' he shouted. 'You think being frightened so that you shit your pants is not important? Jesus Christ. In that case, I'd like to know what *is* important.'

The actors were still standing in the middle of the set, talking together, frowning into the darkness. Some were giggling. The sideshow had come as a welcome diversion from the boredom of filming.

Now another magisterial voice cut across the hubbub.

'What the fuck's going on over there?' it bellowed.

'Oh no,' Loretta whispered. 'That's the director.'

'Perhaps now I've got his whole-hearted attention, he might listen to what I have to say,' said Hugh. 'Hallo? Are you there?'

He strode forward. As he did so, his foot caught in one of the cables, bringing down one of the smaller lights with a crash. There was total silence as the entire company – actors, technicians, director, producer – stared in horrified disbelief as Hugh stumbled blinking into the light. There were one or two sharp intakes of breath and muffled imprecations as the full impact of Hugh's appearance sank in. It was the director who finally broke the silence.

'Jesus Christ, who the hell's he?'

And then the producer himself rose from his canvas chair, ran a lazy hand through his long, elegant, grey locks and said in a quiet, heavily accented voice:

'Will somebody kindly take that man away? He's frightening the actors.'

Chapter Twelve

Early in February, 1941, Hugh returned for the third time to Ashbourne Wood to have his hands grafted with new skin. Although still badly bent into his palms and desperately fragile, they had escaped the extreme effects of fire experienced by so many burnt pilots whereby the fingers became hopelessly locked at the joints and welded together like melted wax. By dint of daily exercise, he had succeeded in almost straightening his two forefingers and one of the middle fingers of one hand. However, further progress was hampered by the slight webbing together of the other two and an uncomfortable shortage of skin on both hands. By separating the two fingers and grafting some new skin from Hugh's thigh onto the back of his hands, Meikle would provide him with far greater possibilities of movement, and with the help of massage and exercises his fingers would begin to recover some of their old strength and deftness.

By now Hugh had devised various methods for performing the majority of everyday tasks. Eating and drinking were no problem (although he sometimes had to ask someone to cut up particularly unyielding meat); nor were washing, shaving, cleaning his teeth and brushing his hair. Buttons and shoe-laces were still beyond him, but the ingenious use of elastic laces and poppers meant that he could usually manage to dress himself without help, and ties were kept permanently knotted and slipped over his head.

His nose had, to his relief, deflated to an acceptable size and pleasant, if somewhat Semitic, shape. His eyelids, though still strangely coloured and rough in outline, were both functioning well, and it was with some degree of confidence that, following his retirement from the film industry, he accepted Lady Downpatrick's invitation to spend a couple of weeks in Ireland.

It was strange, remembering the many houseparties he had attended there before the war, when the great house had been filled with people and talk and laughter and music, to be alone there now with only a tiny, delicate, grey-haired lady and a couple of servants for company. The large sitting room, the dining room and most of the bedrooms had been closed since Lord Downpatrick's death in 1939, and the two of them spent most of their time in front of a log fire in the small, cosy smoking room, reading, playing elaborate word games and eating scrambled eggs and bacon off trays on their knees. Occasionally, they would venture out into the park for a walk by the misty lake with the labradors, but more often than not, the cold wet January weather dissuaded them from such vigorous enterprises, and they happily found the slightest excuse to stay where they were in front of the fire.

Once or twice they reminisced about the old days, but Lady Downpatrick was not a woman who cared for nostalgia and she firmly discouraged Hugh from the habit. 'People spend their lives looking backwards only when they have nothing to look forward to,' she declared, and it was only fear of her disapproval that prevented him from speculating out loud, yet again, about his own future – that, and the knowledge that at that moment Adrian was languishing in some grim German prisoner-of-war camp, suffering Heaven knew what hardships, with little to look forward to except month after month of discomfort, deprivation, bad food, harsh treatment and, for all he or they knew, death.

If Lady Downpatrick brooded on her son's misfortunes she showed no sign of it, and on the one occasion Hugh had raised the subject, she had looked up at him with her wide, blue eyes, her finely formed head erect, and said simply, 'He is in God's hands now. He will do what is best.'

Her courage and her simple faith impressed Hugh deeply and made his own problems seem rather small.

They were, if not the most lively, then certainly two of the most contented weeks he had ever spent, and although reluctant to leave, he returned to England and Ashbourne Wood with the feeling that, for all its uncertainty, life would – in some way that none of them could quite forsee now – turn out for the best.

Meikle noticed the change in Hugh straight away.

'Hallo,' he said with a twinkle in his eye, 'I do believe you've fallen in love.'

Hugh smiled.

'I think perhaps I have a little,' he said.

The pain following the hand operations was as bad as anything he had so far experienced. In the course of separating the two middle fingers, Meikle had had to cut a nerve, which in itself had resulted in almost unbearable pain. In addition, the necessary tightness of the crêpe bandages and the pressure of the soft plastic mould between the separated fingers sent a dull, throbbing ache up his arm and into his shoulder, and however much he tried to manipulate his arm, the pain was relentless. He felt thoroughly wretched, and to make matters worse, some indefinable infection suddenly invaded Francesca Ward, causing sore throats, an unusually high failure rate amongst freshly applied grafts, and a great deal of ill temper all round. Every patient was forced to undergo the shortest back, sides and top of his life, and then to have his scalp washed with special soap and sprinkled with M & B powder. The unfortunate ones upon whom the streptococci had seen fit to settle were at once put onto a course of Prontosil, a drug that had the effect of turning its victims an unhealthy shade of grey, and making them feel permanently sick.

Meikle came round twice a day, removing dressings and examining grafts for signs of infection. Time and again he would curse as he saw his handiwork destroyed. Hugh prayed that the tightness of his bandages would prevent the infection attacking his hands, but on the second day his worst fears were realized. By that evening his face was as grey as the rest, and the pain from his hands so intolerable that he had to be put back on morphine for the first time since Ashford.

Both the grafts had failed to take, but the neatly stitched wounds between his middle fingers had, for some reason, escaped infection. Even so, it was a further four weeks before the crêpe bandages could at last be removed to reveal that the second set of grafts had taken perfectly, and plans could be made for Hugh to return to Bournemouth.

In late March he returned to Ashbourne Wood – this time for a comparatively minor operation to relieve the skin shortage on the left side of his upper lip.

'We can't have you going round sneering at everybody like that any longer,' Meikle told him. 'You're superior enough as it is without rubbing it in.'

Hugh was astounded. He was convinced that in recent weeks, particularly since his time with Lady Downpatrick, he had become markedly more tolerant and well-disposed towards the world. He had made a conscious effort to chat nicely with the nurses, and be polite to Sister Beatty and both matrons – at Queen Mary's and Bournemouth – and be generally helpful and considerate to everyone in the ward. Perhaps rumours of the new-style Fleming had not yet reached Meikle's ears.

'I think you must be thinking of someone else,' Hugh laughed, but Meikle was in no mood for jokes.

'I know you're doing your best to change,' he said. 'I realized that as soon as you came back from Ireland. You asked me once whether I believed suffering built a man's character, and I told you at the time that in my experience more often than not it destroys it. You, I'm glad to say, are one of the exceptions to the rule. You've grown as a man since I first met you at Acton. Then, you could think about nothing but yourself and your own misfortunes, never of others. Over the months you have grown to understand that you alone have not been chosen out of the whole world to suffer; you are not some sort of upper class Jesus Christ. There are others like Ray Andrews and Clive Unsworth – even Dick Barclay – who are faced with agonies of mind so intense that you can only guess at them, and you have gradually begun to realize that intellectually you are in a position to help them. And yet, when it comes to the point, it's that damned superior intellect that always let you down at the

188

last moment. It tells you that humility and a genuine sympathy with your fellow human beings will give you the purpose and peace of mind you are looking for, and yet, like some tragic flaw, it is that very intelligence that causes you to recoil time and again.'

Meikle broke off and laughed.

'You know, I've missed my vocation. I ought to have joined the church. My sermons would pack 'em to the doors.'

'Priests can only cure minds and spirits,' said Hugh. 'You can mend bodies as well.'

'Oh, hell,' snorted Meikle. 'Enough of this mutual mind massaging. It all boils down to whether you love yourself more than other people. If the answer's yes, then you'll remain a superior bastard and probably be unhappy for the rest of your life; if not, then all your worries are over.' He grinned broadly. 'Well, not really. But that's roughly the idea. I tell you, you find yourself a nice girl you really love and who loves you; that's what'll make a real man of you. But make sure she's plain.'

'Why pick a plain girl when there are so many pretty ones to choose from?' Hugh said with a laugh. 'And don't say it's because they're funnier.'

'Because,' said Meikle, and now he was being completely serious, 'knowing you, if you choose a pretty girl, it'll be because you still love yourself, but if you pick a plain one, it'll be because you love her.'

After an uncomfortable and malodorous week the thick dressing across his upper lip, which prevented him from breathing properly and itched like hell, was removed along with the stitches, and Hugh hurried to the bathroom to inspect. The sneer had disappeared to be replaced by an astonishingly white patch of skin, as if he'd suffered an attack of frost-bite. However, when the area had been painted with mercurochrome, it fitted in surprisingly well with the rest of the upper lip. Meikle assured him it was perfectly securely fixed in place, but even so, for the next few days Hugh ate his food and blew his nose with all the daintiness and precision of a middle-aged Victorian spinster.

Three days later, he was sitting on his bed reading, when a nurse arrived to say that Mr Meikle would like to see him.

'Come in, Hugh,' Meikle said cheerfully as Hugh stood in the doorway of his office. 'I'd like to get you started right away on some physio for those hands. Meet Mrs Maybury, your masseuse.'

Hugh turned to find himself face to face with Marjorie.

'The thought crossed my mind that it might be the same Hugh Fleming, but then I dismissed it as being too good a coincidence to be true.'

'At least my name's the same. Mrs Maybury . . . I didn't recognize you at first. You've changed. You're more . . . I don't know . . . complete. No, that's not it. I don't know . . .'

He shrugged his shoulders helplessly.

'Keep still, please.'

Meikle, chuckling with delight at this unexpected reunion, had offered Marjorie the use of his office while he drove to East Grinstead for a meeting with Archie McIndoe. She had begun with a long and careful examination of Hugh's hands.

'They're not as bad as I'd imagined,' she said finally. 'A lot of the muscle tissue has been lost, but there's still a surprising amount of strength left. And there's far more movement than I'd have expected.'

'That's because I've been a good boy and done my exercises,' Hugh said.

'Hmm. I'm surprised this one's straightened out so well, and this, but not this or this.'

Her fingers moved firmly but tenderly over his, feeling, touching, trying.

'I'll need to see you once a week, preferably twice,' she told him.

'Here?' he asked. 'Or where? I'm afraid I still haven't quite understood.'

'Once a week here,' she said crisply. 'Otherwise in London.'

In the face of her deliberate air of quiet professionalism Hugh was beginning to feel like an over-enthusiastic schoolboy, dying to ask a hundred and one questions, bursting with impatience.

'It depends on you,' she added.

'What do you mean?'

'What I say. It depends how quickly you progress, your programme of convalescence, future operations, all sorts of things.'

'Yes, of course,' said Hugh meekly.

Marjorie moved across to the basin and started to wash her hands.

'What an extraordinary coincidence bumping into you again like this,' she said over her shoulder.

'Isn't it?' said Hugh. 'I've thought about you often. How about you?'

She turned off the big tap with her elbow and reached for a towel.

'How about me what?'

Hugh grinned and said nothing.

'You mean, have *I* thought about *you* often?'

'Well . . .' He shuffled in his seat.

Marjorie thought for a while, then said,

'I can't say I have really. So much has happened.'

'I can imagine,' said Hugh brightly in an attempt to hide his disappointment.

'How?' she asked mildly. 'You know nothing about my life, nor I about yours.'

Hugh felt himself flushing.

'No,' he stammered. 'What I meant was . . . well, you're obviously married, for a start.'

She finished drying her hands and threw the used towel into a wicker basket beside the basin. Then she walked across and sat in Meikle's chair.

'Was,' she said.

'Oh?'

'He was killed – about the same time you were shot down I'd imagine.'

'Was he a pilot?' Hugh enquired politely.

'No,' she said, 'he was a solicitor actually. He was several years older than me. Too old to be called up anyway. So he volunteered as a fireman. He was down in the docks one night, dealing with a burning warehouse. A wall fell on him. He was dead by the time they dug him out.

'I am sorry,' said Hugh.

'You'd have liked him,' said Marjorie. 'Alec. He was a beautiful painter. Water-colours mainly; seascapes. He loved the sea. You'd have got on well together. Did you keep up your painting?'

'I haven't really had the time or the inclination since Cambridge,' said Hugh.

'You will one day,' Marjorie told him with a smile. 'You wait and see. If you want to, that is.'

Hugh grunted non-committally.

She said she had to go then, but that they'd see each other again soon. She had to come down again to see some other patients convalescing.

After she had gone, he realized she had asked him almost nothing about himself, nor had he succeeded in eliciting very much information about her. He consoled himself with the thought that they would have plenty of time to talk in the weeks to come. Yet somehow it was not enough. Greedily he had wanted more. At first she had seemed genuinely delighted to see him again. But then her enthusiasm appeared to have waned and she had treated him as politely and impartially as she would any other patient. He had been left with the distinct impression that seeing him again meant less to her than it did to him, and this fussed and concerned him.

He could not imagine why this should be so. Her looks had certainly not improved. Her hair was shorter and curlier, and her horn-rimmed spectacles were a marginal improvement on the round black plastic frames she'd worn at Cambridge, but she still made little effort with her appearance, and her blouse and skirt beneath her white coat were as plain and drab as could be.

And yet, and yet . . . her very lack of interest in her own appearance, and in his too, had impressed itself on him. She had come to the hospital to do a job, not gossip about her recent life with a man she had once known briefly two years before. Was there any reason why she should treat him with anything but polite indifference?

He had expected a reaction from her that he had neither the right nor reason to expect, and her indifference had hurt him. He had, he felt sure, made a fool of himself, and it was largely in order to make amends for his absurd presumption that he anxiously awaited her next visit.

However, by the time that visit came, self-pity had set in and it was an uncommunicative, sullen patient that Marjorie was faced with the following Saturday in the small, bare room to which she had been assigned by Meikle. Hugh had the previous day moved out of the hospital and into the spare room of the Meikles' cottage, three miles away. It had been Meikle's idea and Hugh had accepted the invitation with enthusiasm.

He was the last of the group she had to see that day, and after prescribing and supervising some preliminary finger exercises, she proposed a short outing to a nearby village for some tea.

Hugh grudgingly accepted, and they drove for a while in Marjorie's old Austin through the Surrey countryside, barely exchanging a word, until she spotted a friendly looking teashop overlooking the village green.

Hugh said that it was fine by him and, to the jangling of the door bell and the usual assortment of curious stares, they entered and found a table in the bow window. Marjorie ordered tea and cakes for two and lit a cigarette.

'I don't remember you smoking at Cambridge,' Hugh remarked.

'I don't remember you behaving like a spoilt child,' she replied.

Hugh stared out of the window.

'I'm sorry,' he said. 'I don't think I'm very good company today.'

'I had noticed,' she said. 'In that case, why don't you try and do something about it instead of making both of us miserable?'

'Such as?'

She shrugged.

'Such as ... I don't know ... anything rather than sitting

there with a face like a wet weekend. Or are you expecting me to do all the work? I've given you your exercises, I've driven us both out here, I've ordered the tea, I've made all the conversation. What else do I have to do? Sing and dance?'

He knew he had only to grin to save the situation, but still he said, 'I feel rather mouldy, if you must know,' and stared belligerently at the pattern on the table-cloth.

'I daresay,' Marjorie retorted. 'Who doesn't these days? I've had a splitting headache for three days.'

'I'm sorry,' said Hugh.

'No you're not,' she said. 'You're sorry for yourself. And I bet I know why. At first I thought you might still be sensitive about the way people look at you. I was quite nervous about bringing you in here. But then I saw that you'd largely got over that stage, at least in as much as a good looking man can get over the loss of his looks in a few weeks. You told me last time that you'd thought about me often. It was a nice try, but quite untrue . . .'

Hugh opened his mouth in protest, but Marjorie raised a hand and continued, 'I'm not blaming you. On the other hand, why should you expect me to have pined after you? That's what's upset you, isn't it? That I didn't immediately rush to pick up where we'd left off? You thought you'd buttered me up enough and were thoroughly offended when I failed to return the compliment.'

Hugh said nothing.

The tea arrived and she stubbed out her cigarette.

'I daresay you'd like me to be mother – in more senses than one.'

She poured out the tea and took a cake.

'You'd make a good agony columnist,' he told her, grinning sheepishly. 'Perhaps even better than Meikle.'

'Very plain girls quickly learn to be amateur psychologists,' she said crisply. 'It's part of their survival kit. It helps them to keep sane and it makes them more attractive to men. There's nothing a man likes better than a woman who can explain him to himself. It's the most successful form of flattery I know. Never fails. Well, hardly ever.'

194

She gave him a meaning look.

'There will always be the very immature ones who are dazzled more by beauty than brains. More tea? Oh, you haven't started. Hurry up, or you'll miss all the best cakes.'

Hugh sipped unenthusiastically at the pale, lukewarm liquid.

'We were very happy together that summer in Cambridge,' he muttered.

'Speak for yourself. Oh, for the few brief moments we were together I was happy enough, I suppose. It was quite an event for a girl in Cambridge in those days to find a man who was genuinely interested in the same things as she was. To find a man at all indeed. Like a fool, I really believed you were interested in me as well as the painting and the music. I actually thought something good might come of it. At one time, believe it or not, I managed to persuade myself I was in love with you; that was, until I finally got it through my thick, idealistic skull that the only thing you were capable of loving was that group of superficial friends you never stopped talking about but never let me meet; and yourself, of course. Most of the time I spent in abject misery, if you must know.'

There was no trace of self-pity or regret in her voice; it was a simple statement of fact concerning events that seemed almost to have nothing to do with her. Hugh was disturbed and angry at hearing put into words what he had always suspected but never quite dared admit to himself.

'I didn't realize,' he mumbled.

Marjorie helped herself to another cake.

'This Dundee cake is quite delicious,' she said. 'You really should try a piece. You may not have realized the *extent* of my unhappiness, but you must have known what you were doing. You were quite deliberate about it.'

'You must hate me.'

'Don't flatter yourself. I hardly give you a second thought.'

'I don't know why you're wasting your time on me in that case.'

'Who said I was wasting my time?' she snapped. 'I happen to like driving in the Surrey countryside in early spring and eating tea in village tea-shops. I'd have come here anyway. You just happened to be there and I thought it might make a change for you, that's all.'

'Perhaps we'd better go,' Hugh said with a sigh.

'You can't get your own way, so you give up and take the easy way out. Unless the conversation revolves around you, you lose interest. You've asked me nothing about myself, my life, Alec, how I came to be a physiotherapist, whether I'm happy – nothing.'

'All right, how about yourself?'

'I'm 23; I was married for a year to a rather wonderful man called Alec Maybury until he was killed by a falling building; we had no children; we lived in a flat in a mansion block near Baker Street where I still live and still think about him most of the time; and I earn a modest living from massage which I took up after Cambridge because I like helping people and couldn't think of anything else to do. I think that just about covers it.'

'I doubt it,' said Hugh grimly, 'but since we're swapping life histories, I am a 22-year old ex-Spitfire pilot, with five dead Germans to my credit and a DSO; I am unmarried and unattached; I live in and out of various hospitals and convalescent homes, free of charge, and my service pay is entered automatically into my bank at regular monthly intervals; I have lost my looks, the use of my hands, nearly all my friends, and most of my self-respect; I have no skills and no qualifications and have nothing to look forward to except further operations, followed by long, empty years on a small disability pension – to compensate for which I spend much of my time indulging in aimless nostalgia. I was happy to see you again because you were a link with the days when I was young and life seemed good. However . . .'

'Please,' whispered Marjorie, 'don't go on.' She buried her face in her hands for a while. When she looked up there were tears behind the thick glass of her spectacles. 'I am well rebuked. I didn't really mean half of what I said. I am happy to see you again and I'd like to go on seeing you, in spite of everything.' She stopped and stared down at the remains of their tea.

Hugh took her hand gently.

'Marjorie,' he said softly, 'I just want to say ...

'Not now,' she said with a quick, awkward smile. 'Let's save it up till our next session. Come to London next week. I'll fix it with Meikle. The flat's not exactly Claridges, but at least it's mine. We can talk there.'

Hugh glanced round in time to catch the four middle-aged ladies at the next table hurriedly averting their gaze.

He and Marjorie exchanged smiles. Then she said, 'The trouble is, I think, both of us are feeling rather too sorry for ourselves to say what we really think. We're too anxious to make sure the other appreciates just how hard done by each of us is. Now we've got that out of our systems, perhaps we can begin again on equal terms.'

Hugh nodded.

'I really have been thinking about you,' he said earnestly.

'Maybe,' she said. 'Now let's get the bill and get out of here. I hate tearooms in Surrey villages. And the cakes were absolutely filthy.'

Chapter Thirteen

Bracknell Mansions was a smug, red-brown Edwardian block in a side street to the east of Baker Street.

As Hugh entered the hall on the ground floor, a porter in a peaked cap and toothbrush moustache, bearing a striking resemblance to Hitler, popped out from a cubby hole beneath the stairs, took one look at Hugh and said, 'You'll be wanting Mrs Maybury, I daresay. Fifth floor.'

Hugh moved towards the lift.

'Out of order,' the porter informed him with more than a hint of satisfaction in his voice. 'Been like it for weeks. Can't get the help, see. Ah, well. That's war for you.'

'Yes,' said Hugh.

'You one of them Few, are you?'

'I suppose you could say that.'

'Thought as much,' said the porter gloomily.

Marjorie answered the door in her white coat.

'Can you wait a moment or two,' she said urgently, beckoning him into the sitting room. 'I've still got someone with me.' She darted off along the linoleum-covered passage.

She had been right about the flat. It certainly wasn't Claridges. The armchairs needed re-upholstering, the curtains had seen many better days, and the carpet was wearing dangerously thin in places. It was also rather dark. On the other hand, it was large and comfortable and cosy, like a pair of well-worn slippers, and Hugh felt immediately at home. On a small table behind the sofa, beside a bowl of pink hyacinths, stood a framed photograph of a smiling man with grey hair and glasses. Hugh was peering at this when he heard voices coming down

198

the passage, the door opened and Marjorie entered, followed by Tim Holland, grinning broadly.

'Greetings, old cock,' he bellowed, one misshapen paw extended. 'How's tricks?'

Hugh was so surprised to see him that for a moment he was quite stuck for words. Tim winked suggestively.

'You sly old sod.'

'What do you mean?' Hugh said.

'Come off it, my old fruit-cake. Young Marge here has been singing your praises for the last hour. Hardly got any finger-bending done at all. Not that I'd have thought it made a lot of difference as far as I'm concerned.'

He waved his few remaining stumps in the air and laughed.

'Really!' murmured Marjorie, blushing furiously.

'I'm sure you're exaggerating, Tim,' Hugh said weakly.

Tim winked again.

'Take the advice of one who knows. Once you've found a good'un, never let her go. Some people have to shell out good money writing to agony columns for that sort of advice.'

'How's Nancy?' Hugh asked laughing. 'Decent of you to ask me to the wedding. I think I may have been given your old bachelor suite at the Ritz.'

'Spur of the moment job, old boy,' Tim told him cheerfully. 'Caxton Hall. Just the two of us and a passing War Office type as witness. Couldn't be happier. Small flat opposite Battersea Park, kid on the way, job, three-piece suite – and suit. What else could a man ask for?'

'Congratulations,' said Hugh. 'I can't picture you as a father somehow.'

'Ah well, as I told you before, it's we uglies what gets the gravy these days.'

'What sort of job?'

'Journalist, news hound, green eyeshade and all that sort of thing. I happened to meet Beaverbrook at a party and he offered me a job, completely out of the blue. Mentioned a princely salary, immediately doubled it, then told me to go away and report to some joker in Fleet Street. Of course, the poor fellow knew nothing about it; thought I was pulling his pudding. Who wouldn't? Anyway, it all sorted itself out in the end. I'm still a bit of a back runner in the pencil and pad stakes, and I tend to hit a few wrong notes on the typewriter, but they seem quite pleased with my journalistic gems and I'm enjoying it. And after all, that's what life's really all about when it comes down to it, isn't it?'

'He's very fond of you,' Marjorie said after Tim had gone and they were sitting together drinking tea in front of the electric fire.

'The feeling's mutual,' said Hugh. 'I only wish I were blessed with one ounce of his capacity for life. Nothing seems to bother him. After a few minutes with him, you hardly notice his . . . what should one call it? Disability? Scars? Disfigurement? None of the usual words seem to apply to him somehow.'

'He's had to work at it, you know,' Marjorie reminded him.

'Perhaps,' said Hugh. 'Meikle once said you needed to be a pretty extraordinary man to begin with to pull it off successfully.'

'Not necessarily,' said Marjorie. 'Tim is certainly no ordinary man. On the other hand, he has had the advantage of being brought up in the belief that the world does not owe him a living.'

'Which I didn't, you mean?'

'Evidently not, otherwise you wouldn't have been so convinced that those rich friends of yours at Cambridge were the be-all and end-all of your life. You'd have taken advantage of Cambridge by working and reading and preparing yourself for some sort of career, instead of assuming that you would be spending the rest of your days with your amusing pals, drifting high above the world on a pink cloud, sipping champagne and giggling helplessly at your own jokes.'

'Not much hope of that now,' Hugh said. 'They're nearly all dead.'

'I know, and still you haven't come down to earth. You still believe that doors are going to open, wonderful opportunities are going to present themselves at every turn, and everyone you meet has been put there for the express purpose of advising you and assuring you that you are not really as bad as you think you are. Being looked after is the prerogative of the very sick and the very unintelligent. You are no longer the first and you were never the second.'

She stood up and went across to the window and looked down into the street where men in uniform were clearing away the debris left by a recent bomb. She watched them in silence for a while, then turned and stood with her back to the fading light. 'I remember I went to North Africa during one Long Vac from Cambridge. Morocco. There was a crowd of us, all undergraduates, and one day we drove to a little seaside town; I forget the name now. There was a sort of little square in the middle with cafés round the outside. We were all there drinking wine, watching the world go by, when we heard a strange rumbling noise. It turned out to be a crippled boy of about fifteen going round the tables in a makeshift cart, begging for money. His legs were deformed and twisted out of recognition and he pushed himself along the pavement with the back of his hands which were wrapped in rags. We gave him a few coins, not much, and he continued on his way. We had planned some sightseeing and shopping, but it was very hot so we stayed where we were, drinking and talking. About three quarters of an hour later, we heard the rumbling again, and there was the same boy on his cart asking us for more money. We explained we'd already given him some. To our amazement, he berated us in the strongest possible language, cursing and shouting and telling us how mean we were and how he had a family to support and goodness knows what else. Instead of being embarrassed and giving him more – after all, it wasn't a lot to us – we found ourselves shouting back and telling him not to be so stupid and greedy and to go to hell. Somehow the fact that he was appallingly crippled didn't come into it. He was living life on the same terms as everyone else; he expected no special treatment and received none. When we thought about it afterwards, we all agreed he was an extraordinary fellow; but really he wasn't extraordinary at all by Moroccan standards. He had simply come to terms with what being a member of the human race is all about. Like Tim.'

Hugh's next appointment with Marjorie was at Ashbourne Wood two days later. As soon as they had finished the treatment, she said, 'Now I'd like you to try a new kind of exercise. It's been devised specially for you.' Before he could utter a word, she marched him out to the car and opened the boot to reveal two easels, a large box of paint brushes, another of paints, and two blank canvases. There was also a wicker picnic basket.

'But, I can't . . . I mean, I haven't . . .'

'There's no excuse,' she said laughing. 'Meikle has officially prescribed it. Moreover he has promised me that if you show the slightest signs of intransigence, he will personally drive you down to Bournemouth. Now get in.'

It was noon on one of those early spring days which only seem to happen in Britain, when the warm sun draws from the earth dozens of fresh scents that have been lying there throughout the winter months alongside the green shoots, waiting for the first opportunity to break out.

They drove, singing and laughing, through the Surrey countryside, then climbed to the top of the North Downs, turned left and continued for a couple of miles along the winding green lanes, until they came to an open space above some chalk pits. Below them, as far as the eye could see, lay the fields and woods and hedgerows of Southern England, almost as familiar to Hugh from this high vantage point as they had been from the cockpit of his Spitfire.

'Extraordinary,' he murmured.

'Isn't it just?' said Marjorie. 'On a clear day you're supposed to be able to see five counties – or is it the sea? I can never remember. It's somewhere round here that Queen Elizabeth is supposed to have stopped on her way to or from one of the innumerable houses where she spent the night and said, "What a magnificent realm is mine" – or words to that effect.'

'A lot of remarkable things have happened round here,' said Hugh. Marjorie laughed and ran to the car and started unloading the canvases and easels and the picnic basket which contained bread, ham, cheese, apples, a bottle of cider, and a thermos flask of coffee.

'You're amazing,' Hugh told her.

'Not really,' said Marjorie as she began to arrange the food on a gaily coloured check table cloth on the grass. 'Shall we have lunch now and then paint? Or make a start on some initial sketches and then have something to eat?'

'If only all life's problems were as simple and attractive.'

'Now, now,' said Marjorie. 'None of that talk, if you don't mind.'

'All right then, since you insist on a decision, I say we paint now and eat later. Or rather, I stand with a glass of cider in one hand watching you paint now, and then we both eat later.'

'And no more of this defeatism either, or I'll sneak to Meikle.'

'I'd never speak to you again.'

'That would be a shame.'

Hugh had been joking, but Marjorie clearly meant what she said.

'I agree,' said Hugh with equal seriousness.

And because it seemed the obvious thing to do, he leaned forward and kissed her on the cheek. She did not resist or pull away or give him any indication that she disapproved of what he had done. She just knelt there on the table-cloth in the middle of the picnic, waited till he'd finished, then leaned back and said quietly, 'Some people get everything they want.'

Hugh thought he could detect the faintest hint of a smile. Was she being serious now, or was he being given tacit encouragement to pursue the matter? And, if so, did he want to?

She gazed at him with a steady look. Her eyes seemed to be mocking him. 'You didn't want me before when you had your looks and the pick of all the girls in England,' they seemed to say accusingly, 'but now that you're as ugly as I am, you can't keep your hands off me.' Or was that only his guilty conscience speaking?

'I'm so glad you don't wear a lot of face-powder,' he told her tentatively.

'I forgot to tell you,' she replied. 'Any amorous advances also earn you a trip to Bournemouth.'

'I'll kill Meikle,' he declared, and wondered whether the surgeon had been saying things to her in an attempt to push the two of them together.

Marjorie said, 'You do, and I'll be out of a job.'

They both laughed and the tension was broken, leaving Hugh vaguely dissatisfied – needing answers, but not daring to ask the questions for fear of . . . what? Making a fool of himself? Being rejected? Upsetting the delicate balance of a love-affair in its early, uncertain stages? A love-affair? With Marjorie? Good God, what was he thinking of now?

As she heaved herself to her feet, her grey skirt rode up slightly to reveal plump, heavily stockinged thighs and wide, dimpled knees. Her green Aertex blouse had pulled away from her waistband, exposing white bulging flesh. Her large, rather pointed breasts swung heavily inside the shapeless material. He thought longingly of Bunny and her slim, firm, forbidden body, her tiny round face, her huge green eyes and her wide, greedy mouth. Jean had had a large mouth, too, and had known how to use it. So had that Soho tart. Other women came back to him now – ambitious little actresses, mindless debutantes, the sisters of chaps at school, the two whores in Istanbul, the ones who would and the ones who wouldn't – all in their different ways beautiful and desirable and compliant . . .

Marjorie had set up the easels and the canvases and was getting out the brushes and paint pots. She pushed a lock of hair back with her elbow and smiled at Hugh through her heavy spectacles. It was a smile without suggestion and without allure.

'Have you ever met a beautiful woman with a sense of humour?' Meikle had asked him. Perhaps not. But who went to bed to crack jokes? 'Find yourself a nice girl who you love and who loves you,' he had said. 'That'll make a real man of you.' Hugh looked at Marjorie. He was contented enough in her company, but in no way did she make him feel like a man – at least not in the way that Jean had, or the whore in Istanbul. But then why should she? She still loved Alec; probably always would. And yet he had kissed her, and she hadn't objected.

Oh, to hell with it, he thought. Meikle's right. I *do* think too much.

'Come on. We haven't got all day,' Marjorie called out.

204

She had set up the easels facing the view, but Hugh decided he was going to paint her, with the trees and their first flush of springtime green beyond. At first he found great difficulty in holding a brush at all. His fingers refused to do what he wanted. There seemed to be no feeling there at all, and on several occasions the brush simply dropped out of his hand and onto the grass. After half an hour he had made pitiful progress.

'Oh hell and damnation,' he said. 'I feel like some mentally defective four year old being told to draw a nice picture of an orange. In fact I doubt if I could even do that at this rate.'

He threw himself onto the grass and reached angrily for his cider. Marjorie put down her brush. 'Let's give it a rest and have some lunch,' she said. 'It's far too hot for painting now. We'll go on later.'

Hugh gave a non-committal grunt.

After they had eaten the picnic, they stretched out on the grass, the sun warm on their faces.

'I wonder if I'll ever be able to get a sun tan again,' Hugh murmured sleepily.

'Just as long as you don't get burnt,' said Marjorie.

Hugh chuckled.

'You'd hardly believe there was a war on,' said Marjorie some minutes later. Hugh did not reply. He was nearly asleep. Suddenly, as if in deliberate contradiction of her words, a squadron of fighter planes appeared from behind the trees away to their right, climbing fast, their Merlin engines snarling as the pilots applied full throttle.

Hugh sat up.

'Spitfires,' he said quietly. 'From Woodfold, I shouldn't wonder. It's only a few miles from here; did you know?'

'Yes,' said Marjorie in a vague voice.

'They sound different,' he said. 'More powerful somehow. They must have made a number of modifications by now, of course. Wonder where they're off to? France, I suppose. God, they're beautiful, aren't they? No wonder the Germans were frightened of them. I'd be, too. Wonder if it's anyone I know? Robin, perhaps. On second thoughts, it's unlikely. As a Flight

Commander he'd never let his number two hang back like that. Close up, you lazy sod! That's better.'

The Spitfires climbed away to become insects in the blue sky.

'Do you know,' Hugh said to Marjorie, lying back and closing his eyes against the sun, 'when I used to fly over the countryside like that and look down at the houses and the cars and the people below, I could somehow never quite believe that they were the ones I was risking my life for. They seemed to have nothing to do with me. I wonder if the people down below thought the same about us? Watching those Spitfires, I don't think so somehow, do you?'

'That's because you know the people flying them – or might do. During the battle last summer we watched the planes go up and we saw the fights, but most of us knew nothing of the people in them, what they were feeling or thinking or suffering. When we heard on the news that so many German planes had been destroyed, we cheered, and we were glad that our own losses were so few. But no names were given, and no details – who had died instantly, who had been drowned, who had been burned, who had died bravely and who had been shot down trying to run away. They were scarcely people to us at all.'

Hugh nodded.

'Perhaps that's why pilots find it so difficult to communicate properly with other people – even members of other services. And they with us. My sister once described us as a precious, self-congratulatory bunch. I suppose we are – were; but what can we do about it?'

'Have you ever thought of going back to operational flying?' Marjorie asked him in a casual tone of voice. 'You could, you know. In time. Your hands are getting stronger by the day, and there are precious few left with your knowledge and experience.'

'Almost every pilot I met in Ashbourne Wood kept himself going with the thought that he would eventually be fit enough to take his revenge on the Germans,' said Hugh. 'I couldn't understand it. Still can't really. But when I saw those Spitfires just now . . .'

He shook his head, as if shaking out unwanted thoughts.

'I can't really believe my life was spared just in order that I should go back and be killed. Anyway, all that was in another life.'

Later, they started painting again. Hugh found it easier to manipulate the brushes now, but still they refused to produce on the canvas what was in his head.

'It's no good,' he shouted finally in despair, throwing down his brush. 'I've completely lost my touch, everything. It won't come. I knew I shouldn't have tried.'

'You're behaving like a spoilt child again,' she told him without looking up from her painting. 'Just because you can't get what you want when you want it, you lose heart and give up. Everything came easily to you before, but you had the talent; and you don't lose that, stiff hands or no stiff hands. And that goes for everything else, too.'

Hugh scowled across at her.

'Meaning?'

'You know what I mean,' she said.

They painted on for a while until the sun began to lose its warmth and the colours began to fade. If Marjorie had guessed that all the while Hugh had been painting her, she gave no indication of it.

'It's rough and hard, but it's good,' she said after a moment's solemn consideration.

'Like me,' said Hugh. 'Have it. In years to come, it'll be a reminder of a very important day.'

'Yes,' said Marjorie.

They packed up the car and Marjorie said, 'Look, it's early still, why don't we make a little detour to Woodfold?'

'Oh, I don't think so,' Hugh said at once.

'You might see someone you know. Who knows, they might even want to see you.'

'I doubt it. Anyway, I wouldn't know anyone there now.'

'You might. How about Robin?'

'I think he said something about being transferred.'

'You really do give up frightfully easily,' said Marjorie. And leaning forward, she pecked him awkwardly on the cheek.

'And you're frightfully persuasive,' said Hugh smiling, and

kissed her back, this time properly on the lips. And this time she kissed him back – not passionately, but with an openness and an enthusiasm that left him confused and unexpectedly excited.

It took them longer than they expected to reach the station, but that was because Hugh persuaded Marjorie to drive slowly – the better to enjoy the countryside, he said; really it was to put off the moment of arrival.

At any moment during that half hour's journey he could have told her to stop and turn round and take him back to Ashbourne Wood. He could have feigned tiredness, pain, lack of interest. But he said nothing. He was curious to see the place again. He might very well run into someone he knew – Robin or Dickie Bird or Bill. But more than that, it was a sort of challenge – like getting straight back onto a horse after coming off. It suddenly seemed very important to him to go back.

They trundled in the old Austin along the wooded lanes, past the Green Man and on until a sudden break in the trees, a high bank toppled by a hedge, and a solitary windsock had his heart thumping in his chest. Soon the big black hangars came into view, and the low red-brick Mess, and the grassy mound that disguised the old operations room.

At the gate, a young corporal stepped out of the guard hut, his face already set in an expression of stern discouragement.

'May I help you?'

'Sir, if you don't mind,' snapped Hugh.

'Sir,' said the corporal sulkily.

'And stand to attention when you're speaking to an officer.'

The corporal shuffled his feet and coughed.

'I'm sorry, sir. I don't know you.'

'Pilot-Officer Fleming.'

'I see, sir,' said the corporal narrowing his eyes. 'I haven't seen you before . . . Are you . . .?'

'I was stationed here last summer. I have to see someone.'

'Do you have an appointment, sir?'

'Not exactly, but I'm sure it doesn't matter.'

'Who did you want to see exactly?'

'Squadron-Leader Bird.'

'There's no one of that name on the station, sir.'

'89 squadron.'

'They've moved sir. A couple of months ago or more. North Weald, I believe. Or is it Middleton?'

'So Flight-Lieutenant Bailey's not here any more either?'

'Not if he's with 89, sir.'

Hugh stared ahead as a couple of young pilots in uniform strolled past and the corporal jumped to attention and saluted.

'I obviously should have worn my uniform,' Hugh said to Marjorie. 'You should have warned me.'

Marjorie began to say something, but Hugh was already saying to the corporal, 'If you'd like to ring Squadron-Leader Blades, I'm sure he'll vouch for me.'

'Squadron-Leader who?'

'Blades. He is still the station adjutant, isn't he?'

'Not as far as I know,' said the corporal who was showing distinct signs of enjoying Hugh's growing discomfort.

'And Group-Captain Ocker? I suppose you've never heard of him either?'

'He's on leave just now, sir.'

'At least he exists,' snapped Hugh.

'What exactly was the purpose of your visit, sir?'

Marjorie said, 'We really just wanted to look round, that's all . . .'

'It's none of your business, corporal,' Hugh interrupted her angrily.

'No sir,' replied the corporal. 'Do you perhaps have your i/d card on you, sir?'

'No, I do not, damn your eyes. My God, I've a good mind to report you to your station commander when he gets back from leave.'

Hugh climbed out of the car and walked towards the gate. The corporal hurried after him.

'Excuse me, sir,' he said taking Hugh by the arm, 'but I have strict orders . . .'

Hugh shook him off.

'I'm not planning an armed raid, if that's what you think.

But I would like some fresh air. Or do I need to show you my i/d card for that, too?'

The corporal stepped back muttering.

'I do have my orders . . . how am I to know . . . every Tom, Dick and Harry . . .'

Hugh stared over the gate, breathing heavily, his temper gradually cooling. He felt a hand on his arm and went to shake it off, but it was Marjorie.

'I'm sorry,' she said.

'It was your idea, wasn't it? From the beginning? The painting, the picnic – they were just an excuse, a lure to get me interested.'

'I thought it might give you something to think about – an interest, a purpose. The painting, too. It was just an idea.'

Hugh squeezed her arm.

'I don't know,' he said, 'now . . .' He waved his hand vaguely at the scene in front of him. 'I recognize it all, of course. The hangars, the Mess, the WAAF's quarters. They seem to have rebuilt those; they were terribly badly bombed. But I don't know. In some ways it seems as though I've never been here before in my life.'

'It was just an idea,' she said again.

Hugh pointed to the gap between the hangar and the Mess building.

'Spitfires,' he said. 'At readiness by the look of things. Just like the old days.'

'Excuse me, sir,' the corporal's officious, slightly mocking voice broke into his thoughts. 'But are you planning on staying here long? You can't leave your car here like this, you know. You're blocking the entrance.'

Almost before the words were out of his mouth, from the direction of the Mess building came the urgent jangle of a telephone, followed by shouting, the sound of men running and the first hesitant coughs of a Merlin engine being started up.

'If you wouldn't mind, sir,' insisted the corporal.

Hugh looked at Marjorie.

'Let's go home,' he said in a low voice. 'I don't belong here any more.' Then he added, 'I also feel rather sick.'

Chapter Fourteen

Hugh stayed with the Meikles for the whole of that April. On a couple of occasions he suggested to Francesca, more out of politeness than conviction, that it might be better if he made alternative arrangements. Quite what he thought he meant by this he was not entirely sure, and when Francesca told him he was to do no such thing, he was only too happy to let the matter drop.

Despite the twenty years difference in their ages, he felt as close to them as ever he had felt to Robin or the others. They made no demands on him, nor he on them. Meikle himself had nearly always left the house by the time Hugh came down to breakfast, and Francesca, who acted as her husband's unofficial private secretary as well as running a local WVS station, was often away from the house all day. Once, the Meikle's son Alexander, a lieutenant in minesweepers, arrived down unexpectedly on a 48-hour leave, and the four of them spent a warm, golden evening of music, conversation and excellent food, but apart from that, they were rarely all in the house together at the same time. They made no apologies to Hugh for abandoning him to his own devices, nor did he expect any. He was content to read, sit in the garden in a deckchair, or go for long aimless walks through the bluebell woods with Archie, the Meikles' bouncy Kerry Blue terrier.

Twice a week he drove over to the hospital for his sessions with Marjorie. They consisted mainly of a series of simple finger-stretching exercises and massage with olive oil to loosen the skin. He was achieving more flexibility in his joints every day now and Marjorie declared herself well satisfied with his progress. Often they would go out afterwards for a walk or a drive in the car. From time to time, partly to fit in with Marjorie's plans and partly as an excuse to get up to town, he would arrange to meet her at the flat, in which case she would ensure he was her last patient of the day. When they had finished, she would sit him down in one of the old armchairs with a whisky and soda while she prepared a simple supper for them both. Afterwards they would talk and drink endless cups of tea until it was time for Hugh to catch the last train back to Ashbourne Wood. On a couple of occasions they completely lost track of time so that Hugh missed his train and had to put up in the spare room.

They talked about anything and everything – tentatively at first, anxious not to disagree, then more boldly – questioning each other's assumptions, trying out ideas that had never occurred to them before just to see how far they could take them, exploring each other's minds. Hugh was fascinated by the originality of Marjorie's thinking. Whatever the subject, her ideas were always fresh and unexpected. At times he wondered if she was just being perverse for the sake of it. His own theories seemed in contrast plodding, second-hand, and badly thought-out, and he regretted his inadequate reading. Sometimes their conversations resembled an informal Cambridge supervision, with himself as the keen young undergraduate and Marjorie as the indulgent tutor, listening politely while he expounded some complicated theory on, say, abstract versus representational art and then taking his arguments, and by adding perhaps only one simple idea of her own, making him see the whole subject through entirely different eyes. And yet at no time did he have the feeling she was patronizing him or making fun of him.

For the first couple of visits they both studiously avoided discussing themselves and their feelings, but then one day Marjorie caught Hugh staring at the silver-framed photograph on the table.

'He wasn't a lot to look at,' she said, 'but he was the most remarkable man I have ever known.'

'Alec?'

'Yes, Alec.'

'He had a kind face.'

'He was more than kind; he was utterly good.' She gave an awkward little laugh. 'I know that must sound silly and sentimental, but it's true.'

'Not at all,' Hugh said. 'I think the same way about Robin Bailey. I hope you'll meet him one day.'

'I miss him dreadfully, of course,' Marjorie went on, running her fingers lightly over the top of the frame. 'But more than that, I miss the child we never had. People like Alec shouldn't be allowed to die without leaving something of themselves behind. There was nothing wrong, you understand. It was just that we never got round to it. We thought we had all the time in the world. I suppose everyone does.'

'You're obviously still in love with him,' Hugh said.

'I try not to be,' she smiled. 'It doesn't pay to remain faithful to memories. We've all got to get on with our lives.'

Never having needed to envy another man anything in his life before, the realization that not only did he envy the two of them the happiness they had shared, but that he was actually jealous of Alec, took him completely by surprise.

Until this moment, it had never seriously occurred to him that his feelings for Marjorie were anything other than those of a simple undemanding friendship. Frankly, he had felt rather sorry for her. The thought that he might be falling in love with her both alarmed and excited him.

Suddenly he found he was looking forward more and more to his massage sessions, and devised elaborate excuses as to why he should see her in London rather than at Ashbourne Wood. Almost overnight, it seemed, from being contented on his own in the Meikles' cottage with the dog and his books, time began to hang heavy on his hands, and he found himself counting the hours until he could be with her again. As far as he could tell, she was delighted to see him and always expressed great disappointment when the time came for him to leave to catch his train. And yet, for all the pleasure they had when they were together, that vague sense of dissatisfaction that he had experienced after their first meeting at Ashbourne Wood persisted. To know that she liked him was not enough; he wanted

213

more. If he was going to fall in love with her, he wanted to be sure his feelings were matched, and it concerned him that the more he tried to move towards her, the more distant and self-contained she seemed to become. She had said nothing more about Alec since their earlier conversation, but she had told him enough to persuade him that, whatever she may have said to the contrary, she was using him and their life together as a kind of shield behind which she could shelter in moments of uncertainty and which at other times she could shake in his face as a challenge to his character and his manhood. Hugh had never been used to competing for any woman's affections, certainly not with a dead man as his rival. It was hardly a fair match.

One evening, following a more frustrating session than usual during which it seemed to Hugh that his fingers would never be straight again, Marjorie told him that she had asked some friends to dine with them.

'Gregory and Nesta Parker,' she explained. 'We used to see quite a lot of them. He's a barrister. He would have been a K.C. by now if the war hadn't come along. You'll like them.'

But he hadn't. It was not their fault. They did their best. When they talked about old times, they tried to fill Hugh in on the background to the stories and encouraged him, belatedly, to become a part of the comfortable, unassuming little world they had made for themselves – the golf at Sunningdale, the bridge evenings, the walking tours of the Lake District, the concerts at the Queen's Hall. But the more they explained it and attempted to relive it, the more of an outsider Hugh felt.

'God what a pair of bores,' he said when they had gone.

'I daresay they thought the same of you,' said Marjorie, 'sitting there with a superior look on your face. I could have killed you. They're kind, simple, unpretentious people who work hard and would do anything for anyone. They also happen to be our oldest friends. Amongst other things, we shared a taste for plain food and quiet conversation and milky coffee. If you can't get through an evening without cocktails and pillow-fights and schoolboy jokes, you'd better go and look up your old Cambridge cronies instead.'

214

Hugh gave a hard laugh.

'I would, if any of them were still alive.'

Marjorie walked round the room puffing up the cushions and straightening the chair covers.

'I might be tempted to feel sorry for you, if you didn't feel quite so sorry for yourself.'

'I'm sorry,' Hugh said frowning. 'It's just that . . . well . . . all that talk about Alec and what a wonderful chap he was and what wonderful times you all had together . . . Don't you see? It's not exactly easy for me sitting there, feeling out of place.'

Marjorie rounded on him, her hands on her hips, a strand of hair flopping across her forehead.

'How dare you,' she said. 'What right do you have to come round here telling me who my friends should be and what we should talk about? Just because you and I talk together sometimes, it doesn't mean you own me.'

Hugh stared at her.

'Talking together sometimes?' he said. 'Is that all it means to you? Is that really the way you look at me? As a poor patient who needs chatting to from time to time so he doesn't get too depressed? Was that the way you described me to your friends this evening on the 'phone? "I do hope you don't mind but I've got this patient who will insist on staying on. I haven't the heart to ask him to leave. He's rather sad. One of those burnt pilots, you know. Do try and be nice to him." Is that really all I mean to you after all this time?'

Marjorie looked at him half-frowning, half-smiling. Hugh hauled himself to his feet.

'I'm glad you find it so amusing,' he said, his face red and perspiring. 'For what it's worth, I happen to be very fond of you. In fact, if you must know, I love you. I don't expect you to love me in return, but at least you might have the decency to respect my feelings.'

Marjorie burst out laughing.

'Oh, really, Hugh. You are a sight when you get pompous.'

Hugh glowered at her.

'Look,' she said walking across to him and taking his hands, 'I like you. Despite the fact you treated me so badly at Cam-

215

bridge, I believe you are a good man. I think I could even love you. But that's not something that's going to happen in a moment of blinding revelation. Alec's only been dead a few months, and despite my determination to go on and not to keep harking back, he is still very much in my mind. You will just have to accept that, whether you like it or not.'

'I know,' said Hugh. 'I know.'

'I wonder if you really do,' she said. 'You've become so used over the years to having what you want when you want it that you cannot bear to be told to wait. You say you love me. In your own way I believe you do. But there's more to love than wanting someone, or even needing them. There's patience and understanding, real understanding, and self-denial. Alec taught me that.'

'Now you're talking to me as though I were a small boy,' Hugh said sulkily, working at a hole in the carpet with his toe.

'That's because at times you behave like one.'

'I think I'd better go,' Hugh muttered.

'Where to?' Marjorie asked him. 'You've missed the last train.'

'Oh, hell and damnation.'

Hugh fell back into the armchair and stared unseeing into the fireplace.

'Now I've made a complete fool of myself.'

'Perhaps, but that's another thing you're going to have to learn to do from time to time,' Marjorie sat on the arm of the chair. 'It's part of loving, too.'

She stroked his hair, then laid her cheek against it.

'Poor Hugh,' she whispered. 'You're only just starting to live. Like all of us. The terrible thing is that it should have taken all this pain and death and suffering to show us how.'

Hugh returned to Ashbourne Wood the following morning, resolved not to see Marjorie again for a while. He needed time and space to think, and when he suggested that he should go to Norfolk for a few days, Meikle, though surprised, did not attempt to dissuade him. He added that they both hoped he would feel free to come back to the cottage whenever he felt like it. Hugh told him he thought it was high time he stood on his own feet again, but promised to ring the moment he'd had enough.

It happened sooner than even he'd expected. The weather was warm, the sun shone every day on the marshes, highlighting every dyke and ditch and channel, and the sand dunes glowed on the horizon. But Hugh was overwhelmed with a melancholy that no amount of walking and sitting on the bank in the sun could disperse. Once, he tried taking the Sandpiper out for a sail, but soon found that he couldn't get a proper grip on the sheets, and so had to return after only a few minutes.

Susan had long since returned to Somerset with the children to pick up the pieces of her life, and with them had gone, it seemed, the small vestige of life that remained in the Rectory. Muv and Far seemed to have aged ten years since he last saw them. At first they had been overjoyed to have him home again, expressing surprise and delight at his physical improvement and obviously trying hard not to fuss him. But after a couple of days they had reverted to an unwavering, slow-moving routine of meals on trays, early nights, and domestic trivialities, so that Hugh began to feel even more an invalid than he had on his previous visit. Even Percy had lost interest in walks.

He thought constantly about Marjorie and missed her almost all the time. He said nothing about her to his parents until one day, as they were sitting round the fire after supper, Mrs Fleming said, à propos of nothing,

'Your father and I often wonder when you're going to find a nice girl and settle down. I don't know why you don't marry Bunny. We always liked her. Didn't we, Arthur?'

Mr Fleming frowned slightly and said nothing.

'I have,' Hugh said.

His mother looked up from darning a blue woollen sock.

'What?' she said. 'Married Bunny?' Her voice was full of enthusiasm suddenly.

'No,' said Hugh, and told them about Marjorie. They listened politely.

When he had finished, his father said, 'A physiotherapist, eh? That's unusual.'

217

'Well,' said his mother, 'just as long as you don't go rushing into anything.' And she returned to her sock.

The following evening she said, as she was pouring the tea they always drank after the nine o'clock news, 'Have you thought what you're going to do when your sick pay comes to an end?'

'Not really,' Hugh said. 'I daresay something will turn up.'

'You're leaving the Air Force then?' said his father, his voice undisguisably hopeful.

Hugh gave a short laugh and said, 'I don't think I'd be much use to them now, do you?'

'You could always give Uncle Reggie a ring at his advertising agency,' said his mother. 'I'm sure they could use a good brain.'

'I somehow don't think advertising's quite my cup of tea,' said Hugh.

'I wonder what is,' she said. 'There's no living to be made out of being an ex-fighter pilot.'

'I'll see,' said Hugh irritably. 'Something'll turn up.'

Mrs Fleming puffed up the cushions and collected up the tea cups while Arthur took Percy out for a late night constitutional. It had been another long evening. It was just after half past nine.

Hugh lay on his bed and stared at the ceiling. His bedroom was exactly as it had been for the past goodness knew how many years. The childhood books, the model of the *Victory*, the electric cars – they were all still there on the shelf beside the window, exactly where he had left them after he had last played with them during some school holidays or other. His Eton cricket cap still hung on the wall by a nail, and Percy still scratched to come in in the morning. But it was not his home any more. What was, though? Nothing – unless it was a large, shabby flat on the fifth floor of an Edwardian mansion block just off Baker Street.

The next morning Hugh announced that he had to get back to London. His parents seemed neither surprised nor upset. 'Where will you stay?' his mother asked him. 'Friends,' Hugh told her. She seemed satisfied.

'You know your room is here for you whenever you want it,' she said, but her words carried little conviction.

'Let us know how you get on, old chap,' said his father. 'Remember, we only want what is best for you.' And he awkwardly pressed a packet of Players into Hugh's hand before turning brusquely away in the direction of his study.

As he kissed his mother goodbye and climbed into the taxi for the two mile journey to the station, Hugh noticed that for the first time ever Percy had not come to see him off.

The moment the train arrived at Liverpool Street, he took a cab straight round to Bracknell Mansions.

'Mrs Maybury's gone to the hospital,' the porter informed him. There was a hint of satisfaction in his voice. 'She won't be back till three.'

'I'll wait,' said Hugh and sat on the stairs.

He was still sitting there when Marjorie returned.

'I'm glad you came back,' she said when they were in the flat. 'I've missed you. You might have written or 'phoned or something.'

'Sorry.'

He stood there in the middle of the sitting room, uncertain and helpless. Marjorie moved across to him and put her arms round his neck.

'I was right,' she said. 'You really are just like a little boy sometimes.' And she kissed him lightly on the lips.

Hugh smiled.

'I want you to marry me,' he said.

She looked at him steadily, without moving.

'Are you sure?'

'Of course I'm sure.'

'You're not asking me because you feel sorry for me?'

'No.'

'Or because you feel guilty about jilting me at Cambridge.'

Hugh shook his head.

'Why then?'

He shrugged.

'I suppose I just can't bear not to be with you.'

'That's not a bad reason.'

219

'It's true.'

'I believe you.'

'How about you?'

'You mean, can I bear to be without you?'

Hugh nodded and grinned shyly. Marjorie cocked her head on one side and thought for a while. Then she said,

'Yes.'

'Oh,' said Hugh, genuinely disappointed.

'But then I have a lot of other things to think about; people to meet, cars to drive, trains to catch, appointments to keep.'

'While I just sit on my backside all day, thinking too much. I know.'

Marjorie detached herself from Hugh and perched on the arm of the sofa.

'You needn't,' she pointed out. 'You're perfectly well enough now to do a job. Not flying perhaps, but there are other things that are needed in a war apart from pilots. Let me see your hands.'

Hugh held them out.

'Flex your fingers.'

Hugh did as he was told.

'Now grip my hand in yours, and squeeze as hard as you can.'

Hugh did.

'Come along. You can do better than that. Squeeze really hard.'

Hugh closed his eyes with the effort. Suddenly she uttered a cry and he opened them to see her face contorted with pain. He let go at once.

'I'm sorry,' he said. 'I didn't realize. I'm so sorry.' And moving forward, he took her crushed hand and held it gently between both of his. Then he lifted it to his mouth and pressed it against his lips. After that, he took her face and gently kissed her on the mouth. For a moment she stood there with her arms by her sides; then she lifted them behind his back and held him tightly, sighing softly as she felt him harden against her.

'I want you,' he said at last.

'I know,' she said. 'I want you too.'

'Now?'

'Now.'

And so the two of them, without another word, moved towards the bedroom – the plain, overweight girl, her unruly hair more tousled than usual, her spectacles slightly steamed up, and the tall, slim boy, his deep blue eyes smiling out of his ruined features, one scarred and misshapen hand clasped protectively around her plump shoulders.

After they had made love and slept for a while, Hugh lit a cigarette and said, 'What about it then?'

Marjorie moved closer and clung to his chest, her large breasts soft against his bony frame.

'Already?' she said and snuggled up closer against him.

Hugh laughed.

'Not that, you idiot. Getting married, I mean.'

She propped herself up on one elbow.

'I've got a better idea,' she said. 'Why don't we just live here together for a bit and see how we get on?'

'You mean live in sin?' The suggestion quite shocked him. It had never crossed his mind that girls might propose such things.

Marjorie smiled.

'No, I mean share the flat with me.'

'However delicately you choose to describe it,' said Hugh, 'it's still not as good as the real thing.'

'How would you know?'

'I wouldn't. But if we're going to live together, we might just as well go the whole hog and get married.'

Marjorie lay down beside him again.

'Later,' she said. 'Give me time.'

'How much time do you need?'

'Some,' she said. 'It'll be all right in the end. You see. But please don't press me now for a definite answer. Please.'

'Okay,' said Hugh, stubbing out his cigarette. 'But don't leave it too long or I may go off the idea altogether.'

'That's what worries me,' she said.

For the first two nights after leaving the Meikles' and moving in with his one suitcase and his kitbag, he had, out of some absurd sense of propriety, insisted on sleeping in the spare room. Marjorie had made no attempt to persuade him otherwise, and on the third night, without either of them saying a word, he had undressed and climbed into bed beside her.

For the next few weeks they lived like a newly married couple, dining with Tim and Nancy Holland, playing canasta with Gregory and Nesta, occasionally walking down to Marble Arch to see a film, but otherwise rarely moving out of doors. The only difference was that it was Marjorie who set off for work in the mornings, and Hugh who stayed at home and made the beds and dusted and shopped for supper. At first it was rather fun, but the novelty soon wore off, and after a month, they had begun to fight and bicker like a married couple, too. Three days later, Hugh rang Uncle Reggie.

Chapter Fifteen

At eleven o'clock on a dull morning in late May of 1941, Gwen Maddocks, receptionist and switchboard operator for the firm of Doone, Vesey and Barnes, Practitioners in Advertising, of High Holborn, W.C.1., looked up from the scarf she was over four months late in finishing for her boy friend, and said in a flat, bored voice, 'May I help you?'

Hugh wondered how many times in recent months someone had asked him that question without really meaning it.

'I have an appointment with Mr Reginald Barnes,' he said.

The girl stared open-mouthed at the tall figure before her in his light grey, chalk-striped, double-breasted suit, soft blue shirt, and dark blue tie with a pale blue stripe.

'My name's Fleming,' he said. 'Hugh Fleming. I have an appointment.'

'Oh,' she said, unable to take her eyes from his face. 'Righty-ho. What did you say your name was?'

'Hugh Fleming.'

She fiddled with the wires on the switchboard in front of her, then pressed a switch.

'Oh, Mr Barnes? Reception here. I've got a Mr . . .?'

'Fleming.'

'. . . a Mr Fleming here who says he's got an appointment with you. Is that right? Oh, I see. Righty-ho, Mr Barnes. Two minutes.'

She unplugged the wire and looked up at Hugh.

'He says he'll be with you in two minutes. Would you like to sit down?'

Hugh smiled and shook his head.

'Can I get you anything? A drink of water or anything?'
Her voice whined with anxiety. Hugh shook his head again.
'No, thank you,' he said.
'Are you sure?' she insisted.
'I'm not ill, if that's what you're thinking,' he told her
pleasantly.
'I didn't know,' she murmured. 'I wasn't sure. Only I couldn't
help, you know, noticing . . .'
'Of course. It's quite understandable.'
She ran a pink tongue round her bright red lips and pushed
at her hair at the back of her head with the palm of one hand.
'How exactly did it happen?' she asked. 'Your . . . er . . .?'
'I got shot up in a Spitfire,' he replied with a smile. 'Un-
fortunately the thing caught on fire. I didn't get out quite fast
enough.'
'Strewth,' said the girl. 'I bet it didn't half hurt.'
'Oddly enough, I didn't feel a thing at the time. It wasn't so
nice later. In hospital and so on.'
'Did you have to have a lot of operations?' she asked,
genuinely interested.
'Lots,' he said.
'How do they . . . you know . . .?'
'They wait till it's all healed up, then they cut little bits of
skin from different parts of your body, and where the face
has got too badly burnt, they stick them on.'
'Strewth, 'said Gwen. She leaned forward to get a better look.
'You'd never know, what with it all being wrinkled, if you
don't mind me saying so.'
'No, I don't mind,' Hugh told her cheerfully. 'It is all rather
a mess, isn't it? It'll look better eventually.'
'I hope so,' said Gwen earnestly. 'You've got lovely eyes, and
it seems such a shame somehow.'
'I don't mind,' said Hugh. 'I did at first, but I've got used to
it now. You can get used to anything in time.'
'I know what you mean,' said the girl, warming to the subject.
'When you first came in, it gave me quite a turn, know what I
mean? Well, you don't expect it somehow, do you, in the middle

of London? But now that we've been chatting for a bit, it hardly notices at all. Funny, isn't it?'

'I'm glad,' said Hugh.

The girl grinned.

'I could quite go for you,' she said, 'if I wasn't already promised.'

Hugh leaned forward until his face was close to hers. She was really a very pretty girl.

'Me too,' he said.

'You really have got lovely eyes,' she murmured.

'So have you,' murmured Hugh.

'When you've both quite finished.'

Gwen Maddocks's face dropped with horror, and she hurriedly sat up and began busily adjusting her headset. Hugh turned and grinned.

'Hallo, Uncle Reggie,' he said.

'Good morning, Hugh,' said his mother's brother. 'You haven't changed your ways, I see.'

'Oh, yes I have,' said Hugh. 'More than you'll ever know.'

Uncle Reggie ushered Hugh up a narrow wooden staircase, along a corridor and into a large, panelled room, heavy with oak and leather. A series of advertisements mounted on cardboard were propped against the wall on a side table. At the far end, beneath a high window, was a large, round table surrounded by several matching chairs. A grey-haired woman wearing a severely cut dark suit, rimless glasses and a bun, marched in with two cups of coffee on a tray.

'I'm afraid it's instant,' she remarked to no one in particular.

Uncle Reggie waved Hugh into one of the deep leather armchairs that were ranged round a low coffee table in front of the heavy stone fireplace.

'This is our Miss Powell,' he said. 'I don't know what we'd do without her. Miss Powell, this is my nephew, Hugh Fleming, who might be coming to work with us. He has the DSO.'

He fingered his yellow bow tie as if in some way claiming personal responsibility for the award.

'Indeed,' said Miss Powell, smiling thinly and addressing an invisible person somewhere between the two of them. 'I'm very glad to hear that, I'm sure.' And she turned and walked crisply from the room.

'Doesn't say much,' Uncle Reggie confided to Hugh, 'but a heart of gold.' He tapped his chest. 'One of the best.'

Hugh smiled politely.

'I don't know quite what Muv told you on the 'phone,' he said, 'but the fact is I'm not as yet in a position to accept any post you might offer me. I'm still a serving officer in the RAF. At least until the RAF decide what to do with me.'

'My dear boy,' said Uncle Reggie expansively, tucking a pair of chubby fingers into the pocket of his drum-tight waistcoat, 'I perfectly understand. No rush, no rush at all.'

'I'm afraid I know very little about commerce.'

'Commerce?' exclaimed his uncle. 'We are not in commerce. We are all artists here. Our job is the communication of ideas. We are the Wordsworths and Constables of the age, bringing a little light and magic into this dark and unhappy world.'

'Really?' said Hugh politely, not sure whether the little man was being serious or not.

'If you have any doubts about it, come and spend a week in the place and try your hand at a little communicating of your own. No obligation on either side, and I won't breathe a word about it to your C.O.'

Uncle Reggie winked and tapped the side of his chubby nose. Then with the same finger he made a number of funny little pointing gestures at different parts of his face.

'Sorry about your ... mm ...' he muttered. 'Nasty business. Jolly bad luck. Ah well. The fortunes of war.'

After they had drunk their Camp coffee, Uncle Reggie took Hugh along a narrow corridor, up some narrow wooden stairs and into a tiny room overlooking a dingy courtyard. There were two plain wooden desks in the room – a large one by the window, covered with dried blobs of spilled paint, and a smaller one in the darkest corner on which were an Underwood typewriter and a great many sheets of paper, some with typing on them.

The front edge of the desk was decorated with a series of

226

cigarette burns, each about an inch long. Beside the plain upright chair with its green leather seat was a metal waste-paper basket, half-filled with balls of screwed-up paper. A metal reading lamp cast a dim light over the debris, attracting a thin line of blue smoke which rose from a cigarette that lay smouldering in an already full ashtray.

Uncle Reggie sighed deeply.

'Where's the fellow gone this time?' he muttered. 'Surely the pubs can't be open yet?'

At that moment into the room shambled a large balding figure in a bulging brown corduroy suit. Such hair as he possessed was long and dishevelled, and a pair of tiny round tortoise shell spectacles was perched halfway down his nose.

'Ah, there you are, Mr Douthwaite,' said Uncle Reggie sternly. 'This is Mr Douthwaite,' he told Hugh. 'He's the copywriter whose evocative words and ringing phrases you would be illustrating. I daresay you're pleasantly surprised.'

'Should I be?' Hugh asked.

'You mean to say the name doesn't ring a bell?'

'I'm afraid not.'

'Eric Douthwaite? The poet?'

'Oh yes, of course,' Hugh lied.

'Liar,' said Douthwaite in a low mumble.

'You know his work well,' said Uncle Reggie. 'The bread ads? "As good as the countryside of England"? Of course you do.'

Hugh smiled faintly but the poet said nothing. He sat down in front of his desk and carefully stubbed out the burning remains of his cigarette.

'Mr Fleming is considering a job as your new art director,' Uncle Reggie explained to him, as if trying to mollify a bad-tempered child. Douthwaite looked up. 'You poor bugger,' he said with evident feeling.

Uncle Reggie hurried his nephew back to the office.

'The job pays £400 a year,' he told him, fingering his bow tie and running his fingers over his plump jowls. 'An hour for lunch, half day Saturdays, two weeks holiday a year, and we also run our own little personal retirement pension plan if

227

you're interested. As I say, give it a week's trial; see what you think.'

Hugh stared at him in silence. It was not the sort of information he was capable of absorbing quickly.

'May I let you know my decision tomorrow?'

'Take your time, my dear boy,' said his uncle. 'Take your time. We artists should never be rushed.'

'It's funny,' Hugh told Marjorie later that day, 'but I'd always thought of advertising as a young man's business – finger on the pulse of the nation and all that. The people at Doone, Vesey and Barnes must spend half their time wondering if they're going to survive the day. I feel I've aged thirty years since this morning, and I was only in the building for half an hour.'

'All the young ones are off fighting for their country, I suppose,' Marjorie said. She was kneeling by the book-case under the window, re-arranging a collection of Penguins.

'Don't remind me.'

She knelt up on her heels.

'Oh Hugh,' she said. 'We've been through all this. You decided you couldn't go back. I agree. You really must stop brooding on it. Your war's over. You've got more important things to think about.'

'Like brown bread and cornflakes?'

'Like making a living. If we're ever going to get married, we really can't live on my pay and your miserly pension.'

Hugh went across to Marjorie and kissed her.

'I'm sorry, my darling,' he said. 'I do make a fuss, don't I? But if you'd seen the people I'd have to work with . . .'

He shook his head. Marjorie stood up and put her arms round his neck.

'Look at it this way,' she said softly. 'You'd be earning a living at something you like doing anyway. The salary's not at all bad and the hours are reasonable; and you'd be doing something of real benefit to people. How many other unknown artists can you think of whose work is seen by millions? It's important

228

work and I think you should try it for a few days and then make up your mind. Not for my sake, but for your own.'

Hugh squeezed her around her waist and kissed her nose.

'The really maddening thing about you,' he said, 'is that you're always right.'

A week later, at eight o'clock sharp, Hugh stepped out of the front door of Bracknell Mansions, acknowledged the crisp salute of the Hitlerian porter with a lazy lift of his rolled umbrella, and taking a firm grasp on his attaché case (which contained two rounds of cheese and pickle sandwiches and a copy of the *Daily Express*), he set off boldly in the direction of Baker Street station.

By the time he returned, soon after six, he had eaten his sandwiches, read his *Daily Express*, sketched out and rejected six ideas for typical English rural scenes to illustrate Eric Douthwaite's new campaign for brown bread, had another flirtatious encounter with a breathless Gwen Maddocks in Reception, drunk two glasses of dry sherry with Uncle Reggie in his office and three pints of warm beer with Alfred, a young, mournful copywriter from the next office who was exempted from the forces because of his flat feet. It could, he reminded himself as he climbed the stairs of Bracknell Mansions, have been worse.

It was a phrase he was to repeat to himself frequently in the days that followed.

Having fondly supposed that copywriters and artists in advertising agencies were expected to produce a new advertisement every day at least, it came as a surprise to find that most of his day was spent with his feet up on the desk, smoking cigarettes and drinking bottled beer while he and Douthwaite argued over the merits of Yeats, Eliot and Auden. Occasionally they would break off to stare mindlessly out of the window at the building opposite, or else resume an elaborate and long running word game with Alfred and his Eton-cropped art director, Naomi.

One day, an advertisement was actually completed, whereupon Hugh and Eric trooped up to the next floor for a meeting with Dennis, a small, harassed man with a dry, nervous cough. Dennis suggested a couple of changes to the copy which Eric said he was buggered if he was going to do. This was followed by a couple more suggestions about the illustration which Eric said he was buggered if Hugh was going to do. After that, Dennis announced gravely that he would present it to the client and let *him* decide. But evidently the client had better taste than Dennis, since the advertisement did not come back, and Hugh and Eric happily resumed their word game with Alfred and Naomi.

The following day, Eric received a visit from Dennis, who announced that the client wished to see him in Mr Barnes's office.

'Both of us?' asked Eric.

'Mr Barnes said just you,' said Dennis.

When he returned twenty minutes later, Hugh asked, 'Did I miss anything?'

'Not,' said Eric, 'unless you have a secret penchant for conversations with uneducated nobodies in spats who don't know the difference between a past participle and a hole in their bottom.' Hugh laughed, but still he was sorry not to have been asked.

He mentioned this to his uncle, who hurriedly dismissed the matter with an airy, 'Oh, art directors never meet the client.' But Naomi did, and the art director with the goatee beard in the office next to that.

'What's the betting Uncle Reggie thinks I'd frighten the clients into removing their accounts?' Hugh said angrily the next morning over breakfast.

Marjorie said mildly, 'Now then. Enough of that.'

'Perhaps I should go to work in my uniform, with my DSO ribbon lit up in coloured lights,' he went on.

Marjorie managed to laugh it all off as usual, but the thought had occurred to him frequently in the few days he had been going to the agency. He said nothing about it to Marjorie, but the looks on the faces of his fellow passengers as he travelled to and from High Holborn still hurt him. In uniform, with a pair of silver wings and a flash of ribbon on his chest, he might

230

have been able to face them with more confidence. People knew about burnt fighter aces now, and the mere fact of being a pilot automatically denied the possibility of failure. Dressed in a suit like everyone else, he felt a constant need to explain himself. Time and again he wanted to stand up in the crowded tube train and shout at the top of his voice, 'Don't keep looking at me like that as though I were some sort of leper. I got this by defending you bloody lot. So let's have a bit of respect and gratitude.'

There were times during that week at Doone, Vesey and Barnes when he felt that, if it hadn't been for Marjorie, he might have cracked up completely. He realized he was relying on her more and more for her common sense, her gaiety, her wisdom, and above all for her apparently limitless store of patience and understanding; and yet she asked for nothing in return. Worse, he seemed to have nothing to give.

Despite his best endeavours, he was still as possessive and jealous as ever. One weekend they had driven down to Marjorie's parents' home in Suffolk – a small, rather dark, Victorian house with a little walled garden in the middle of a long, straggling village.

Mr and Mrs Fisher had reminded him of his own parents. Marjorie's father was a tall, slightly stooping man in late middle age. He wore a thin, grey moustache, and smoked slightly scented tobacco in a small, blackened pipe that was held together with a length of red rubber tube. He was the managing director of a small firm in Stowmarket that made electrical components for farm vehicles. His wife, a plain, ample woman, an older version of Marjorie, taught classics at a nearby girls' school.

Hugh got on with them both at once, largely because they were the first people he had met who discussed his injuries in a genuinely interested and unselfconscious way. They were particularly fascinated to hear about Meikle and his work at Ashbourne Wood, and they appeared to know almost as much about massage as their daughter.

'Oh, Marjorie often used to bring patients down for the day,' said Mrs Fisher by way of explanation, when Marjorie was out

231

in the kitchen preparing the tea. 'Of course, that was before she met Alec. Since his death, she has preferred to spend time on her own. There have been one or two, mostly Air Force boys like yourself, but not so many.'

Hugh, his stomach twisted with jealousy, would have pressed her for further details, had Marjorie not appeared at that moment with a tray of tea cups and cake and sandwiches.

Unable to contain himself, he raised the matter in the car driving back to London. Marjorie replied that they were nothing more than patients and that anyway, it was no concern of his.

He found it hard to believe that one woman could have so much love in her that she could share it out amongst so many, and cursed himself for wishing to keep it all for himself. He realized now that he had never really loved anyone in his life before, and probably never would again; yet at the same time he was afraid that he might never find a way of expressing it.

But then how could he possibly hope to make Marjorie happy unless he was happy too? It would have been a simple enough matter to resign from the R.A.F. on a disability pension, and accept Uncle Reggie's offer of a permanent job at the agency. The work was not especially well-paid, but it had the advantages of being amusing and undemanding. The fact that his uncle saw fit to confine him to a small back room whenever the client was in the building rather than run the risk of losing business was certainly insulting and demoralizing. On the other hand, how much more of an insult and a blow to be turned down for a more illustrious job elsewhere? Not everyone was anxious to employ a man whose only qualification was that he had killed a few Germans. His mother had been right: there was no living to be made out of being an ex-fighter pilot, especially a burnt ex-fighter pilot. He should take the job and be thankful. The days when he could afford the luxury of sitting back and weighing the respectability and suitability of different careers and occupations were over for him. Soon, if all went to plan, he would have a wife and children to support, holidays to pay for and school fees and new clothes, a house in the country with staff and a few acres of land – all the pleasures of life for which he had blithely declared he was fighting this war, and for which someone, he had presumed, would pay. That someone, he now realized, was himself.

And yet, he kept telling himself, there had to be more. Surely he had not survived the last few months in order to spend his days in a small back room in High Holborn, drinking beer and playing word games? The opportunity that Robin had talked about had surely not yet arrived.

The weekend following his trial period at the agency they spent with the Meikles.

On the Saturday evening, Angus and Francesca threw a party for some of the patients from the hospital. Noel Mackinnon was back with a brand new left ear and the sad news that Russell Johnson had died – but not before first marrying his little VAD. On the whole, though, it was a cheerful gathering, with Meikle at his ebullient best, and Francesca moving through the throng with her usual quiet dignity and gentle smile, dispensing food and drink, and exchanging confidences with everyone in the room in turn.

The following morning, they drove over to the hospital. Clive Unsworth's face was at last beginning to acquire some sort of human shape; but Ray Andrews still had many weeks of waiting before he would be ready for an operation. Victor Szepezy had returned to his squadron. Hugh did not know any of the others.

Meikle insisted on carrying out an examination on Hugh before they left. He congratulated Marjorie on the progress she had made with his hands, and made Hugh promise he would let him have a go soon at the lower half of his left ear.

Just as they were getting into the car, he took Hugh's arm and said quietly, 'I was right. You're beginning to grow into a man at last.'

Hugh grinned sheepishly.

'And you're beginning to turn into quite an elder brother.'

Meikle snorted and told him to be off with him, but he was clearly pleased. That night, Hugh made up his mind to apply to be invalided from the RAF and join his uncle's firm.

The next morning, he found a letter waiting for him in the

233

hall. It was a moment or two before he recognized the hand writing as Robin's. He was itching to open it all the way to Holborn, but forced himself to wait until he had reached the comparative peace and privacy of his office. He was pleased to see that Douthwaite was late again. He tipped his chair back, placed his feet carefully on his desk among the papers and pencils, and began to read.

'My dear Hugh: I have been meaning to write for many weeks now, ever since receiving your letter. Was it really as long ago as March? But we've been so busy lately with constant sorties over France and trying to train new pilots that I don't seem to have had a spare moment. I'm really more tired now than I was at the height of the battle last August.

I was sorry we missed each other at Woodfold. I thought you knew we'd been posted. (We have got dreadfully out of touch lately, haven't we?) But your description of trying to break in past the duty corporal at the gate almost made up for it – although I don't suppose it was all that amusing at the time. Dickie Bird would have appreciated your account, but sadly he was killed in a sweep over France almost as soon as we got here. We all miss him dreadfully, but we couldn't have a better replacement than Bill Carmichael. Did you know that he'd got the DSO?

I'm still trying to lick my section into something vaguely resembling a professional fighting force (I sound more like Sergeant Gillespie every day!), but the boys they're sending us now are no more than school children, and I don't have the heart to shout at them. Many of them have never been away from home in their lives and I gather that one or two even cry at night from homesickness.

It's funny to think that less than a year ago we were as green and frightened as they are, and looked up at people like Dickie and Bill with the same mixture of awe and fear that new boys regard school prefects. They seemed to have all the answers while we fumbled about trying to keep up

234

and make a good impression; they stayed alive while we long-haired boys were shot down in flames one after another. How could we ever have thought we were any good?

And yet here I am, more as a result of luck than good judgement, a veteran of 21, who's supposed to have all the answers and know the secret of keeping alive, as much a professional to these children as Dickie and Bill and the others were to us. And in a way they're right. I was never trained to shoot down enemy planes like they were; it was never my life, as it was never yours. Yet, through a mixture of aptitude, good training, experience and luck, it has become my life – at least, it's the only thing I'm any good at.

Several times in the last few months it has been suggested that I should give up operational flying for a bit and join some training unit, or retire into a safe desk job. I've been strongly tempted, I can tell you. And yet something tells me that I am more use here, trying to keep some of these young pilots alive a bit longer than most of us were, and I know now that I shall remain operational until they force me out, or the war ends, or my luck runs out – whichever comes first.

I'm ashamed to say that I have very little idea of the progress of your recovery, nor of your future plans. I know that when I last saw you at Ashbourne Wood you were not contemplating going back to flying, and I can understand that. Nor would I attempt to change your mind. Few of us, thank God, have had to go through what you've gone through. On the other hand, the RAF can ill afford to lose talent and experience like yours.

I told you last autumn that when the right opportunity presented itself, you would recognize it and seize it. I do not expect you to decide anything one way or another purely on the strength of this letter, but I am suggesting that, if you have nothing better to do, you might consider coming down here to see us, and see what we are up against. It might just give you some food for thought.

Apart from anything else, I feel desperately lonely much of the time and would welcome your company, if only for a few hours. As I think I have said before on more than one occasion, there are very few of us long-haired boys left.

Yours affectionately,

Robin.

Hugh put the letter down and stared out of the window. A light, grey drizzle had started to descend, and one or two lights had come on in the building opposite.

There was a knock on the door and Dennis stuck his head round.

'Eric not in?' he said with a little cough.

Hugh peered about under his desk in an exaggerated fashion.

'Not unless he's hiding in one of the drawers.'

'Ah,' said Dennis. 'I was just wondering if you've had any ideas yet for the new bread campaign. Only the client's in this morning, and it occurred to me . . .'

His voice tailed away pathetically.

'No,' said Hugh, 'I'm sorry. I haven't.'

Chapter Sixteen

The next morning, Hugh donned his uniform and instead of changing trains at King's Cross for Holborn, travelled on to Liverpool Street. There he telephoned Gwen at the office to say that something had come up and that he would not be in. He then caught the 9.35 train to Middleton. It pulled in to the little Essex station forty minutes later.

'How far to the RAF station?' he asked the ticket collector.

'Half an hour's walk,' he replied, 'or five minutes by taxi from the station yard.'

'Thanks.'

'Here,' he called after Hugh. 'If you're planning on giving Jerry a kick up the arse in the near future, give him one for me, too, would you, sir? I owe it him on account of my boy.'

'Yes,' said Hugh. 'If I get the chance.'

It was a warm day and Hugh decided to walk. The hedgerows were white with Queen Anne's Lace, and the martins were busy putting the final touches to their little mud homes beneath the eaves of the cottages and farmhouses along the way. Hugh whistled a few snatches of 'If I Only Had Wings'. He was sweating profusely by the time he reached the Station's main gate three quarters of an hour later.

'Good morning, sir. May I help you?'

Hugh acknowledged the copy-book salute.

'I have an appointment with Flight-Lieutenant Bailey,' said Hugh. 'My name's Fleming.'

He reached into his inside pocket and produced his i/d card. He handed it to the sentry who examined it, looked at Hugh, looked back at the photograph, pulled a slight face and handed it back with a rueful smile.

'Thank you very much, sir. The Mess is straight through and to your right.'

Hugh ducked under the barrier and walked slowly across the tarmac until he reached the perimeter of the airfield. Fifty yards away to his right a number of pilots were sitting in chairs outside a low yellow-brick building, their parachute packs by their sides, laughing and talking. Three sections of Spitfires were dispersed nearby on the edge of the runway. As Hugh approached the pilots, they broke off their conversation and looked up enquiringly.

'Good afternoon,' Hugh said.

'Good afternoon,' they replied politely. They did, as Robin had said, look ridiculously young. 'Are you looking for anyone?' one of them asked. The faint trace of a blond moustache was beginning to show on his upper lip.

'I was looking for Flight-Lieutenant Bailey actually. Is he around anywhere?'

The pilots looked at each other, as if waiting for someone to take a lead.

'Well,' said one of them at last. 'That depends.'

'On what?' said Hugh with a laugh.

A big man with dark, straight hair and a heavy, black moustache came through the doorway, squadron leader's stripes on his sleeve. 'What's the form?' he said.

'Chap here asking for Robin Bailey, sir,' said one of the pilots.

'Bill,' exclaimed Hugh. 'Bill Carmichael. You old devil.'

The big man peered at Hugh and frowned.

'Hugh?' he said tentatively. 'Good God! What are you doing here?'

Hugh grinned.

'Robin suggested my coming down to see what you're all up to. I think he's hatching a plot to get me back into Spitfires, but he's got a job on his hands. How are you, Bill? I'm told you're leading the squadron now. Congratulations. Keeping these chaps in order, I hope? How is Robin? Is he around? I didn't ring first. Thought I'd give him a surprise.'

Hugh beamed at Bill but he did not smile back.

'I'm sorry, Hugh,' he said. 'But I'm afraid Robin's dead. Yesterday afternoon. A couple of 109s jumped him over Rouen. There was nothing he could do about it. It was over in seconds.'

He stared at Bill for a long time while the news gradually sank in.

'I am sorry, Hugh,' Bill repeated.

'Would you like to sit down or anything?' one of the young pilots said, gesturing towards one of the deck-chairs.

Hugh knew he had no right to feel anger at the young man. He probably did not mean to sound as though he were addressing an old man, but then in their eyes that was just what he was: a veteran, a survivor of the old school – what was it they used to call them? The weekend pilots? There was another expression; something to do with long hair. Poor old fellow, give him a chair. Who is he? Don't know; friend of Flight-Lieutenant Bailey's from the old days presumably. From the Battle of Britain days. Come back to re-live past glories . . .

Oh, hell. That probably wasn't what they thought at all Either about him, or about Robin. It was just him feeling out of things, wanting to explain himself again – wanting to say, all right, so you think you're a great bunch of pilots; you know it all. But you're just a lot of little pip squeaks compared with men like Robin and Peter Hemingford and Jimmy Macdonell and Pat Lumsden. By rights they should be sitting in those deck-chairs, laughing and joking and reading comics and talking about women, not you.

Hugh looked round at the array of anxious, boyish, puzzled faces. Was he really once as young and fresh and innocent as them? And was it really only a year ago? And then he realized what it was about them that had angered him. It wasn't just their self-confidence, nor the feeling that they were humouring him, nor even that he missed his old friends more badly than he had realized. It was that he himself was not sitting in one of the deck-chairs – not instead of them, but *with* them; not harking back constantly to the old days, but living in the present, being a part once again of the only real world he had ever known, speaking the shop that was the only language in

239

which he had ever really been fluent, and flying Spitfires which was the only thing he really knew how to do well. For better or worse, the time had come to throw himself back into real life, instead of standing aloof and superior on the sidelines, expecting life to come to him. That was the way to exorcise the old ghosts, and that was what Robin had been hinting at in his letter.

Susan had been right. He had used, or rather misused, Robin's words at Ashbourne Wood to justify his own indecision and inactivity. He had declared that his only duty was to himself and perhaps a little to the memory of his dead friends. Now he knew better. It had taken Robin's death to convince him that his duty was not to the dead but to the living.

Long ago, in the Anglesey Arms in Halnaker, the day Hugh and Pat had been made operational, Robin had said that the long-haired boys had to stick together, because they'd be needed after it was all over. Well, it wasn't all over yet, but he was the last of that group of long-haired boys left alive, and they were damned well going to need him whether they liked it or not.

'What will you do now?' Bill's voice cut across his thoughts. Hugh smiled.

'I think I'll have a beer,' he said.

Chapter Seventeen

That evening, Hugh told Marjorie he had decided to go back to flying.

She nodded dumbly. When she finally spoke, her voice was low and calm, but there were tears in her eyes.

'So now I'm to lose you, too,' she said.

Hugh took her hands in his and stared down at them.

'I doubt it.' He looked up at her and smiled. 'If the great squadron-leader in the sky had really wanted me to go, he'd have made a thorough job of it the first time.'

'That's not funny.'

Hugh sighed. 'I'm sorry. I was only trying to cheer you up. In fact I've never been more serious in my life. I have to go back, don't you see? I'm the last one left. I must have been spared for something better than a second-rate advertising company in High Holborn.'

Marjorie got up and walked across to the window, her arms clasped tight round her body, as though trying to keep herself warm.

'Oh, I understand all right,' she said, unable to disguise the bitterness in her voice. 'You feel you've got to prove to yourself that you're really a man after all. But going back to the Air Force is not the answer. That's the easy way out.'

Hugh gave a short laugh.

'Oh but it is,' Marjorie said. 'All right, so you've persuaded yourself that it's your responsibility to carry on the work of training young pilots where Robin left off. That would have been perfectly understandable a year ago, when you didn't know anything else. But things have changed since then – for you and for others. You've undertaken new and different responsibilities. Life is going to go on after this war is over. That's what you should be concerned with now. You can do something useful there. Leave the business of fighting to those who are properly suited. You've done all you can do.'

Hugh went across to her and took her in his arms, but still she kept her own arms clasped firmly across her body.

'Look,' he said gently. 'We can go on arguing this thing rationally till the cows come home. Don't you think I haven't come up with every reason why I shouldn't go back? I'd be more useful on the ground; I'm only trying to prove something to myself; I'm not really up to it, physically or mentally; I'm trying to live up to my hero image; my duty should be to make you happy . . .'

'Well? Shouldn't it?'

'Darling, I have never loved anyone as much as I love you, and never shall again. I realize you don't really believe me, and I can understand why. I'm a difficult, spoiled, selfish, possessive person, and I've got a long way to go yet before I can really say I love you in the way you should be loved, and once were, by Alec. I also know very well that you do not really love me either. Perhaps you never will. But I want you to, more than anything else in the world – in spite of everything I have done to convince you otherwise. We have already travelled such a long way together that we must not fail. But to love someone truly, you must love yourself first. I think I am at last beginning to. But I cannot succeed without self respect. I must be true to myself, and I just know I must go back. Reason tells me I am wrong, but instinct convinces me that there is no other way. If I fail myself now, I shall fail you, too. Please say I'm doing the right thing. Please . . .'

Marjorie unclasped her arms and brought them up round his neck. Tears were streaming down her cheeks and chin.

'Oh, Hugh . . . ,' she began, and caught her breath in a sob.

'Without your strength I don't think I could go on.' He, too, was weeping now but for what he was not quite sure. For his dead friends? For his lost youth? For the pain he knew he was inflicting on her? Perhaps just because she was weeping.

242

'Of course you must go back,' she said at last. 'It's just . . . it's just . . . I couldn't bear to lose you. That's all.'

'You won't,' he said. 'You can't. Not if we really love each other.'

'No,' she said. 'That's right.' She stood sobbing against his chest.

'Our hearts may be breaking now,' he said, 'but they'll soon mend again, and when they do, they'll be stronger than ever, because they'll be as one.'

He bent forward and kissed the top of her head, then he kissed her red nose and her damp eyelids, and then her soft, frightened mouth, and their tears mingled and flowed together.

On a warm, overcast day in early July, 1941, Hugh went to Buckingham Palace with Marjorie to be invested with the DSO. Afterwards, as he was coming out of the gates, a reporter ran forward and asked him what the King had said to him, but he couldn't remember a thing about it. He'd been thinking about Robin at the time, but he didn't suppose the reporter would be interested in hearing about that, so he just smiled and walked on.

A press photographer happened to snap his camera at that moment, and a rather over-inked picture of Hugh appeared in the early edition of the *Star*, with the caption DSO FOR BURNT HERO.

That evening, he cut the picture out and put it in an envelope to his parents, with a short letter. After telling them of his decision to return to flying, he added:

'At the risk of sounding rather pompous, I just want to tell you how grateful I shall always be for your unfailing sympathy and kindness to me in the last year, especially when I least deserved it. I realize now that I must have been a terrible disappointment to you, and I am sorry for any pain I may stupidly have caused you. I only hope that it is not too late to show you how fond I am of both of you. My decision to go back to the RAF may seem at first sight thoroughly selfish, and I can imagine the pain it will cause

243

you. However, you must believe me when I tell you that I have thought about it for a long time, and I ask you, as I have asked Marjorie, to have as much faith in me now as you always shown in the past. God bless you both, Hugh.'

A week later he attended an RAF medical board. A number of mono-syllabic doctors impassively submitted him to a series of tests, and Hugh handed over two letters in support of his application to be returned to operational duties: one was from his surgeon at Ashbourne Wood, the other from his masseuse.

It was perfectly obvious to all the doctors that he was not yet ready for operational flying. The decision was passed on to him ten days after the board by a kindly air-commodore who told Hugh that he admired his determination and guts and hoped he'd apply again in a few months' time.

Hugh said that he couldn't wait that long, and suggested that in the meantime it might be possible for him to join a Training Unit as an instructor. The air-commodore said he would think about it and let him know his decision in a week or two.

When Hugh rang Meikle in a state of deep gloom to deliver the news, the surgeon made little effort to disguise his relief. He told him that it wouldn't do him any harm to wait until his hands were really strong again, and that anyway he'd like to have another go at the skin on he back of his right hand.

'One or two of the fellows from here, on our recommendation, have been posted to' A.T.A.,' he said encouragingly. 'You could do worse than try for that.'

'A.T.A.?' Hugh said.

'Air Transport Auxiliary,' Meikle told him. 'You know, moving planes about from one station to another, that sort of thing. Not permanently, of course; just for six months or so to see how you get on. Then apply again for operational flying in a few months' time.'

'Anyone can shunt planes about,' Hugh said. 'I want to work with young pilots. I've got the skill and the experience. I'm up to more than A.T.A. and you know it.'

'Of course I know that,' said Meikle. 'But do the squadrons?

There's more resistance than you might think to taking back men who've been burnt. Bad for morale and all that.'

'So rather than hurt young pilots' feelings, they let them be killed instead?'

'I also, believe it or not, don't want you killed either,' Meikle said grimly. 'And neither, I daresay, does Marjorie.'

'Look, Angus,' Hugh said, 'for the last nine months I've been relying on others – you, Marjorie, Tim, my parents, my sister, everyone in fact – to live my life for me. Who knows, perhaps I've been doing it all my life. All right, if I hadn't been such a bloody fool as to chase that 109 last summer, I probably wouldn't be where I am now. In fact I'd probably be dead like the rest of my friends. But none of us asked for this war. The great decisions are made by a tiny handful of men, and the rest of us have to make the best of it and risk getting hurt in the process. Well, given that I am still alive and in reasonable command of my various faculties, and given that the war will grind on to its inevitable conclusion, I have the right at least to decide whether I am going to take part in it or sit back and let others do the job for me. Of course I may be killed in the process, but rather that than have to live the rest of my life knowing I never once took the responsibility of deciding what I should do with it. I know Marjorie would agree, and so would you. After all, isn't that what being a man is really about?'

Immediately after speaking to Meikle, he rang the Air Ministry and asked to speak to Air-Marshal Hoggart.

'He may not remember my name,' he told the ADC. 'In which case mention Sir Walter Monckton and a film called *The Boys in Blue*.'

The following day Hugh had a long conversation with the air-marshal over lunch in his club. He described his brief career as technical adviser to *The Boys in Blue*, and explained what he had in mind next. Air-Marshal Hoggart listened gravely. He did not say much, but as they folded their napkins and prepared to leave, he told Hugh that he would have a word with a few people and that he'd ring him in a few days and let him know the form.

245

'You'd settle for a training unit then.' It was a statement rather than a question.

'Yes, sir,' said Hugh.

'Naturally, I can't promise anything,' the air-marshal said, 'but I don't foresee any serious problems. You're obviously a young man who's used to getting his own way.'

'Yes,' said Hugh.

On a hot, sunny day in the middle of July, Hugh and Marjorie were married in the church in the Suffolk village where her parents lived. This was particularly convenient for Mr and Mrs Fleming since it meant they could drive down and back in a day without using up their entire month's supply of petrol coupons.

The Meikles came, much to everyone's delight, bringing with them Tim and Nancy Holland, whose baby was due at any moment. Susan came up by train with Joanna and Timmy, who made an endearing, if fidgety, page-boy and made everyone titter nervously by asking Hugh, in the middle of the service, if he could have a uniform like his when he grew up.

Everyone remarked on how attractive Marjorie looked in pale yellow with a matching hat, and it was generally agreed that Hugh looked very handsome in his uniform with his new DSO ribbon.

At the modest reception Marjorie's parents had laid on in the garden of their house, Arthur Fleming said to Hugh, 'It's very interesting, this physiotherapy business. It's obviously a highly-skilled profession. She must be very clever, your wife.'

'She is,' said Hugh.

'She's such a sensible girl, that's what I like about her,' said his mother.

Hugh smiled and kissed her on the forehead.

Marjorie's mother said at one point, 'Look after her. She's the only one we've got.' And her father said, 'Come and see us often.'

Hugh smiled and promised he'd do his best.

Later, Tim got rather tight on champagne and had to be taken indoors for a talking to by Nancy. The sun dipped behind the church tower.

The shadows began to lengthen in the garden. The air was heavy with the scent of roses, and from somewhere high in the copper beech came the soothing, slightly mournful cooing of a turtle dove.

The Meikles were the first to leave.

'Whatever the decision,' said Meikle, 'I want you to promise me you'll come down soon and let me have another look at that hand.'

Hugh promised.

'I still wish you'd wait a little longer,' Meikle told him.

'Don't worry, Angus,' Hugh told him. 'I'm not going to get myself killed for a while yet.'

Soon afterwards Mr and Mrs Fleming left, taking Susan and the children with them.

'God bless you both, my dear,' said Mrs Fleming and had a little cry; and Arthur said, 'The great thing is never to expect too much out of life,' and pressed a plain white envelope into Hugh's hand. Timmy jumped up and down and begged Hugh to come and visit them soon.

'Please do,' urged Susan. She kissed him with a sudden, awkward movement. 'You always were the lucky one,' she murmured.

Hugh and Marjorie drove back to London later and spent the night at Claridges. It was Tim and Nancy's wedding present.

'It isn't exactly my flat,' said Marjorie when they were shown into the awe-inspiring suite, 'but it'll do for tonight, I suppose.'

The next morning, they set off for a little hotel in South Devon for a week's honeymoon, but not before Hugh had remembered to ring Air-Marshal Hoggart's secretary with the phone number, just in case there should be any news.

They arrived at six-thirty to be told by the girl at the reception desk that somebody had called half an hour earlier from the Air Ministry and would call back in a couple of hours. 'A man,' she added. 'Quite old. He had a nice voice.'

'Was there any message?' Hugh asked her.

'Not really,' she said, 'but he sounded very cheerful. Almost perky you might say.'

'Good,' said Hugh.

'Shall I have the call put through directly to your room?' she asked.

'Please.'

Hugh was making love to a girl when the telephone rang. She was young, a little on the plump side, and extraordinarily compliant.